FROM EARTH Z WITH LOVE

FROM EARTH Z WITH LOVE

DIE AGAIN TO SAVE THE WORLD™ BOOK FOUR

RAMY VANCE

MICHAEL ANDERLE

THE FROM EARTH Z WITH LOVE TEAM

Thanks to our Beta Reader

Rachel Beckford

Thanks to the JIT Readers

Veronica Stephan-Miller
Deb Mader
Jeff Goode
Jackey Hankard-Brodie
Paul Westman
Zacc Pelter
Debi Sateren

If we've missed anyone, please let us know!

Editor
The Skyhunter Editing Team

LMBPN Publishing
PMB 196, 2540 South Maryland Pkwy
Las Vegas, NV 89109

Version 1.00, August 2021
ISBN (ebook) 978-1-68500-428-6
ISBN (paperback) 978-1-68500-429-3

DEDICATION

For my mom ... who let me 'RePeat' so many of my mistakes

—Ramy Vance

To Family, Friends and
Those Who Love
to Read.
May We All Enjoy Grace
to Live the Life We Are
Called.

— Michael

CHAPTER ONE

Earth-Z
(Where the twisted, older Rueben-Z is from)

"Run!" Rueben-Z shouted.

"What have you gotten us into?" Rueben yelled as he concentrated on hopping across the tops of the cars across the street. Rueben-Z was in front of him, leading the way, and Buzz was behind him, panting.

Some of the car roofs and hoods dented when they stepped on them. One time, Buzz cried out behind Rueben and almost fell, but Rueben caught him, and together they rushed forward after Rueben-Z.

Behind them, the sloughing sound of dust continued to slide over the empty cars lining the New York City street like a dry waterfall.

"This was supposed to be a simple sample grab!" Buzz said. "Not a horror movie!"

"Can we kill that thing?" Rueben yelled. He gripped a

semiautomatic rifle, but he wasn't about to turn and use it when he needed to focus on running.

Rueben-Z called over his shoulder as he leapt to the next car. "Nah. But bullets hurt it. Once we chase it off, you can grab your sample."

Buzz gulped. "We're gonna die."

Up ahead, on the sidewalk on the other side of the car-clogged street, Rueben-Z abruptly stopped and turned, tilting his machine gun up. "No one's dying today." He gritted his teeth as his gun spat bullets.

Rueben grabbed Buzz by the wrist and yanked him off the last car and onto the sidewalk.

Buzz gasped. "That man is crazy."

Rueben sucked in air as he stopped to glance back at the monster pursuing them. His mind referred to it as a monster because that's what it looked like: a giant panther of dust with hollow eye sockets and teeth and claws. It didn't move like a monster though—it was too fast, too fluid. It cascaded over the tops of the cars like a raging rapid. Before that, it had descended from the sky like a storm cloud. A massive, sentient storm cloud.

Rueben considered raising his rifle, but he didn't trust his aim after sprinting over the cars. As Rueben and Buzz caught their breath and glanced behind them, Rueben-Z's bullets punched into the dust monster in a roaring stream. Dust-like material sprayed up from the monster's skin where the slugs impacted, and its giant beast-like head writhed and turned as it approached. The thing took up nearly the entire width of the street. It was huge.

"Can you explain this?" Rueben shouted to Buzz as he gripped his best friend's shirt and tugged him down an alley. He could shoot later if he had a chance to rest a moment.

Now, it was in their best interest to keep moving. "Is it alive?"

Buzz shook his head. "It shouldn't be. This is amazing. And pants-shittingly terrifying."

Rueben breathed hard as they ran down the alley. The gunfire behind them had stopped, only to be replaced by Rueben-Z shouting for them to run faster.

"The virus," Buzz continued, out of breath, "must have found a way to transmute into different forms. Based on how it interacts with Rueben-Z's blood, and how it feeds on time warps, who only knows how many times it's mutated since it first devoured this Earth..."

Rueben-Z sprinted between them and threw his arms out wide to grab Rueben and Buzz by the shoulders. He must have tossed his machine gun to the side when he ran out of bullets. "Keep moving. It's wounded."

Rueben snuck a glance over his shoulder. "Doesn't look like it." As he said that, he noticed the black goo trailing down the creature's dusty hide. Was it the monster's version of blood?

Rueben-Z smirked. "Oh, I hurt it. It's pissed." Then Rueben-Z retracted his hands from Rueben's and Buzz's shoulders and sprinted ahead of them, not winded in the slightest. "Try to keep up. We've got it on the run."

Buzz and Rueben exchanged glances and struggled to pick up their pace. "That future parallel version of you is a real badass," Buzz said.

"I know. I kind of hate him."

Rueben might have been a time warper, but he was also lanky and out of shape. And this was the longest alley ever. *I'm going to start running after this is all over...*

From ahead of them, near the end of the alley, Rueben-Z

called, "My grandma runs faster than the two of you combined. And she's dead."

Rueben considered stopping, raising his rifle, and blowing the man away. Or lobbing one of the grenades jangling in his pockets. Buzz awkwardly cradled a pistol in his hands as he ran beside him. Judging by the look on his face, the scientist was thinking the same thing.

"This is why I don't go in the field," Buzz said. "From here on out, I'm staying in the lab."

"Oh, come on," Rueben said between panting breaths, snapping out of his funk. "You enjoy this a little. We're basically superheroes."

"I'm not the one who can warp backward in time if we die."

"Are you forgetting that I can't warp now? Now that we know the monster feeds on time warps."

"We don't know if it feeds on your time warps—only Rueben-Z's time warps because he's infected. I have to run some more tests to confirm first. When I get back to the safety. Of. My. Lab."

They rounded the corner at the end of the alley and came out on a sidewalk. Rueben-Z had stopped there and waved them on while he pulled out two grenade pins with his teeth and spat them to the side. "Take that," he grunted as he tossed the grenades, then annoyingly caught back up to Buzz and Rueben as if it was nothing.

"How much farther do we have to run?" Rueben tried to keep up with Rueben-Z as they raced down the sidewalk.

Twin explosions rocked the city behind them, and a monstrous howl split the air.

"Not much farther. There's a place up ahead where we can make our last stand."

Buzz gasped. "Last stand? This wasn't supposed to be a suicide mission."

"Oh, I don't plan on dying," Rueben-Z said. "Between the three of us, we have enough firepower to scare that thing off. See, I think it feels pain, the same as us."

Rueben shook his head. "How? And why does it bleed?"

Rueben-Z cracked his knuckles. "If it bleeds, we can kill it," he said in an Arnold Schwarzenegger accent.

Rueben's eyes widened. "Earth-Z has an Arnold Schwarzenegger?"

"You mean the Terminator? Hell yeah. In our universe, he becomes president." Rueben-Z scratched his chin. "Come to think of it, that could still happen on Earth-A."

Buzz shook his head. "Focus, guys. To answer your question, I don't know why it bleeds. Evolution shit. My best guess, the time virus found a way to manipulate the dead 'dust' cells of the withered life it killed. Then developed a sense of unity or hive consciousness or something."

"I'm no scientist," Rueben said, "but that's not how viruses work."

Buzz coughed to clear his throat. "I am a scientist. Sometimes discoveries are made, and science contradicts itself."

Rueben-Z scoffed. "In case you haven't noticed, this ain't your garden-variety virus. Pretty sure it was man-made. It's the only thing that makes sense."

Rueben shook his head. "Sounds too science fiction-y to me."

"I don't know," Buzz said. "It would make sense if the designer of the virus was familiar with Repeaters. But only a handful of people know about Repeaters, let alone how their time-warping powers work."

They were approaching an overturned semi lying perpendicular to the street. Behind it, a row of crashed cars formed a makeshift step up to the semi's long metal flank. Rueben-Z climbed atop it. "Enough talk, boys. Time to blow shit up."

The dust monster was nowhere in sight, but judging by its agonized howl, it was still coming for them, careening down the alley.

They all clambered up on top of the overturned semi and waited, crouching as they laid out their extra gun magazines and grenades before them. The grenades all had a tiny yellow LED on them. Were these some kind of special Earth-Z grenades? Even with all the weapons at their disposal, Rueben doubted they could wound the monster enough to make it flee. From their spot, it was a good hundred yards to the alley's opening, and they had a perfect view of the entire length.

"Catch your breath while you can. Don't fire until you have a good shot. We can't afford to waste any ammo." Rueben-Z looked like a mercenary or soldier as he unslung the two submachine guns from his shoulders and trained them down the street.

Rueben was glad the man was here, but not so much about the part about Rueben-Z knowing what they were walking into when they arrived here. "Why didn't you tell us?"

"Tell you what?" Reuben-Z growled. He set down one of his guns to line up his grenades on the surface in front of him.

"About the friggin' monster that awaited us when we traveled back here."

Rueben-Z shrugged. "Oh, that. Well, you needed a sample of the super-evolved virus. That thing has your sample."

"It's a sentient monster dust cloud."

"Meh. An obstacle to overcome. Nothing more."

"An obstacle?" Rueben said.

A bestial howl erupted from the alley's opening. Buzz glanced down at the pistol shaking in his hands.

Rueben-Z grunted. "It's not gonna bite you. The safety is already off. All you gotta do is point and aim. And pull the trigger."

Buzz gulped.

"Line up the top sights, and you got this. I've seen your shooting before—well, this Earth's version of you. You're a natural killer."

Rueben flashed Buzz a look to show his agreement.

"It's coming…" Buzz's words were soft.

Rueben-Z picked up his other submachine gun. "Look alive, boys."

Earth-A
(Where our Rueben is from)

"You think I'm paranoid, don't you?"

Aki shook her head, turned her attention away from Martha, and returned to the live satellite feed she was viewing in Buzz's lab. "No. It's just that they've only been gone for a few minutes."

Martha sighed. "You're probably right. I'm sure they have everything under control."

"Of course." Aki drummed her fingers on the desk. "Rueben and Buzz are accompanied by a parallel-Earth-twenty-years-older Rueben doppelgänger that we've very uncreatively named Rueben-Z…"

"Ugh." Martha grabbed her head in her hands. "Now you have me worried about that variable. You don't think Rueben-Z will try anything funny, do you?"

"There's no way to tell." Aki's smirk tightened as her eyes focused on a portion of the satellite feed showing the Catskill Mountains in upstate New York. With pursed lips, she zoomed in on a cluster of trees on one of the green-covered rocky slopes.

"Oh, shit." Martha leaned in over Aki's shoulder for a better look at the screen. "Did the time virus escape the lab after all?"

"I…don't know."

A cluster of trees gently swayed as if swept by a strong wind.

Martha nudged Aki's shoulder. "What are we looking at? Besides trees."

They both watched for a few moments, but nothing happened.

"I don't know. I guess it was nothing."

"Well, what did you think you saw?"

Aki sighed. "I thought I saw some trees disintegrating. You know, withering away into dust like how we saw in Buzz's greenhouse experiment."

"And?" Martha prodded.

"You can see for yourself. There's no rampant spreading. No outward expanding circle of withering death. I think we're in the clear." Aki wiped her forehead while Martha continued to stare at the screen.

"These trees on the side do look a little funny. Almost like a part of them was chopped off."

Aki chuckled nervously. "Don't take this the wrong way, but I think we're seeing things."

Martha stared for a bit longer at the odd-looking trees and drew a deep breath. She stood to her full height, then sank into a chair. "Yeah."

The two women sat in silence for a few minutes, watching the satellite feed and seeing no sign of the virus. Even if they did see virus activity, there wasn't much they could do. The virus was all-consuming and fed on all living things, instantly withering them and rendering them to dust. If the virus had somehow survived, this world was done for.

Aki continued their conversation as if they hadn't had an interruption. "There's nothing to worry about. They all took Buzz's time virus vaccine. According to Rueben-Z, Earth-Z is all dust. What's the worst that can happen to them?"

Martha sighed. "Yeah, you're probably right. I'm sure they have everything under control."

CHAPTER TWO

<u>Earth-Z</u>

With a screeching cry, the monster burst from the mouth of the alley. It had to condense itself to fit through the alley, but it now enlarged as it emerged. Dust scraped off the sides of the passage, sprinkling to the sidewalk and asphalt like sloughed off dead skin. Maybe it was only Rueben, but he thought he saw tentacles flapping above the monster's back and sides.

The monster's hollowed-out eye sockets tightened as they locked in on their position. Then it opened its dark, dusty maw and howled.

It surged forward.

"That form," Buzz said hurriedly, his scientist's brain taking over as he gripped the pistol in a two-handed grip. "How curious that the virus is posing as a…Cthulhu panther or something—"

"Let's save the philosophical waxing for the after-party, shall we?" Reuben-Z said. "Now. Fire!"

They let loose with everything they had, and for what it

appeared, their shots were taking a toll on the beast. Black goo spilled out from the wounds that racked its dusty hide.

It pressed onward.

Rueben fired his rifle with precise shots, striking the monster in the facial area. He hit it in the nose, the cheek, the forehead, and even in the eye socket. Rueben-Z's spray of submachine gun fire ripped along the creature's bulging neck, shoulders, and front legs, while Buzz was firing away at the incoming monster, most likely missing with each shot even considering the monster's size.

It was now almost halfway to them. It was moving much slower than it had been, almost dragging itself along. Were they going to be able to defeat it?

The first to run out of ammo was Rueben-Z. He deftly reloaded each submachine gun and then brought one up to begin firing again. Buzz's handgun emptied next, but the genius didn't seem to notice as he kept pulling the trigger long after he'd run out. When Rueben's rifle emptied, he ejected the magazine and shoved in a replacement, firing until the creature started to get dangerously close to their position. Still, it charged toward them in sporadic limps and bursts of speed. Although wounded, the beast threw up its head and blasted them with an enraged howl that made Buzz drop his gun.

"Shit!" Rueben muttered. Maybe this fight wasn't almost over after all…

He had reached the end of his second magazine when Rueben-Z called, "Grenade time!"

Black goo drenched the monster's entire front side. It screamed and pushed on.

Rueben-Z ripped out the pins from two grenades and lobbed them into the monster's path.

Rueben did the same, hoping that Buzz wouldn't fumble and blow them up. They had only one shot at this, or else Rueben would have to warp back in time, and he didn't know if that was safe yet or not.

Rueben-Z threw two more grenades. Buzz managed to fling one, but it was such a terrible throw it was comical even given the dire circumstances.

Chuckling, Rueben-Z continued to chuck grenades. Rueben and Buzz did their best to keep up. Directly in front of them, the monster was nearly right on them, its torso and back end trailing back to the alley it was so big. Dark tendrils whipped wildly above its body like something from a nightmare. Suddenly, Rueben realized that none of the grenades had gone off yet. Were they defective?

With the monster looming up right in front of them now, they were screwed.

Rueben-Z turned to them and ordered in a drill instructor's intense tone, "Get the fuck down!"

The grenades went off seemingly all as one as the monster's head swooped over the semi right toward them.

Rueben clenched his teeth. Then his body was shoved sideways off the semi as about a ton of dust collapsed upon him and Buzz and Rueben-Z, completely burying them on the street below.

***

Dust covered the street like a dune.

A moment later, Rueben's hand shot up through the pile. His fingers searched the air as another hand reached down and gripped the flailing wrist, ripping Rueben up from the grainy depths.

Rueben coughed to expel the dust from his lungs as he watched Rueben-Z calmly drop to his knees and start digging beside where Rueben had been. Eventually, Rueben-Z glanced up at Rueben, irritation on his face. "You gonna help?"

Buzz.

Rueben dropped and started to scoop the dust aside. It wasn't long until they'd uncovered Buzz's shoulder and arm. With a grunt, Rueben-Z grabbed Buzz under the arm and hauled him up and on top of the dune. Black goo spotted the giant dust pile. Fortunately, it didn't have a smell, considering it was a mass of withered, dead organisms infected by the time virus.

Buzz sat up and sputtered, spitting out a glob of the black goo. "What the hell is this stuff?" he whined.

"The virus' equivalent of blood," Rueben-Z said.

"It's messed up, is what it is." Buzz straightened his shirt collar. Then childlike glee showed in his eyes as he ran his hands through the dune. "Wait, what am I saying? This is incredible. I must study it—"

His words cut off as Rueben-Z smacked him on the top of the head like a misbehaving dog. "No time. Grab a sample. Quick."

"Huh? What's the rush?" Buzz said. "The monster is gone."

The dust pile they were standing in was starting to shiver.

Rueben shook his head. "Looks like we're still in that horror movie after all."

"I'm going to be sick." Buzz drew a glass vial with a locking rubber cap on it from his pocket. Luckily it hadn't broken. He wasted no time in scooping up some of the dust into the vial, twisting the cap back on, and pulling the extra rubber cover down over the seal.

The dust all around them no longer shivered but tremored like an earthquake.

Rueben turned to Rueben-Z. "Now what? We fight it all over again?"

Rueben-Z scoffed. "I don't know about you, but I'm down to my combat knife. No. We run."

"Run?" Buzz and Rueben both whined.

"Back to the space and time capsule. Follow me."

They reached the space and time capsule, a metal and glass dimension-traveling vehicle reminiscent of something out of *Superman*. It would take them back to Earth-A and safety, for the moment at least.

They popped the lid and climbed inside as the dust monster howled from a few blocks behind them. They were strapping themselves in when the monster burst around the street corner and rushed toward them in a giant writhing mass.

"Where are we going?" Rueben asked as he shut the lid above them with a *click*. Beside him, Rueben-Z punched in a command on the center console. The capsule started to vibrate. Through the glass lid, the time virus monster hurtled toward them in the shape of a massive sharp-toothed jaw. The vehicle winked out of existence.

Earth-A

The lid *clicked* open, and the fluorescent light of Buzz's lab washed over them.

As Rueben climbed out, Buzz was saying, "Oh, home sweet

home," over and over again. Rueben stumbled out and caught himself against the side of the capsule as Aki rushed over to him.

"Are you okay?"

The warmth of her hands steadying him felt so comforting. "Yeah. We're fine—"

"You're bleeding." Aki pointed at Rueben's scraped arms and cheek. She straightened his shirt, and dust fell to the lab floor. "What is that?"

"Oh, only the time virus." Rueben ran a hand back through his hair. "We kind of…got attacked." He whipped his gaze over at Rueben-Z, who had silently exited the space and time capsule and was rummaging through his futuristic body armor laid out on one of the lab tables.

Aki gave Rueben an incredulous look. "There were survivors on Earth-Z?"

"The time virus is the only survivor," Buzz clarified. He raised a hand. "Don't ask me the specifics right now. Or why there was oxygen for us to breathe without any trees. I have much to study."

"Study?" Rueben said. "You're not coming back to Earth-Z with Rueben-Z and me to collect the ground zero virus sample?"

"Fuck that." Buzz lovingly cradled the sample of the super-evolved virus in his hands. "I think you two have it covered."

Rueben glanced down at the dust filtering onto the lab's floor from their clothes. "Speaking of being covered, this stuff isn't going to come to life, right?"

Buzz scratched his head and studied the vial in his hand. The dust sample was swirling around violently inside the glass. He turned his gaze back to the dust on the floor, which looked like dust. "Guess not. The world hop must have reverted the active virus to dormant, or maybe it killed it outright since the Earth-Z host was already dead."

"So creepy," Martha said, entering the room. "I was in the bathroom. What did I miss?"

Rueben patted some more dust from his pants. "Where to start? A giant time monster attacked us—"

"Can we save the memoir for after we grab the other sample?" Rueben-Z impatiently interrupted as he climbed back into the space and time capsule.

"Can't we wait a minute?"

"Best we get this done as soon as possible. Don't want the virus mutating further and finding a way to hop worlds on its own now, do we?"

"Okay, okay." Rueben turned to Buzz. "You got any more of those special glass vials?"

Buzz indicated the capsule, and Rueben-Z raised a padded bag containing two vials.

"One for each of you," Buzz said. "In case something happens to one of them."

Rueben nodded.

Buzz continued, "The virus at ground zero might not be visible to the human eye like this super-evolved dust version of it. In fact, you might have to swab a sample up and put that in the vial. I don't know, though. Maybe you'll get lucky, and ground zero will be a biohazard spill or something visible."

"How will we know where ground zero is?" Rueben asked.

"The virus detector should light up like crazy," Buzz said.

Rueben-Z raised the cell phone-sized, Gauss meter-like device in one hand while he irritably tapped the space and time capsule's center console. "Yes, yes. We already know that. Now can we please get going?"

Rueben turned to leave but faced Aki before he got in. "I

love you, and I'll be back." For a moment he got lost in her dark eyes. Then they kissed, long and hard. He didn't want to leave her.

When he pulled back from her, he saw the same longing in her eyes.

"You sure you have to go back?" she asked. "What if something goes wrong and you can't return to this Earth?"

Rueben looked down at the floor, then back at her. "I'll be okay. I wish there were another way, but we have to get the other virus sample so we can destroy the virus."

"I know." Aki reached up and trailed a finger through Rueben's hair. "Seriously, be safe. Okay?"

Rueben nodded with a smile. Then he got into the capsule. As he was harnessing himself in, Buzz stepped forward again.

"Some important cautions before you go back to Earth-Z and warp back to find ground zero. Whatever you do, do NOT engage with young Rueben-Z or anyone else who's part of Team Z. You could inadvertently affect the future timeline on Earth-Z. Okay? Got it? No visiting Earth-Z's version of ourselves."

Rueben nodded seriously. Buzz turned to Rueben-Z.

"Yeah, yeah," Rueben-Z said. "Scout's honor and all that bullshit."

Rueben shook his head. "It's okay. I'll look after Rueben-Z. He might not have told us about the virus monster waiting for us on Earth-Z, but he did save our asses. I'm not sure we would've gotten that first sample without his help. Anything else we need to be wary of?"

"Yes," Buzz said. "Absolutely NO warping until I finish some tests."

Rueben-Z smirked. "I thought you guys took away my

warping powers." He laughed. It annoyed Rueben. Hopefully, he didn't kill Rueben-Z on this little mission.

Buzz disregarded Rueben-Z. "No warping. Okay? Under no circumstances can you die and warp backward until I do my testing. We want to undo this virus—not mutate it further! Can you imagine if the virus learned how to warp back in time?"

"Got it," Rueben said. "How about we formally add two more rules to 'Buzz's Rules for Repeaters:' one, no dying for either of us, especially Rueben-Z, and two, no dying."

Buzz scratched his forehead. "Buddy, that's only one rule."

Rueben chuckled. "Yeah, but you know, *Fight Club*? The two rules, but they were the same thing."

"I don't have time to watch frivolous movies," Buzz scoffed.

Rueben tapped his fingers on his lap, turning serious again. He swallowed. "This 'no warping thing' sucks big time." He caught Martha's eye from across the room next to the monitor displaying the satellite feed. "Hey, how do things topside look? The virus still isn't on this Earth, right?"

The brief look of concern that Martha and Aki exchanged worried Rueben, but then the two women smiled and shook their heads.

"All good, babe," Aki said.

Martha scratched behind her head. "Yep. Thought we saw something earlier, but it was nothing. Just some weird trees."

Whew. "That's good to hear."

"Can we stop talking and start hopping?" Rueben-Z growled.

"Oh, and one more thing," Buzz said. "Once you hop to Earth-Z and time jump back to before the tanker incident in the space and time capsule, if for some reason shit hits the fan, you two are basically on your own. To get a message to us, you'll need to go to Earth-Z's version of the *Paper Warriors* newspaper office and send a message out to all the worlds by punching the green button."

"Green button?" Rueben asked.

"Yeah. I called the *Paper Warriors* office yesterday. Man, those workers are complete morons. Don't even know how the printing press works. They make copies of the papers it spits out from other worlds and sell them.

"What I was able to ascertain from both your and their descriptions of the machine, all you have to do is make sure the date and time configuration is set for today on Earth-A and presumably, hit the green button." Buzz scribbled down the current Earth-A date and time, adding a few hours for Carolyn and Marshall to arrive at the newspaper office. "Also, my tests should be conclusive by then on whether or not you can safely start warping again."

Rueben nodded. "Good to know. I never thought I'd say this, but I'm itching to die."

His friends all made sour faces.

"It's okay," Rueben said. "We don't plan on anything going wrong."

"No one ever does," Buzz said. "No one ever does."

Rueben-Z growled and turned to Rueben. "Ready, cowboy?"

Rueben bid his team a final goodbye and reached up to close the capsule's lid.

"Remember, no warping and NO interacting with yourselves."

Rueben-Z smirked at Buzz. "That sounded...dirty."

Everyone in the lab shook their heads as the space and time capsule's lid clicked closed.

"Why?" Martha asked, her voice muffled by the glass lid. "What would happen if they interacted with their Earth-Z selves?"

"That," Buzz said, "could mess up the future on Earth-Z, which could in turn have consequences in regards to how the virus first infected Rueben-Z. Also, it sounds like a bad idea. We don't know if there could be any other consequences we haven't thought of. Stay away from Earth-Z's versions of ourselves unless it's the absolute last option. Okay?"

From inside the capsule, Rueben nodded. Aki rushed forward and pressed her palm against the capsule's outer glass window, and Rueben matched hers against his side of the glass. For a long moment, they met each other's eyes. Then Buzz pulled Aki backward.

The space and time capsule began to vibrate.

Then it was gone.

C H A P T E R   T H R E E

Earth-Z

With Rueben-Z operating the controls, they hopped first to Earth-Z's present time—which was twenty years in the future by Earth-A's standards—and promptly warped back in time on Earth-Z before the time virus monster could find them.

At least, that's what Rueben-Z had said he was doing. Pitch blackness pressed in on the glass lid of the capsule.

"Are you sure you know what you're doing?" Rueben asked. "You didn't warp us back to before the Big Bang or something, did you?"

"Ha. Ha. We're good."

Rueben waited as the capsule's vibrations ceased. He tried to discern where they were through the glass lid, but he still couldn't see anything. Were they inside a building or a thick forest at night or something? What the hell?

He turned to Rueben-Z. "What did you do? Is this some trick? What happened?"

Rueben-Z laughed. "Don't get your panties in a bind. We're good."

"We're good? What the hell is that supposed to mean? Where are we—" Suddenly, a fat drop of sludgy water smacked the top of the capsule's glass lid. Another drop fell, then another.

Rueben-Z smirked as he withdrew two penlights from his pants pockets.

Rueben accepted his light and played it at the windshield. They were in a dark, stone-walled enclosure and brownish liquid was dripping on top of them. "Are we in a sewer?"

"Very perceptive. Yes. We are."

"That's disgusting."

"It's also one of the safest places we could store the space and time capsule. We don't want people snooping around it, now do we? If they tampered with it, you could be trapped here. Nobody's coming down in this section of the sewer except the rats."

Rueben scratched behind his head. It was a rather smart place to appear in the past on Earth-Z. It would have completely blown their cover if they had appeared on the sidewalk somewhere as they had on present-day Earth-Z. "If I get shit dripped on my head when I climb out of this capsule…"

Rueben-Z made a dismissive gesture. "Look, if you decide to stay in this line of work on your Earth when this is all over, you'll have a lot worse than shit dripped on your head."

"What's that supposed to mean?"

"Shit isn't so bad, is what I mean. Now shut up and get out. Don't forget to take the virus detector and your glass vial."

Rueben growled. Who did this prick think he was, taking control like this?

"Don't forget—this is my Earth," Rueben-Z said as if reading Rueben's mind. "I know my way around better than you. You might want to follow my lead."

Rueben raised a hand irritably. "You're the biggest..." He let his breath out in a big sigh. "Fine. You get to lead. As long as you remember what Buzz said: absolutely no interaction with your old friends and family. They can't know we're here or the virus timeline might get messed up beyond repair."

Rueben-Z nodded solemnly and made an X gesture across his chest. "Cross my heart and hope to die, yada, yada, etcetera. Now come on."

"Wait," Rueben said. "We went back to before the tanker incident. So how many years ahead in the future are we, compared to Earth-A?"

"About fifteen years. Now come on."

They popped the lid and climbed out of the capsule. Rueben grabbed the virus detector and his vial and handed Rueben-Z his vial. Luckily the equipment was small and easily concealable in their clothes.

Clothes... As he closed the space and time capsule's lid, Rueben briefly wondered what people wore on Earth-Z since they were technically fifteen years in the future in regard to Earth-A. Ahead of him, Rueben-Z lit the way through the sewer with his penlight.

"Coming, Princess?"

Fuck this guy. Rueben hurried after the man.

"Where are we going?" Rueben observed the stone of the sewer tunnel as they walked. So far, Earth-Z looked the same as Earth-A. Not that Rueben ever frequented the sewers on

Earth-A, but it looked like an ordinary sewer. He wondered if the people on Earth-Z would look different. Would there be any other differences here since the timeline on Earth-Z was twenty years ahead of Earth-A?

"First off," Rueben-Z said, "we're going to get a change of clothes. Then we're going to follow up on a lead as to where ground zero might be."

Rueben scoffed. "We just got here, and you already have a plan? And a lead?"

"I've been at this for a long time."

"Being an asshole?"

"Hah. Funny. What I mean is I'm well trained and know how to run a good op. It's something you'll eventually learn if you stay with the CIA. Also, Aki will teach you a lot too. Being a Special Agent, she has a lot of experience."

Rueben-Z sighed and added almost as an afterthought, "The other thing I mean is that I've been planning for this day for a long time. I knew that once I found a Buzz on a parallel Earth that could help me defeat the time virus, I'd have to eventually come back to Earth-Z before the virus' wanton destruction. Let's just say you're lucky to have me. I have all my ducks in a row."

Rueben ran one of his hands along the perspiring stone wall beside him. "I'll have to take your word for it. For all I know, you're stringing me along. Bullshitting me."

Rueben-Z turned and faced Rueben in the dim sewer, their penlights the only source of light. He jabbed his finger into Rueben's chest. "This mission is about saving my family. I don't bullshit about family."

"Okay. Okay. Lead on. It's just, how do you know we're far enough back in this Earth's timeline before the time virus mutates? How far back did you even go?" Rueben-Z had insisted on manning the controls since he was the only one of them who had ever piloted a space and time capsule.

Rueben-Z started walking. "Buzz said he thinks my infection most likely took place before the tanker mission, which is the first distorted place in my nanobot footage. Today is currently five days prior—"

"You think that's enough time? What if the incubation period is longer than five days? What if young Rueben-Z is already infected?"

Rueben-Z spun. "Don't question me. All right? And can we stop referring to me or this Earth's younger version of me as Rueben-Z? It's degrading."

"What do you want me to call you? If we each call each other Rueben, that might get confusing."

"How about God?"

"What about RZ?" Rueben asked.

Rueben-Z considered it. He laughed. "Simple. And badass, like me. How about we go with Z? And we call this Earth's younger version of me Young Z?"

"Those sound like rapper names."

"Who said I'm not a rapper?" Z gave a tight sneer.

"Me. Because I'm you and I don't rap."

"Please," Z barked. "You're a parallel knockoff of me. We're not the same person. We're from different worlds, with our own destinies."

Rueben crossed his arms. "Whatever, asshole. Prove it."

"What? That I can rap? I don't have to prove shit to you."

Rueben made a fist and released it. "Can we please keep moving?"

"No."

"No?"

Z pointed at a metal ladder welded against the sewer's stone wall. "We're here."

They replaced the heavy sewer grate at the top and surveyed the room they were in. Rueben thought they might emerge on the street somewhere, but they were in a dark room filled with pipes, ventilation shafts, and HVAC equipment.

"Where are we?"

"Follow my lead, okay?"

"I don't like blindly following a man who once kidnapped me, put me in a coma, and locked me in a basement for three days."

"Can we let bygones be bygones?"

"No!"

Z threw his hands up. "I was out of my mind. Okay? The time disease was screwing me up inside. You want to blame me for my actions? Fine. But it's all spilled milk."

"That's rich," Rueben said.

"That's rich," Z mimed.

"Asshole."

"Bitch."

Rueben growled, and Z laughed. "I'll toughen you up yet—"

Rueben lunged forward with a fist, and Z easily caught it and shoved it to the side. Z had an easy opening but didn't take it. Rueben, however, followed up with a surprise left hook and caught Z on the mouth.

Z pulled back his lips to reveal blood sluicing over the whites of his teeth. He swallowed the blood. "Nice one. I deserved that—"

Rueben took another swing. Z sidestepped and caught the fist, maneuvering behind Rueben and twisting his arm up. When Rueben grunted, Z chuckled. "I'll let you have that first one. But you're not going to get another one. We're on the same team, remember?"

Don't remind me, Rueben thought. This mission couldn't be over soon enough for him. He hoped he didn't kill Z first.

There was a metal door up ahead. Z stepped toward it and placed his hand on the knob. "You ready to meet Earth-Z?" He threw open the door.

CHAPTER FOUR

Earth-Z

People milled past the door in dense groups. Families. Teenagers. Mall cops.

"Mall cops?" Rueben squinted against the sunlight pouring in through the skylight. "Your sewer exit led us here? We're in a mall?"

"What better place to get clothes so we can fit in?" Z inhaled deeply. "Ah. The smell of giant soft pretzels, fresh baked cookies, and—"

"Overpriced kiosk perfumes?"

"You're no fun." Z entered the throng of people coursing back and forth in the mall complex.

Rueben recognized the layout of this exact mall from Earth-A, but most of the stores had different names—not surprising considering they were fifteen years into the future. Also, this was a parallel Earth so there were bound to be some small differences.

He turned his attention to the people and noticed most wore

fashionable jogging-style pants and form-fitting hooded jackets. Many of them wore sleek-looking sunglasses even though they were inside a building. Rueben glanced down at his and Z's clothes, which had been contemporary on Earth-A. Yeah, dressed like this, they'd only draw attention to themselves.

Z seemed to know where he was going so Rueben followed him through the mall until he stopped in front of a soft pretzel vendor tucked into the wall. Z turned to Rueben. "Buy me a pretzel, will you?"

"I'm not buying you a—"

Z thrust out his hand and dropped some bills into Rueben's hands. "Get you something too. Don't want to work a mission on an empty stomach, right?"

Rueben felt there was something more to the request. Was this a test? "We need clothes. Not food."

Z shook his head. "First food. Then clothes."

Rueben sensed he wasn't going to be able to reason with the man so he stepped up to the pretzel vendor.

"What can I getcha?" a teenage boy asked from behind the stand. He wore a red and white striped uniform, a red baseball cap, and a cheesy smile.

"Two pretzels."

The boy grinned as he grabbed some parchment paper to wrap around the pretzels. "You want some hot cheese dipping sauce for 'em?"

Rueben glanced at the order sign to make sure he had enough money in his hand for the two pretzels. As long as the sales tax on Earth-Z was about the same as on Earth-A, he'd be fine. "No. Just the two pretzels."

"You got it, sir. Two fresh warm pretzels, coming your way." The boy negotiated two of the pretzels from their metal rotating perches and into paper wrappers. He told Rueben the price.

"Geez, tax really went up, didn't it?" Rueben said. He barely had enough money.

When he tried to hand it over, the boy chuckled. "Nice joke." When Rueben didn't pull his hand back, the boy's smile faltered. "But it does get rather old. A few people try that every week."

"Um…"

The boy's face now turned serious. "You can pay for these, right? You've got a digi-card?"

A digi-what? Rueben turned back to Z, who had conveniently disappeared. An older woman who'd stepped in line behind him pushing a baby stroller held up a plastic card. "Digital money. Cash went out of style over a decade ago. Get with the times. And hurry up—Grandma's hungry."

Silently cursing, Rueben apologized to the pretzel kid and walked off, hoping the boy wouldn't call mall security on him. He should have known better than to trust Z.

Speaking of Z, where the hell was he? Once he was a safe distance away from the pretzel vendor, Rueben stopped walking and surveyed the mall's interior for any sign of Rueben-Z. There were too many people milling around as well as potted plants and ornamental trees in the mall's center aisle. He didn't see the man anywhere.

Then he had a thought. Before they had gotten into the space and time capsule for the first time, Buzz had given Rueben and Z a tracking chip so that they could find each other in case they got separated in a dust storm or something on Earth-Z.

He drew his smartphone from his pocket and was unsurprised that he had no cell service—he was on a different Earth after all. But that wasn't what he needed right now. He opened Buzz's "tracker" app and watched his screen as two tiny red dots flashed on a sonar-like display. One of the dots was him, and the other was Z. The man was close, somewhere off to his right.

Rueben started walking in the direction of Z's tracker blip, ignoring the weird looks that people gave his clothes and the archaic smartphone he was holding in his hand. A teenage girl laughed and pressed on the display of her wristwatch. A hologram of another girl popped up over the watch, and the two girls shared a laugh.

Ignoring them, Rueben continued toward the red blip, stepping under the entrance alcove of some expensive-looking surfer-style clothing store. The entrance was dark, and a lounge chair sat out front beneath the store's name lit up in bright green neon.

The blip on the tracker app was pulsating as if he was right on top of Z. Rueben stepped up to the lounge chair. According to the tracker app, Z ought to be sitting right there...

That's when Rueben spotted the chip sitting on the lounge chair's armrest. Sensing something was wrong, he started to turn, but something hard had already poked against his ribs from behind.

"Your money, or your life," a harsh voice whispered in his ear.

The speaker had muffled it, but Rueben had heard it enough times to know it was Z. He spun, caught Z's arm by the elbow and slammed into him, trying to headbutt the man, but Z pulled back and Rueben's head connected with Z's chin. With a grunt, Z slipped from Rueben's grasp and shoved him through the entrance to the darkened surf store.

Rueben caught himself on a center stand filled with t-shirts. He didn't much care for the darkened interior lit only by green neon lights. He also didn't like the fruity perfume saturating the air. Did people wear that stuff on this Earth? At least there didn't appear to be anyone inside at the moment.

Rueben got his bearings as Z stepped confidently into the store without a sound. Shirts, pants, and surfing memorabilia lined the store's interior.

"I knew I couldn't trust you—" Rueben started, but Z cut him off with a growl.

"It was a joke."

"A joke? A joke?" Off to Rueben's side was a tall *fifteen percent off!* sign connected to a metal post. He picked it up and made to swing it at Z when a man in his early twenties stepped into the darkened store wearing flip-flops, cargo shorts, and an opened button-up shirt. "How can I help—dude! Put down the sign. We don't need those vibes in here."

Z was on Rueben in an instant, his fingers gripping Rueben's wrist like claws, and the sign dropped from his grasp. Z deftly caught it and set it on the floor with a soft clatter. "Sorry about that. My associate—"

Rueben kicked out and struck Z in the crotch, and he bent over.

"Dude! What are you doing? I'm going to get fired…get out. I'm calling security."

Rueben huffed. His eyes darted to the object leaning against the far wall. "Fine by me. I'm going to beat my 'associate' half to death with that surfboard."

"Dude! No, you're gonna get me fired…"

Rueben started toward the wall when Z recovered and sneaked up behind him, jabbing two fingers into the side of his neck. Rueben instantly felt lightheaded and as his legs wobbled, his vision blacked out.

When he woke, he was sitting in a lounge chair. Sickly sweet perfume tickled his nose. He blinked. Z was crouching in front of him.

"You bastard," Rueben started.

"Calm the fuck down. You're gonna get us kicked out of here."

"Yeah, because you tried to give me the slip!"

"Keep your goddamn voice down. People are starting to stare."

Rueben glanced out at the people walking by who had stopped and pointed their watches his way. Most had holograms floating above them with Rueben's and Z's images in them. The devices each had a red flashing light on them, which probably meant they were recording the scene through some kind of camera built into them.

"I wasn't trying to 'give you the slip,' I was testing your reflexes."

"Testing my reflexes?"

"Yeah, you're not supposed to die on this world, remember? You can't let your guard down, even for a moment."

"But we're on the same team—"

Z hushed him. People were still watching them. "Get up and act normal. These simpletons will forget all about you then."

"Me? What about you?"

Z smirked. "I'm not the one who looks drunk before noon."

Rueben clambered to his feet, and the two of them walked off. As Z had said, the people soon grew bored and turned back to their watches or resumed chatting with each other.

Rueben rubbed the back of his neck. "What did you do to me back there in the store?"

"Hit one of your pressure points. Dropped you like a log. I'd show you but then…well, you might get the idea of using it on me."

"I wouldn't have to if you didn't pull stupid surprise stunts like that. You're the worst partner ever."

Z nudged Rueben's arm with his elbow. "I'm the best partner you could have. I know thirty ways to kill a person with a toothpick, I can blend into any crowd, and normally I can warp back in time if I want. I'm the full package deal."

"You're an asshole who's full of himself."

Z stopped walking in front of a clothing store with mannequins in the front window wearing normal-looking casual clothes. "Before we get into another fight, how about we get some clothes so we blend in with the locals?"

"Oh? With what money? Don't tell me you've got a digi-wallet or card or whatever and you're only now telling me."

Looping his thumbs into the pockets of his pants, Z grinned smugly. "I don't. But we need clothes, and we need them now. So you're going to steal them."

CHAPTER FIVE

<u>Earth-Z</u>

"Steal them? I'm not stealing anything. I've never stolen anything before in my life."

"There's a first for everything."

"I'm not a bad guy. I don't break the law."

"You never smoked weed in college? I know I did."

"Look, I'm not doing it. Under no circumstances will I do it."

Z sighed. "Then don't think of it as stealing—think of it as paying with a credit card. I'll pay for your clothes once we save the world from the time virus. If we don't do that, stealing one measly pair of clothes won't matter, will it?"

"One pair? What about your clothes?"

Z scratched his chin. "I'm going to go 'shopping' at another clothing store. This one looks more up your alley."

"Why didn't you steal some clothes from that surfing place?"

"We can't exactly change the past now, can we? Oh, wait..." Z chuckled.

Rueben fidgeted.

"You need to change your perspective. You're not doing this to be a bad guy. You're doing this for your country, for your world. For Aki and the future the two of you might one day have." Z checked his watch. "We're wasting too much time. How about this? I'll show you how to incapacitate with two fingers if you get the clothes."

"Why can't you steal both of our clothes? You're the expert badass commando guy."

After staring at Rueben for a few moments, Z shook his head. "I'm only trying to toughen you up. Give you half a chance at becoming the 'badass' that I am." He paused. "Fine, I thought you'd like to know the two-finger trick. They don't teach it in the CIA..."

"Fine, fine, I'll do it. Then we're going to track down the location of ground zero for the virus."

"That's the plan. Now, after you finish, change in that bathroom over there, and we'll meet up."

Rueben met Z's eyes. "If you try anything funny again..."

"Who, me? Never."

Rueben prepared to exit the clothing store, feeling more than a bit dirty and guilty for what he was about to do. He'd gotten a dark lightweight hooded jacket with an eagle on the front, a pair of jogging pants that looked like jeans, and a sleek pair of sunglasses that everyone seemed to be wearing these days.

He'd never shoplifted before so he tore the tags off and discreetly hid them among the various piles of folded clothes. He thought there might be an anti-theft device in them that only the cashier could remove, but he couldn't find any. Was shoplifting this easy on Earth-Z? Was it this easy on Earth-A?

The store had been moderately crowded so he felt safe that none of the store's employees were watching him as he slid the clothes under his shirt. They were surprisingly thin and didn't extend his stomach too much. Also, he couldn't see any security cameras in the building. That was strange, wasn't it? Should he be doing this?

Before leaving, he checked his phone, and it looked like Z was in the bathroom they'd agreed to meet in. He saw the bathroom across the mall's walkway from inside the clothing store's entrance. He was so close. Still, if an alarm went off as he left, what was he going to do? He wasn't supposed to warp backward in time until Buzz confirmed if it was safe to do so.

Drawing a deep breath, he exited the store, feeling quite sure that this was a trap or trick. When no alarms went off and no employees yelled at him, he drew another breath and strode into the bathroom. Several stalls had occupants, but Rueben couldn't tell if Z was in any of them. He stepped into a vacant one and changed.

When he stepped out dressed in his new pants and jacket and shades, he saw an old hobo leaning against the sinks with his arms folded across his chest. He wore old jeans and a tattered rain jacket with the hood up. A pair of discolored but sleek sunglasses covered his eyes.

"Snazzy," the hobo drawled. "Did you steal those?"

"Huh?" Rueben narrowed his eyes at the hobo and groaned. "Are you serious?"

The hobo threw back his hood to reveal that he was Z. He waved for Rueben to follow him. As they exited the bathroom, Z glanced at R's attire. "I bet those pants feel pretty comfortable."

"They are breathable," Rueben said. "And lightweight. But what the hell? Where did you get your clothes? The dump?"

Z shook his head. "On Earth-Z, there are boxes in most public places for people who have more than they need to donate their clothes and objects for those in need. I fished these out of the box at the front of the mall."

Rueben stared at the man. "You're kidding. Right?"

Z smirked behind his shades. "Nope."

"You made me fucking steal from a store—"

"I didn't *make* you steal anything. I said we needed new clothes and simply suggested that you could steal them. That was an option. Now that I know you're not averse to stealing, I've learned something about you."

"You're the worst person on this Earth!"

"Says the thief."

Rueben made a fist. "I think I'm going to kill you."

"Can we at least wait until we find and collect the ground zero virus sample first?"

Z's sarcasm made Rueben see red. He no longer cared if people were watching or recording him with their fancy high-tech watches. "You know what? I don't think you have a fucking clue where to go next."

"Of course I do." Z checked his watch and made a clicking sound with his mouth. "Follow me."

Z started walking. "Big place, this is. But I know where I'm going." A minute and a half later, he stopped about thirty yards away from the entrance to a Chuck E. Cheese establishment.

"What? This is it? This is your big lead?" Rueben shook his head.

Z meanwhile muttered to himself. "I guess we could go outside and come in through the side entrance...but then...nah." He thumbed his chin. "The fibbie routine might work..." He glanced down at his clothes, then at Rueben's.

"The what?" Rueben asked.

Z walked toward the Chuck E. Cheese entrance. "We'll try it. Come on. Don't mess this up."

Rueben trotted up and fell in line with Z. "Might be hard considering I don't know what we're doing going inside a children's party play area."

"Chuck E. Cheese is a magical place. Or so they say." As they approached the entrance, Z reached into his jacket and withdrew two identical black wallets. He waited until he reached the door and then handed one to Rueben. "Follow my lead."

Z opened the door and stepped inside. For a moment, Rueben felt sick to his stomach from the flashing lights and the smell of sweat and cheese. He couldn't believe he'd ever wanted to come to such a place when he was a kid—not that he'd ever been allowed to. It was too "dangerous."

As Rueben's eyes adjusted to the flashing, brightly colored interior, he fumbled with the wallet Z had given him. "If this is some sort of trick—"

"It's not a trick. Come on."

Rueben had barely managed to open his wallet when someone in a giant rat costume said, "Well, golly gee, welcome to Chuck E. Cheese!"

Z stared at the talking rat.

"Would you...like to schedule an upcoming party?" the rat said.

Z flashed his wallet. "FBI. Detective Wilson." He jerked his head at Rueben. "Detective Brown, he's new. We were off duty. Got called about a possible missing child in the mall. Parents said the child was a big fan of this place." Z paused as he raised a calming hand. "It's probably nothing, but you know, gotta check our bases, especially where kids are concerned."

The rat stammered. "Holy shit. Um, let me get my manager."

"Much appreciated," Z said. "We'll wait right here."

"Um. Right. I'll...go find my manager."

Z nodded politely. When the mascot had disappeared through a side door, Z started forward and waved for Rueben to follow. "Nice job, kid, you didn't botch the job. Now come on."

"You just...and then...what are we..." Rueben closed his fake FBI badge. "Where did you even get these from?"

"My body armor back in Buzz's lab—concealed in a hidden pouch. A good badge comes in handy. Thought we might need them."

"But they're not real. They don't even have our pictures on them."

Z smirked. "The key is the angle of how you flash the badge and the confidence with how you talk. People will believe anything if presented correctly."

"Whatever." Rueben pocketed the badge and slid the virus detector from his other pocket. "I don't see any sign of the virus."

"Oh, it's here."

"Jesus. You think ground zero is in a Chuck E. Cheese? That's demented."

"The world's a demented place."

While Rueben chewed over Z's words, Z held up a hand. "Wait here." Z walked off and disappeared around a corner.

For about a minute, Rueben stood against the wall, staring at the décor. Off to the side, he noticed an emergency exit. He waited another minute and thought, *What the hell am I doing?* and followed Z. He bit his lip when he rounded the corner.

Z was crouched and talking to a little girl. She might have been ten or twelve and appeared to have come from the bathroom. She wore a cone-shaped party hat on her head and an energetic grin. They seemed to be having a deep conversation as if they knew each other, which was good, Rueben supposed, since the alternative was that Z was a pervert. At intervals, Z glanced at a sign on the wall with an arrow pointing down a hallway toward the party room.

Rueben considered what this was all about. Was the girl Z's virus lead? He thought about confronting the two of them but decided to wait off to the side and observe. He cringed when Z pointed back at him, and the little girl waved at him excitedly. Rueben awkwardly waved back.

Z made a gesture for him to come to them, and when Rueben didn't, Z stood and guided the girl his way.

Shit. Was this man abducting the girl?

On instinct, maybe because Z was wearing his sleek sunglasses, Rueben donned his jacket's hood as well as his new shades. Z and the girl chatted as they approached Rueben's position. They had nearly reached him when the sound of footsteps echoed from the direction of the party room.

A woman emerged from the hallway. She walked briskly over to the bathroom door and peeked inside. "Emma? Emma, are you okay?"

Rueben froze. He recognized that voice.

Suddenly, the woman turned his way. She looked about fifteen years older than on Earth-A, but he was certain who it was.

Aki-Z.

CHAPTER SIX

Earth-A

As he waited for his computer to spit out the test results, Buzz could've been sitting on a stool with his chin resting in his hands. Instead, he was standing at another desk, already preparing to run another test. His eyes scanned the monitor as his fingers raced across the keyboard. He was in a flow state.

The first test would show the analysis on whether or not Rueben could safely warp back in time without affecting the time virus. Once he found the answer, he'd call Marshall and Carolyn, who should almost be to the *Paper Warriors* newspaper office. They would then let the Ruebens know on Earth-Z through the intergalactic printing press.

The second test was a deep dive into the super-mutated time virus' evolutionary growth. He was reasonably sure he could find a way to de-evolve it into a harmless form once he had the ground zero virus sample. He hoped to have most of the process mapped out before that. Then, it was only a matter of—

Beep!

Buzz swiveled away from his current computer and darted back to the first one to analyze the results. His eyes widened.

"Oh no. No, no, no…"

Footsteps sounded, and Martha peeked into the lab. "You good?" she asked.

Buzz grimly shook his head. He didn't look up from the results.

"I guess it's still not safe for Rueben to warp?"

"It's not that," Buzz said. "The computer is still working on that. This is something else."

Martha looked worried. "Is this concerning Rueben? Should I go get Aki?"

"No, no. Not Rueben. Well, kinda Rueben, but mostly Rueben-Z. It looks like my initial understanding of time warping is all wrong. I mean, way wrong."

"Go on." Martha gave an impatient wave as she stepped into the lab and leaned against a counter.

"I've had my programs analyzing everything we know about time warpers as well as the time virus. It looks like, well…after time simulations both forward and backward in time…once accounting for real-time—"

"Buzz," Martha said. "Just say it."

Buzz grabbed his head. "I used to think that hopping worlds reset the virus back to dormant. Now I've realized that instead of resetting completely, the virus gains another level of genetic material. Sort of like the rings on a tree."

"Is that bad?"

Buzz heaved a sigh. "It proves that my conception of warping back in time once you're on another parallel Earth is all wrong. Well, it's the space and time capsule that complicates things. To be more precise, time jumping back in time with the capsule. That's the real problem."

"Goddamnit," Martha said. "You mean we have to add another rule to your list of Buzz's Rules for Repeaters?"

"Looks like. I'll have to tack it on to the end. *Rule n+1:* If you use a space and time capsule to hop to your original Earth from another Earth, then time-jump backward to before you initially left in the capsule, you will essentially 'break' the timeline, and there will be an extra copy of yourself, existing outside of space and time."

Martha placed her hands on her hips. "English, please."

"It means, well, Rueben can come back to this point on Earth-A, and everything will be fine. But Rueben-Z, on Earth-Z, well, he's currently a duplicate of himself. Even if he's able to go far enough back in time to fix the virus, he..."

"...won't be able to stay?" Martha finished. "Because there will already be another Rueben in existence."

"Exactly. Shit. I wonder if Rueben-Z knows this. If not, I wonder how he'll take the news. I mean, he can't return to be with his family because the younger version has already replaced him in the timeline."

Martha massaged her temples. "He's a pretty smart guy. My intuition says he already knows."

Now Buzz started to massage his head. "Ugh. The human variable."

"The what?"

Buzz narrowed his eyes at her. "Humans are the hardest living beings to predict behavior for. Unlike most animals, plants, bacteria, fungi, and protozoa, they don't always act in a rational manner."

"You're saying Rueben-Z could go rogue and try to visit

his family on Earth-Z? And screw up the timeline for his world."

For a moment, Buzz didn't say anything. "Yeah. Without his warping powers, the man has only one life to live. He's essentially a loose cannon. To make matters worse, he's the only one who knows how to pilot the space and time capsule. Which means, if he goes rogue, he has my best friend trapped with him on his Earth."

Martha shook her head. "Shit."

CHAPTER SEVEN

<u>Earth-Z</u>

Standing there with Aki-Z squinting at him from across the hall, Rueben was thankful for his hood and sunglasses. They were the only things keeping her from recognizing him and blowing the whole operation.

Still, the hood didn't make him invisible. If anything, it made him look more suspicious.

He couldn't help but notice how sexy Aki-Z looked, even with the tinge of sultry weariness under her eyes. She had longer hair than Aki-A, toned arms, and a flat belly that showed no sign that she'd ever had any children. It stunned Rueben how intoxicated by her presence he was, no matter the Earth he was on. He couldn't wait to spend a life with Aki-A back on Earth-A, hopefully—

Z sprinted up and clapped a hand to Rueben's shoulder, turning him around. "Time to go," he grunted, searching for a way out.

Rueben wanted to punch the man in the face but now

wasn't the time. "Follow me." He took the lead and headed for the emergency exit up ahead. As they ran, he said, "You bastard, you heard what Buzz said about interacting—"

A woman standing near the door cupped her hands over her child's ears and gave him the stink eye. Rueben rushed past her and pushed open the emergency exit. Luckily it was the kind of door that didn't sound an alarm when you opened it. They emerged in an alley.

"You are such a bad influence," Z said.

Rueben glanced left and right. "Oh yeah? I'm blaming you."

"You're blaming yourself?"

Rueben took off down the alley. Up ahead they could duck into a side alley running between two warehouses, but first, they had to navigate past multiple alleyway obstacles. "You said yourself that we're not the same person."

Z shrugged as he kept pace with Rueben. "If it helps you sleep better at night. You dirty thief."

"Fuck you."

"Spoken like a true thief. It's a good thing Aki's into bad guys…"

Rueben hopped over a crate of junk on the ground and entered the side alley between the warehouses. "Speaking of Aki—"

The emergency exit door crashed open from the main alley behind them.

"Who the fuck are you creeps! I'm going to kill you!"

Z grinned. "That's my wife."

Rueben maneuvered around a fire escape ladder. "This is bad. Why the hell did you have to see them? You said this was a lead."

"Calm yourself. How about we get out of here, and I explain."

"Calm myself?" Rueben skirted a large potholed section of the alleyway. "What if younger Rueben-Z—"

"Young Z," Z corrected.

"What if Young Z is back there in Chuck E. Cheese and comes out and warps back in time to stop us before we go inside?"

"A non-issue."

They were nearing the end of the alley. A high chain-link fence blocked it. Twisting to the side, Rueben noticed a warehouse door ajar. The two of them slipped inside, closing the door behind them, right before Aki-Z entered the side alley screaming, "Where the hell are you?"

The warehouse's interior was empty aside from a couple of forklifts, a bunch of metal shelves, and pallets laden with bubble-wrapped products. The workers must've been on their lunch break. "A non-issue?" Rueben whispered as he dashed past a fork truck. His working plan was to hide behind some of the metal shelving.

As if sensing Rueben's plan, Z grabbed his collar and yanked him to the opposite side of the warehouse toward a heap of discarded bunched-up bubble wrap. "It's a non-issue because I'm not in this memory."

Rueben followed Z and waded into the mess of bubble wrap. There was a lot of it, and it was so thick it was nearly opaque. "You missed your daughter's birthday party?"

Z pulled up some bubble wrap, and they both hid underneath it, being careful not to pop any of the plastic bubbles. The several layers of clear wrap on top of them allowed enough light in so that the two Ruebens could faintly see each other but not too far into the warehouse. They could see only the vague outline of the warehouse door to the side alley, and Rueben figured it would get hot under there before long.

Z grunted. "Yeah, okay. I missed my daughter's birthday party. Some tourists got kidnapped down in Havana. I was saving their asses."

"Oh."

"This power. It takes a lot from you. Responsibility and all that."

Shit. Rueben hadn't considered how family life might be impacted by having superhero-like powers. Of course, he didn't have a family yet. This mission was to stop the virus so he could have one back on Earth-A.

There was a *clang* on the other side of the warehouse door, and suddenly it was ripped open, but no one entered. A moment later, Aki-Z darted inside in a crouch, a concealable handgun in her hands. "Where the fuck are you two?" she demanded as her eyes scanned the warehouse's interior. She started toward the far end of the warehouse.

"Man, I love this woman," Z whispered.

"She's going to find us," Rueben said. "Is that what you want? Are you on some personal mission?"

"No. I'm not. She won't find us. I know her."

Rueben was about to protest when he heard Aki-Z's footsteps stop on the far side of the room, then grow louder as she approached their spot. Was the opaque-ish mass of bubble wrap amassed on top of them thick enough for her not to see them? It concealed them, but all she had to do was peel back the bubble wrap.

That would blow the mission because even if they subdued her without getting shot by her, she would see their faces and know something was up. Then she'd tell her husband Young Z, and that was one big fat time mess they didn't need to deal with. If worst came to worst, Rueben could die and warp back, but they didn't know from Buzz if that was safe or not yet. Both alternatives were terrible, but one was going to happen if she found them. Aki-Z wasn't an idiot. Rueben held his breath, reminding himself to be still and not pop any of the bubble wrap.

Through the thick bubble wrap, Aki-Z's blurry form appeared in front of Rueben's face. He tensed. Then he felt Z's grip tighten around his wrist, and he focused on breathing silent shallow breaths.

A moment passed and surprisingly, Aki-Z turned and took a step away from the bubble wrap pile. Her blurry form bent and silently plucked something up from the floor. As Rueben wondered what it was, her cell phone suddenly rang.

Aki put it on speaker, her voice loving and warm. "Rueben?"

"Hey babe," a gruff voice said that Rueben recognized as Rueben-Z's, which meant that it was Young Z on the other end.

"Are you okay? How did things go?"

"Oh, you know. Saved the world again. All in a day's work."

Aki-Z sighed. "That's…good. I'm glad you're safe. You didn't take any unnecessary risks, did you?" Her footsteps sounded against the warehouse floor as she stepped away from the Ruebens' location.

"Of course not. Heh. Still got all my limbs. I miss you. Where are you?"

Aki-Z's footsteps stopped. She drew a long breath. "Our daughter's birthday party."

There was a pause from the other end of the line.

"Chuck E. Cheese? That was today? Fuck me. I forgot."

"I know. You've had a lot on your plate lately."

"Shit. I mean, you know how it is. All the terrorist attacks of late."

"Yeah."

"Babe, I'm sorry. But the world needs Buzz and me."

Aki-Z sighed. "I know."

What Rueben guessed she wanted to say was *Emma and I need you too.* He glanced over at Z hiding beside him, but the older man wouldn't meet Rueben's eyes.

"Look, it's not right," Young Z said. "I'll make it up to you, okay? I will. Swear."

Aki-Z's words lacked conviction. "Okay. Sure."

There's no way he's getting out of that doghouse...

Young Z's words were smooth and confident. "On my way back home, I'll pick up that wine you love. The dark chocolate rosé wine."

Aki-Z's voice warmed. "Oh?"

"Yeah. It's expensive. But you're so worth it, babe. If I'm not mistaken, it's what we were drinking around the time you conceived Emma..."

Aki-Z headed toward the warehouse door. "Rueben Peet, what am I going to do with you?"

"Forgive me?"

She laughed.

"Hey, babe? You sure you're at Chuck E. Cheese?" Young Z chuckled. "Sounds awfully quiet in there."

Rueben tensed under the bubble wrap. They weren't in the clear yet. If Young Z suspected that something was up, he could still warp back and possibly find the two alternate Ruebens and mess up the timeline. Lost in his thoughts, Rueben repositioned himself under the bubble wrap, and his palm crushed a plastic bubble. It popped like the cork of a champagne bottle.

Aki-Z spun and gazed at the warehouse interior.

Under the bubble wrap, Z whispered harshly, "Nice job, you nincompoop."

Rueben bit his lip. This was it. Aki-Z was going to find them.

The next few moments passed in silence.

"You still there, babe?" Young Z said over the phone.

Aki-Z tilted her head down at whatever was in her hand that she'd picked up from the warehouse floor. What had it been? Would she say something to Young Z?

Then she turned toward the warehouse door and opened it. "Oh, just stepped out for a second. The smells were starting to get to me. Martha is watching Emma and the others." She left and closed the door behind her.

The two Ruebens let out relieved breaths but stayed in their concealed position in case Aki-Z came back. A few minutes later, Z punched Rueben's arm and started to stand under the bubble wrap.

Rueben grabbed Z's wrist and tugged him back down. "What the hell, man?"

"What?" Z pulled his hand away, and Rueben grabbed the man's jacket at the throat.

"You know what I'm talking about. We're not supposed to interact with ourselves. We'll mess up the timeline on your Earth."

Z scoffed. "Look, that's only an educated guess on Buzz's part. Plus, I'm not the one who popped the bubble wrap." He smacked Rueben's hand away from his jacket collar. "Now, I'd appreciate it if you kept your hands to yourself."

Rueben made a fist but kept it at his side. It was getting hot under the bubble wrap.

Z started to rise again, pressing up against the bubble wrap as if it was a cocoon, and Rueben lashed out with his foot and caught Z around the ankle. Then he lunged forward and grabbed the back of Z's jacket, pulling him off balance. Z thrashed as he fell, trying to hook Rueben with his fist, but Rueben had already maneuvered around him, jabbed him in the side, and now had the crook of his elbow wrapped around Z's throat.

"Why, you little—"

Rueben cut off Z's words and easily anticipated Z's next action. As Z formed two fingers tight together and shoved them back at Rueben's neck, Rueben positioned himself out of the way.

Z grunted. "You're gonna pay for this."

The heat under the bubble wrap was becoming unbearable. One of Z's palms slapped against the floor, and his boots stomped as he tried to wriggle out from Rueben's grip.

"I've had a lot of training, too," Rueben said. "I'm done with this 'pushing me around' shit. Either you're on my team, or you're not. This is my story—not yours, you asshole."

Z's body started to go slack, but Rueben didn't let up on his applied pressure. He wasn't as strongly built as Z and had only managed to get him in this vulnerable position due to the element of surprise.

When he was reasonably sure that Z was out cold, Rueben relaxed his grip. He didn't want to kill the man. Only Z knew how to pilot the space and time capsule, and they needed to get back to Earth-A after they recovered the second virus sample.

Rueben was scooting back away from Z when Z's fist flew at his head. Rueben raised an arm in defense, and the blow caught him on the shoulder with a *pop*.

"Damnit," Rueben grunted, his back and head pushing up

against the bubble wrap enclosure. His foot stomped the floor, bursting more of the bubble wrap. Sweat dribbled down his face and chin and stained his armpits under his form-fitting jacket.

Z twisted over onto his hands and knees and pounced.

Rueben sidestepped in an awkward crabwalk maneuver made possible only from his old ballroom dance training days. Z missed him, and Rueben delivered a satisfying blow to Z's chin. The older man collapsed onto his chest, blood leaking from the corner of his mouth.

A few moments of silence ensued, punctuated only by their heavy panting.

Finally, Z let out a long groan. "Fucking A, that was a good punch."

Crouching a few feet away from Z, Rueben remained on guard. "Don't patronize me. I can see through your tricks."

Z spoke slowly as he raised himself to his hands and knees again. "I underestimated you. Props." He wiped his mouth with the heel of his palm. "I hear you. I hear you. I've treated you like a kid. Anything else you want to say to me?"

Rueben was silent for a moment. Then he angled his gaze at Z's tattered jacket. "You smell like shit."

Z chuckled and started to stand, and his stomach rumbled. "Look, infiltrating Chuck E. Cheese wasn't some rogue careless action."

"But we can't change anything! I'm fighting for the future I want to have back on Earth-A."

Z grunted in agreement. "I'm fighting for the past I want to protect here on Earth-Z."

"Holy shit," Rueben said suddenly. "We should call ourselves Team Alpha and Omega."

Z dropped his head and raised a hand in protest. "I lost

that cheesy sense of humor shit after the birth of my daughter. You can keep that left hook, but you have to lose those jokes."

"Don't mock my humor. Not when you almost blew our cover."

"True enough," Z said. "You have to take risks in life. This one paid off big time. Check this out..." He drew a tiny listening device from his pocket. He turned up the volume, and Aki's voice came over the device's speaker. Emma's voice and Martha-Z's voice also came through. There was some sort of celebration going on in the background and kids were cheering.

"What..." Rueben said. "Did you plant a bug in Chuck E. Cheese?"

Z grinned. "Nope. Emma did. This is going to be our big lead to the virus' ground zero. Now how 'bout we grab some lunch and I'll explain?"

Rueben stood and warily eyed Z as they searched for the way out from under the bubble wrap. This man would never cease to surprise and perplex him. Maybe that's how Aki-A felt about him? Oh well, Rueben was hungry too and would rather eat than fight with this asshole.

They found their way out from under the bubble wrap and emerged into the warehouse to find a foreman with a pencil tucked behind one ear and a clipboard in his hand staring confoundedly at the two of them. "The fuck you two doing in my bubble wrap?"

Z cut loose with a raucous belly laugh and slapped the man on the shoulder as he passed him on his way toward the door. "Some real primo bubble wrap you got." He turned back to Rueben. "You coming? That is, if that's what you want to do. Partner."

Rueben ignored the warehouse foreman's bewildered look and nodded at Z. Recognition as an equal felt good. "Let's go. You know a good place to eat on your Earth?"

"I don't know about you, but I'm in the mood for some fried chicken."

CHAPTER EIGHT

<u>Earth-A</u>

"What kind of cockeyed contraption is this, anyway? Certainly wasn't made in America, I'll guarantee that."

The three stooges—as Marshall called them—all cried out for him to stop messing with the machine.

Marshall stepped back from the printing press and wiped the back of one sweaty arm across his forehead. "I'll stop messing with it if you tell me how to work the inky sonofabitch…"

He stopped his rant as Carolyn placed her hand on his arm.

Marshall grimaced. It had been a long drive from Buzz's underground hideout in the mountains back into NYC, and he was more than a bit cranky. That, and his hip was acting up. Winking at Carolyn, he turned back to the men. "Gee, boys. I'm sorry for hurting your 'feelings.' I haven't had my Snickers bar yet. You got any?"

One of the three young men who worked at the *Paper Warriors* news office raised his eyes. "Sugar? We don't keep such harmful food products here. Sugar is so detrimental to your health. Not to mention all the other ingredients."

Marshall glanced down at his girth and back at the three newsmen. "Well, they taste good."

"On one Earth," the tallest of the three newsmen said, "the government banned sugar. I wish I lived on that Earth."

"Too bad it's all made up," the third newsman said.

Carolyn hooked him with her gaze. "What do you mean? Not real?" She glanced over at the clippings of news headlines of aliens and Bigfoot plastered at intervals on the walls surrounding the room.

The first newsman shuffled his feet. "They make good stories. But they're not real. I mean, parallel Earths? It's ridiculous."

"Our customers sure eat it up, though." The second newsman pushed his glasses up on his head.

Marshall snorted. "If you don't believe the shit in your papers, why do you sell it?"

All three of the men threw their arms up exasperatedly. "Because it's what the people want, and you gotta give the people what they want."

Marshall took an intimidating step toward them. "Let me set this straight for the record." He gestured a hand at the newspaper clippings on the wall. "All this alternate world bullshit is real, and my son is on another Earth, and we're gonna get this thing set up so we can send him a message if we need to."

The smallest man all but squeaked. "Okay. Okay. Just don't hurt us. We pay our taxes and stuff like everyone—" One of the other newsmen jabbed him in the side, and he shut up.

Marshall sneered. "Oh, you better. I used to be a cop. I know some people."

The three newsmen cowered back a step. The bravest of them cleared his throat. "Fine. Fine. Just have at it. Please, try not to break it though?"

"I swear," Marshall said. "If you guys had a boss, I'd slap him silly for hiring you three idiots." He turned his attention back to the printing press and all the metal struts and levers and knobs.

After a few moments of searching, he located the green button they had to press to send a message, as instructed by Buzz.

"Here are the time controls," Carolyn said from a little farther down the machine. She was pointing at some revolving time and date stamps.

Marshall trudged back to where she was standing and inspected it all. "All right. Now we're talking. How do we write the message to send out to the other worlds?"

He flashed an inquiring look at the three newsmen who were conversing near the wreckage that used to be their desks—they'd been destroyed by one of Buzz's hacked robots when Rueben and Aki had come here. One of them looked up. "We don't know! We don't know how it works."

With a grunt, Marshall started to inspect the rest of the printing press. His deductive mind said that if this machine was somehow receiving transmissions from other Earths, there had to be some sort of scientific explanation. There had to be a computer or something to communicate with the other worlds.

His eyes narrowed at the sight of a thick wire snaking down the back corner of the machine. Although the cable disappeared into the floor, Marshall's instincts traced its probable path back to a suspicious-looking cabinet at the back of the room. Luckily that robot hadn't destroyed this side of the room or the printing press itself.

As he marched up to the odd cabinet, he saw the lock securing it. There was also a sign on one of its doors. *Do not open under penalty of...* The rest of the text had worn away too much to read. It almost looked like someone had purposefully filed it down. He could faintly make out some company's logo at the bottom of the message, but he couldn't quite read what it said.

Carolyn stepped up beside him and tugged on the cabinet doors. They didn't budge.

"Hey, darling," Marshall said. "Can you get me a chair?"

Carolyn batted her eyes at Marshall. "Please?"

"Please?"

Grinning, Carolyn found a sturdy chair the robot hadn't destroyed and carried it over to Marshall. He kissed her on the cheek. Instead of sitting on it, he positioned it so he was between the cabinet and the chair back. Then he braced his meaty palms on the chair top and bent over it, lifting one leg. With a grunt, he kicked out, the heel of his dad shoe bashing against the cabinet door. There was the splitting sound of cheap wood and Marshall carefully lowered his foot. Carolyn helped to steady him. "Thanks, darling." He kissed her again on the cheek and wiped the sweat off his forehead from the exertion.

"Don't open that," one of the newsmen said. "Under penalty of..."

Marshall cocked his head back at the man. "Under penalty of what?" He took hold of the cabinet doors and pried them off one by one. Housed inside was a futuristic-looking computer screen and keyboard. "Aha." Marshall tapped one of the computer keys, and the screen flashed to life. On it was a blocky template with sections for newspaper headlines and columned news stories. Everything already looked pre-formatted—all you had to do was type.

Carolyn pushed the chair up behind him so he could sit. "Think you can figure it out?"

Marshall grinned and sat. "I remember some stuff from back in my computer information systems days." He interlaced his knuckles and popped them. "There is one thing I could use though."

Carolyn eyed him curiously.

"A drink."

One of the newsmen hurried forward with a glass mason jar filled with what looked like green sludge. "Green smoothie? It's organic."

"Oh hell no." Marshall shook his head, and Carolyn laughed.

He spent a few minutes playing around with the computer. There was no mouse so he had to figure out how to navigate the newspaper template with only the keyboard. It was pretty user-friendly though. When he was confident he had it figured out, he turned his head and searched for Carolyn. She was reading some of the newspaper clippings on the walls and sipping the green smoothie.

"Hey," he said, finally.

She glanced back at him over the rim of the glass.

Man, I love this woman. How lucky he was that she had come back into his life. You didn't let a woman like that get away twice. He swallowed. "Martha and Aki haven't called yet. That must be good, right?"

"No news is good news, I guess. We have to wait. Hopefully, the Ruebens will get back and not need our help."

Since when were things ever that easy? Marshall shifted on his chair. "It's all this waiting. I don't much like it."

She smiled at him. "You know what they say. Waiting's the hardest part."

"Ain't that the truth of it."

Carolyn continued to smile at him. "Maybe you should try a green smoothie. It's good."

"Ah, I don't know…"

"Try it for me?"

Marshall glanced at his watch, tapped one foot against the floor, then sighed. "Ah hell. Fine. I'll try it."

Only for this woman. He stood from his chair to find one of the three stooges. He needed to get up and move around anyway. It would take his mind off the waiting.

CHAPTER NINE

<u>**Earth-Z**</u>

"Sir, do you want the Galactic Flamethrower Chicken or the Homestyle Honey Mustard Chicken?"

Rueben shifted his gaze between the fast-food restaurant employee and the food menu. The bright dazzling colors of Hurley's Chicken—It's Intergalactically Good! disoriented him and he was hungry, which didn't help him to think either. On the walk here, Z had promised that he would pay for the meals—this wouldn't be a repeat of the pretzel stand scene.

Now Rueben and Z stood at the restaurant's counter. Behind them in the restaurant, kids cried out, and people laughed. Fried chicken *crunched* as people bit down. Diners slurped sweet tea and swallowed.

"Go with the Flamethrower Chicken," Z said seriously.

"Homestyle Honey Mustard," Rueben said.

The employee nodded and gave them their total. In response, Z glanced at the kitchen employees and then leaned forward over the countertop. He spoke in a conspiratorially low voice to the worker. "Is Jim in?"

The employee's face lit up. "Jim Hurley?"

Z nodded.

"Umm, no, I haven't seen him today."

"Damn." Z turned away from the countertop.

"Umm, sir, you are going to pay, correct?" When Z didn't answer, the employee turned hopefully to Rueben.

"Are you kidding me…" Rueben started, then the door chime rang, and Z was chuckling.

"Look at you, you son of a bitch, how are you?" Z was holding his arms wide. Rueben watched, stunned, as the homeless man Organic Jim strode up with a beaming smile and embraced Z. Except, that it wasn't the Jim Rueben knew from Earth-A. The man had the same ruddy face and wiry frame, but his hair was tamed and greased back neatly over his head, and his clothes were, well, his clothes were nice. Khaki chinos and an untucked trim-fitting royal blue button-up shirt. Vitality and clarity gleamed in the man's perceptive eyes. He looked…healthy. And sane.

Z and Jim separated. Then Jim saw Rueben, and he laughed jovially. "Rueben. And…Rueben. Two of you—it's a pleasure. A real treat!" He stepped up to Rueben and stuck out his hand. Rueben shook it. "Nice clothes," Jim said, and Z smirked at Rueben over Jim's shoulder.

There was a sly grin on Jim's face as he turned to the Hurley's employee behind the counter. "These two gentle-men's meals are on the house." Jim laughed and threw his arms around both Ruebens' shoulders and guided them away from the counter to a high circular table with three stools around it. The table was next to a window that looked outside to the sidewalk. "My friends, sit. Let us talk and be merry."

Rueben gave Z a confused glance, and Z laughed. "Just go with it."

Rueben took a seat and stared at their gracious host. "Uh, Jim?"

Jim flashed a mouthful of perfect white teeth. "Yes, my friend?"

"What's two plus two?"

"Four."

"What's my mom's name?"

"Carolyn."

"Say a tongue twister."

Jim studied Reuben with a curious glint in his eyes, then shrugged. "Peter Piper picked a peck of pickled peppers."

Rueben blinked. "Who…are you?"

Jim took a seat on his stool and fluffed the chest of his dress shirt. "Why, Jim Hurley, of course. And you must be… Rueben-A, I think you call yourself."

Rueben's mouth dropped open, and Z made a miming gesture to close it. "H-how do you know all this?"

Jim grinned. "My déjà vu power, I think you call it on your Earth."

"How? Why aren't you…"

"Crazy?" Jim arched his eyebrows. "Not all of us are crazy. Oh, that poor fellow on Earth-A. He's pretty messed up. See, we all can see parts of futures that never happened when time warpers—called Repeaters on some Earths—warp back in time. We can also see glimpses into the timelines on the other Earths although some of us have greater clarity in our visions." Jim's shoulders sagged. "Some of us Jims…have cracked under that mental strain. It's unfortunate, but the way of the world."

"Way of the world?" Rueben said. He shook his head to clear it. "I don't think time warping and déjà vu is the way of the world. Especially not when only Carolyn, Z, and I are the only three in all the worlds that can warp. We are the only three warpers, right?"

Jim nodded. "As far as I'm able to tell. You three are intergalactic superstars to us Jims."

There was a brief silence, and Z grunted. "Shit. I know that look on your face. What's on your mind?"

Rueben expanded upon his thoughts. "It seems…like too much of a coincidence that the three warpers and you are all located in New York City. Not to mention my friend Martha who sort of has the déjà vu power. Luckily she hasn't gone crazy yet."

"Oh, Martha," Jim said. "I'm sure she'll be fine. In most worlds, her ability fades away. But she's as mad as a bat in some worlds. She ran off and married a punk rocker chick in one of them."

Rueben snorted. "Martha?"

A Hurley's employee stepped forward and placed steaming fried chicken meals in front of the three men at the high table. "Have an intergalactically delightful day," she said with a cute smile.

The scent of mouth-watering chicken and honey mustard wafted up Rueben's nostrils. "Wow. This smells amazing."

Jim grinned as Rueben brought his chicken to his mouth and bit in with a satisfying *crunch*.

Z did the same and waited for Rueben to sip his drink. "Whatcha think?"

Rueben swallowed. "I wish the Hurley's on Earth-A was this good."

Jim shook his head sadly. "Jim-A…poor chap." He turned to his meal, half a plate of Maple Syrup Fried Chicken and a big salad.

Rueben thought of something. "Jim-A once said he could travel to other Earths by going through Hurley's restaurants."

"Only in his mind, I'm afraid," Jim-Z said.

Rueben met Jim-Z's eyes. "You don't have any idea how or why we have these time-warping powers, do you?"

"You don't think we were born this way?" Jim said cryptically.

"Honestly," Rueben said, "I don't know what to think anymore about anything. I mean, first a time virus. Now a time monster—"

Jim gestured with his fork. "Yeah, you better stop that. As Jim-A says, it's both of your 'quests' to defeat it and bring order to the multiverse."

Quest... So that's what Jim-A had meant by that word. Too bad Jim-A wasn't as clear-headed as this entrepreneurial and culinary genius.

"Look, can we please enjoy this meal?" Z asked.

They ate for a few minutes in silence. Rueben didn't think he'd ever had a better meal before. Still, as he ate, doubt crept in about whether or not Z had a lead on the virus' ground zero or if the man was savoring the delights of his world one last time: this mouthwatering meal, and before that seeing his daughter and wife and getting to hear their voices.

Suddenly, another terrible thought rushed through Rueben's mind, and he slammed a hand upon the table, his fork gripped in his fist.

Z jumped. "Jesus. What's wrong with you? People are enjoying their meals here."

Rueben pointed his fork at the man. "You and me. We need to talk. Now." He jerked his head at Jim, who grinned delightedly and wiped his lips in anticipation of some drama between two time warpers.

Z glanced down at his partially eaten plate. He forked some mashed potatoes into his mouth.

"I'm serious." Rueben stood from the table. He turned to Jim. "This will only take a moment."

Jim only smiled. Rueben was starting to find it a little creepy.

Z wiped his mouth and stood brusquely. "This better be good. My chicken's getting cold."

Rueben led Z to the door, and they both stepped onto the sidewalk outside the restaurant. Before the door had even closed, Rueben said, "I can't believe you."

"You got something against free meals? What's the problem?"

"The problem is that Jim clearly knows about Young Z. Now he knows about you and me. What's to stop him from telling Young Z and blowing our cover?" Rueben glanced through the restaurant's window and was a little uneasy to see Jim waving back at him, a wide smile painted across his face.

Z shrugged. "Oh, that. Jim's fine. Me and him go way back. I've been back plenty of times after the virus destroys this world. He's sort of my inside man, I guess, when I need things like a free meal. Or gadgets. Believe me, he doesn't want us to fail our 'quest.' He's not going to tell Young Z about us."

Rueben processed this. "What about running into your family in Chuck E. Cheese? Is the bug really to help you find the virus?"

"Of course." Z chuckled. "When I told Emma what I wanted her to do—"

"Emma knows about the bug?"

Z gave Rueben an odd look. "Yeah. She's a smart girl. I knew I could trust her."

Rueben groaned. "What part of 'don't interact with your family' do you not get?"

"Look, Buzz is a genius, but he doesn't know everything about the world. When you're in the field, you have to go with your gut, especially when the fate of something much bigger than yourself is on the line. I thought I could trust Emma, and I was right."

"How do you know?" Rueben said. This situation kept getting worse and worse. Z was like the ultimate con man with killer instincts and muscles. "Emma could be telling Aki right now about us."

Z scoffed. "You don't know my Emma. But hopefully, one day you do. 'Course, then she won't be my Emma but your Emma. You should've heard her when I told her you and I had come from Earth-A and were on a mission to save the multiverse."

Rueben rubbed his forehead. "I know she's a kid, but she believed you?"

"Yep. She said she suspected as much that a multiverse existed. She said one time at Buzz's place, after he'd had too many beers, he let that fact slip. Also, Emma said she's watched all the Terminators. She's trustworthy."

"What? Why would you be glad that your twelve-ish year-old daughter watches R movies?"

"Because she agreed to put the bug inside Aki's phone. It's so small, Aki will never know it's there. Now we'll be able to listen in on Team Z to see all the places Young Z goes over the next days so we can get to ground zero before he does and stop the time virus from infecting him. If memory serves, I undertook quite a few missions over the upcoming days. There's a high probability that I unwittingly got infected on one of them. You still have the virus detector, right?"

Rueben fished the device out of his pocket and checked it for the hell of it. The virus wasn't anywhere nearby. "Shit," he mumbled and ran a hand through his hair. It was almost too much to take in, but Rueben had to admit that Z's "plan" was their best shot. He hated that so much of the mission's success depended on Z's information and knowledge of this world. He was tired of feeling like he was only along for the ride.

"Are we done with twenty questions?" Z said. "No one likes cold fried chicken."

"What did Aki-Z find on the floor of that warehouse? Why did she lose interest in our hiding spot?"

Z smiled. "A dried cherry blossom petal. One of the items I took from my body armor back in Buzz's lab before we came back to Earth-Z. It's my babe's favorite flower. Figured she'd see it as a sign from the universe that all was good. That we didn't mean any harm."

"What if it had backfired and she thought we were stalkers?"

"Sometime, you have to learn to trust your gut and not to question the universe. Without my warping ability, I have no do-overs left. I figured it had a good chance of working. And it did." He paused. "Now, for fuck's sake, can we please go back in and finish our chicken?"

Rueben stared at Z for a moment and nodded. He turned to go back into Hurley's Chicken when his gut told him to freeze. A split second later, he understood why.

Standing at the counter placing his order with his back to Rueben was Young Z.

CHAPTER TEN

<u>Earth-Z</u>

"What else could go wrong?" Rueben said as he pushed Z away from the restaurant's glass door and down the sidewalk.

"I didn't see that coming." Z peeked over Rueben's shoulder. "Young Z must've snuck in through the back entrance."

"I know you're not an idiot, but you didn't account for Younger You coming to the very restaurant we were inside?" They were nearing a crosswalk full of people waiting for the light to change.

"I completely forgot I came here after the Havana gig. Plus, after all the Earth-A food I've had to eat of late, I was craving some Hurley's Chicken."

Rueben stopped at the crosswalk, joining the crowd already gathered. At least in their Earth-Z clothes, they fit right in. Donning his sleek shades, he turned to Z. "Well, I'm glad to see you were 'trusting your gut.'"

Z frowned, then slowly shook his head. "Rueben. On Earth-Z, you're not allowed to make dad jokes until you're a dad."

Rueben smirked. "Shut the fuck up." Some commuters glanced his way, but he didn't care.

Z chuckled. "All right, all right. I flubbed. I admit it. I should've remembered."

"The main thing is we made it out without Young Z seeing us. If he had, he'd have confronted us by now."

"You're not wrong about that."

Rueben thought it over. "Of course, we do resemble a younger and older version of him. If someone in the restaurant mentions that to Young Z, Jim will cover for us, right?"

Z grinned. "Oh yeah." He rubbed his hands together as if to warm them. He grinned. "You know what? I think we're finally starting to jive as a team. We're starting to think on the same page now."

Rueben shrugged. The traffic light changed, and they started to cross the street. When they had nearly reached the other side of the street, something *beeped* under Z's jacket. Z reached inside and pulled out his listening device. He raised it to his ear, and his eyes tightened. He waved Rueben off to the side out of the flow of traffic where there was less noise.

"This might be our big break," he said when they were standing next to an old brownstone apartment complex. "This is a live conversation between Buzz-Z and Young Z with Aki-Z's bugged phone patched in as well." Z adjusted the speaker's volume.

"...and the arms dealer," Buzz was saying, "is in your vicinity. Security footage shows he has a briefcase with him. No idea what's inside. Could be drugs. Could be a bioweapon. The local police don't know what they're up against. Think you can stop him?"

Through the listening device's speaker, it sounded like

Young Z crunched into some fried chicken. "You know, Buzz, I hate cold chicken," he said.

"Choices. Cold chicken? Or lots of innocent dead people in New York?"

Young Z groaned. "I'll be on my way in a moment. What's the exact address?"

Buzz-Z gave it, and Rueben and Z met each other's eyes.

"That's really close," Rueben said.

"And that briefcase might contain the virus." Z slid the listening device back into his jacket. "It might be how I get infected. This could be ground zero."

"Then we better get there before Young Z does."

Earth-A

In his lab, Buzz was pointing out the protein coating of the super-evolved virus to Martha on his computer screen. He'd hit a dead end and so had his supercomputer. He found in his line of work that sometimes, trying to explain the problem to a layperson helped achieve a breakthrough.

Martha groaned and ran a hand through her hair. "I don't understand. Viruses aren't living beings?"

"Huh? That's all you absorbed from my lecture? That's not even the point I was trying to make."

While Martha rolled her eyes, he huffed out a breath and thought back to the time monster he'd faced on Earth-Z. It was both incredible and terrifying how fast it had evolved into that state. And to think, what if it mutated to the point where it developed the ability to warp back in time or hop to different parallel Earths?

Surely that was a long time away, but the very notion was

the urgency behind why Buzz needed to figure out how to defeat it.

Buzz turned back to Martha, who was looking at him like he was a very weird person. "Sorry. I didn't mean to snap on you. But this is important—"

He was interrupted by the lab door being flung open. In flew Aki, breathless and red-faced. She was clutching a laptop showing the live satellite feed of the mountains outside Buzz's hideout.

Buzz eyed her serious demeanor. "Let me guess, this isn't about the cable going out, is it?"

"It's out," Aki sputtered. "It somehow survived and escaped."

"The time virus?" Martha asked.

Aki turned the laptop around. Its screen depicted an overhead view of the green mountain. Except now there was a big growing circle of withering death expanding outward from around the hidden base.

Buzz couldn't believe it. Well, he could, but it had looked like they were in the clear…

Martha tugged on his sleeve, and he turned to her. "Buzz, we're good, right? With that vaccine or whatever you injected us with. We're not going to wither and die?"

Buzz fanned his shirt collar, recalling the hasty anti-viral concoction he'd whipped up before he and the two Ruebens had first headed to Earth-Z. "Yes. In theory."

Aki spoke up. "We've got to get a message to Rueben and Rueben-Z."

"Would that even help?" Martha asked.

Buzz grimaced. "Once they get the ground zero sample, they'll need to hop back to our world but before the virus starts…" He gestured at the laptop screen in Aki's hands. On it, trees and other vegetation continued to die in an outward expanding radius. The three of them watched as plant life and any animal, fungus, and bacteria turned to dust, their essences warped forward at an accelerated rate.

"This is horrible," Martha said. "There must be something we can do. Call in a biologic warfare threat to the FBI?"

Aki turned to Buzz. "I can call the CIA…but what would it take to stop the virus? A ring of nuclear bombs around the mountain?"

"That might work…" Buzz mused.

Martha shook her head in disgust. "Surely you have some idea. A new experimental robot in the basement, maybe?"

Buzz chewed on his lower lip. "Nope. Look, I'm thinking, okay. This is a hard nut to crack. We're talking about a time-warping virus." He glanced up at the ceiling. "Call Carolyn and Marshall. Have them contact the Ruebens by the printing press. In the meantime…" He shook his head. "I'll try to figure out what our options are."

CHAPTER ELEVEN

Earth-Z

It was a meetup of some sort. That much was clear. The arms dealer paced the alleyway, the thick metal briefcase in one hand handcuffed to his wrist. He wore a sleek gray sport coat paired with dark pants and sported a tight military haircut. Vigilance hardened his face.

Rueben drew a deep breath and lowered the expandable monocular from his eye. He relished its high-tech design and the way it collapsed into a flat circle that you could slip into a pocket. Handing the scope to the Z, Rueben said, "We can take him."

"Damn right we can." Z raised the futuristic monocular to his eyes for another look.

They were two blocks away, completely concealed behind a dumpster. The arms dealer didn't know they were surveilling him. Rueben wondered if the man knew what was in the briefcase or if he'd simply purchased it from one party to sell to another.

"I think we should move in," Rueben said.

"Nah." Z lowered the binocular. "We gotta wait for Young Z to enter the scene. Got to deal with him first so he never gets infected with the virus in the briefcase."

Rueben consulted the virus detector. It still registered no trace of the virus. "If it's even in the briefcase. We don't know for sure that it is."

Z raised his monocular again. "I'm pretty sure it is. It fits. No such thing as coincidences, you know what I mean?"

Rueben still wasn't convinced, but he hoped Z was right. They needed to wrap this mission up quickly and get back to Earth-A so they could figure out how to save all the worlds from the time virus.

He mentally reviewed their plan. Z had lived through this event before so he knew the direction from which Young Z would come. According to Z, it was as simple as incapacitating Young Z before he could confront the arms dealer, then swapping out the virus with something less lethal so Young Z wouldn't get suspicious of time warper interference. As for how they were going to incapacitate Young Z, Z had taken more than the monocular from his body armor back at Buzz's lab—

Z held up a compact tranquilizer dart gun. "It only has one dart in it so I'll have to make it count." He handed Rueben the monocular. "It's about to go down. Watch and learn, grasshopper. Watch and learn."

Z disappeared around the street corner.

For the moment, Rueben decided he needed to trust Z and his plan. He brought the monocular to his eye and focused on the pacing arms dealer in the alley. A few minutes later, he glimpsed movement on the roofline of one of the buildings forming the alleyway. Rueben swiveled the monocular up in time to see the outline of Young Z creeping up to the roof's edge. The man peered down at the dealer.

Crap...

As Rueben watched through the monocular, Young Z went through the process of silently attaching some sort of rappelling line to an AC unit on the roof. When he finished, he tugged the line and leaned forward over the building.

Rueben kept his eye on Young Z through the monocular, wondering where the hell Z had gone. Had he abandoned the mission? Had he gone rogue?

A moment later, Young Z slapped the back of his neck and tipped back and forth before collapsing on the roof. One of his arms slid over the edge. He lay still.

Then Z appeared near him, raising the dart gun in one hand victoriously. Rueben shook his head. "Nice," he muttered.

A couple of minutes later, after dragging Young Z away from the edge, Z regrouped with Rueben at ground level. The man hadn't even broken a sweat.

Rueben studied him. "You don't think he'll wake up, blame foul play, and try to warp back?"

"Nah," Z said. "That kind of dart doesn't leave a mark. Most likely, he'll think he passed out due to overworking himself. I was a busy man during this period of my life."

"I can't believe that worked."

Z smirked. "Not just a pretty face." He tossed the spent dart gun into a dumpster.

As he did, Rueben studied Z's face scar. "How did that happen, anyway?"

"Stopping terrorists aboard a plane." Z grunted as he buried the dart gun under some trash. "Flying over the ocean. Small private jet. Had enough room for three—two guys, a pilot, and a whole lot of explosives. I managed to disarm all the bombs. Then the bad guys and even the pilot started shooting at me—in a friggin' plane. I threw the three of them out and tried to fly the plane to safety. The controls were jammed though from a rogue bullet. The plane went down."

Z lowered the dumpster lid and turned back to Rueben. "Needless to say, the plane crash-landed, and I expected to die and warp back. Instead, I woke up tangled in the plane wreckage on a desert island with a badass facial scar." Chuckling at the memory, Z motioned for Rueben to follow him through the alley toward the perpendicular street separating them from the pacing arms dealer.

He continued with his story. "I thought, what the hell. Aki would give me hell for it, but I survived a fucking airplane crash. That was a better story than 'I died and warped back to before the plane crashed and safely landed it on a desert island.'"

Rueben smirked. "You ask me, both of those are pretty badass stories. You sound way more badass than I could ever be."

"Yeah, if you think like that."

They picked up their pace to cross the street while the crossing light was on. The alley with the arms dealer was only thirty yards away now. "Don't underestimate me," Rueben said.

"I already have. Now, you ready to take this asshole down?"

"Wait." Rueben stopped Z with a hand on his jacket. "What about your hip? You have a hip replacement of some sort. Was that from the plane crash too?"

Z squinted at him from the mouth of the alley. "How'd you know about my hip?"

"You hide it well, but my team and I figured it out when we were trying to stop you from bombing the World Summit."

"Oh." Z rubbed the back of his hand across his mouth. "My hip...I don't want to talk about it. Now come on, focus."

Halfway down the alley, the arms dealer was now leaning against a stack of pallets. When he saw the two Ruebens approaching, he straightened. The metal briefcase *thudded* against the side of his knee. His eyes flicked all around as if searching for some hidden danger.

"Wonder what's got him so spooked," Rueben whispered as the arms dealer continued to search for a threat.

"Yeah," Z said. "It's like he's expecting something to go wrong with the trade..."

Rueben was starting to question the effectiveness of this plan. According to further listening to Buzz-Z over the listening device, they were early for the meeting. They didn't know who the arms dealer was meeting, but they had to make their move in the next few minutes before the deal went down.

The goal was for everything to go smoothly so they wouldn't have to warp. With Young Z out of the picture, surely this would be a cakewalk for two men of Rueben's and Z's skills and intellect to pull off.

The spooked arms dealer cleared his throat. He brusquely raised a hand. "You can stop right there." His voice was sharp and gruff, his eyes full of distrust.

The Ruebens stopped.

"Let me see the money."

Z nodded seriously and nudged Rueben. "What?" Rueben whispered.

"You heard the man. Give him the money."

Great plan, Rueben was thinking. He didn't have any money on him.

Sensing something was off. The arms dealer bared his teeth. "What is this? You think I'm playing here?"

Z turned to Rueben and shoved him back a step. "What the hell, man? You didn't bring the money?"

Anger started to flood Rueben's head. Then he caught the glint in Z's eyes to play along. "What? No. I didn't forget." He turned to the arms dealer, about ten feet away now. "I brought the payment, digital currency like you asked. I'll make the transfer if you give me your account number."

Z smirked, his eyes saying *thatta boy.*

"What?" The arms dealer's expression screwed up now. "That wasn't part of the deal—"

"You want USD? Bitcoin? Ethereum?"

"Are you fucking crazy? That's not what we agreed—"

Z made his move then, rushing forward and clearing the space between him and the dealer. The dealer reached under his suitcoat right as Z was on him. Z threw a vicious swing that took the man across the cheek. He slumped backward to the alley floor with a sagging sigh.

Z threw a glance over his shoulder. "Now that's the way you—"

There was a coughing, spitting sound, and Z clutched his gut with a frown. The slumped-over arms dealer gave a bloody grin, a pistol equipped with a suppressor in his raised hand.

Z kicked him twice. The first sent the pistol clattering against the alley wall. The second knocked the man out as he connected with his chin.

Rueben dashed to Z's side. "Are you okay?"

Z shrugged him off. "Yeah, yeah. I'm fine. It's just a flesh…"

Then Z collapsed, right beside the fallen arms dealer. Blood leaked out from his abdomen onto the ground.

Rueben fell beside him. "Shit. Hang in there. You're not dying on me." He opened Z's jacket and pulled up his shirt to get a better look at the wound. It didn't look good.

Z grunted and lifted his eyelids. "You've...got this. You can..." Then he exhaled and lay still.

CHAPTER TWELVE

<u>Earth-Z</u>

"Come on. You can't die. You can't."

Rueben slapped Z lightly across the cheek, but the man didn't stir. He felt for a pulse on his neck. There was none.

Shit. Shit. Shit...

He ran his hands through his hair while Buzz's words echoed through his mind: *You can't warp. You can't warp...*

There was a chance that if he warped, the time virus in Z's blood wouldn't be affected. There was also a chance that warping would mess things up with the virus.

Shit...

He sat there on the ground next to Z for a few moments, trying to find some clarity in his mind. When he couldn't, he checked Z's wrist for a pulse. Nothing.

Z was his guide here on Earth-Z. Now Rueben was trapped. What were his options? Seek out Buzz-Z and try to explain his situation?

Rueben thought about what Buzz-A would say. *Don't warp. Something about the importance of science...*

He thought about what Z would say. *Trust your gut.*

Rueben trusted his gut and immediately found the arms dealer's gun. He picked it up and turned the barrel around. Before he could second-guess himself, he pulled the trigger.

Earth-Z
Three minutes earlier

"Now, you ready to take this asshole down?" Z asked.

It took a few moments for Rueben to realize he had gone back in time and for him to get his bearings. It seemed like it had been forever since he'd last warped. Glancing around, he saw that they were outside the mouth of the alley where the arms dealer worriedly waited.

Rueben grabbed Z's jacket. "This is a stupid plan, and it's not going to work."

Z arched his eyebrows. "What? You don't even know what it is."

Quickly checking the virus detector, he saw no trace of the virus. That was good. He'd have to hope he hadn't triggered the virus to activate inside Z's blood. He lanced Z's eyes with his. "I do know your plan, and playing it cool with the arms dealer until you have a chance to lunge at him doesn't work."

"How do you know—"

"He has a gun under his coat."

"Of course he probably does. He's an arms dealer—"

"He shoots you."

Z was silent for a moment. Then he silently whispered, "Fuck. You died and warped, didn't you?"

"Didn't have much choice. I don't know how to pilot the space and time capsule. You're my ride out of here."

"What about the risk of messing with the virus?"

"I'll have to live with those consequences." Rueben hoped there wouldn't be any.

"Did you open the briefcase to make sure the virus was inside?"

"No. I didn't. I was too busy focusing on if I should risk the multiverse and save your sorry ass. Besides, the virus detector isn't going crazy." He leaned in close. "Now listen up, this is how this is going to go down…"

Rueben stepped into the alley with both hands thrust in his pockets. With his sleek shades covering his eyes, he bet he made a decent enough looking bad guy.

"Stop right there," the dealer called.

"No." Rueben continued walking.

The dealer slowly reached toward his suit coat.

Rueben shook his head. "I wouldn't."

"Huh? Why? You working for him?"

Him? Who was this guy talking about?

"I asked you a question. You working for him?" The arms dealer glanced paranoidly over both shoulders and up at the sky.

Rueben formed his fingers into a fork and gestured at his eyes. "Look at me. No, I'm not working for him."

"I…I don't believe you. I knew I shouldn't have come. I shouldn't—" he reached under his jacket, and Rueben threw up his hands.

"I don't have a weapon. I'm on your side."

"Huh?"

Rueben could see the man was confused, but some part of

the man wanted to believe him. Just who the hell was this guy afraid of?

Rueben cleared his throat. "I don't like him either. Let's, uh, cut a deal."

"A deal?"

Rueben glimpsed Z over the arms dealer's shoulder at the opposite end of the alley. He had to keep this man talking long enough for Z to sneak up and do his thing.

"Yeah. You know," Rueben said. "Something mutually beneficial to both of us." He'd never done this kind of undercover work. Although his armpits were sweating profusely, he kinda liked it.

"I don't know…" The arms dealer regarded Rueben carefully, then reached for his gun again.

"Don't." Rueben held out an arm. "I am not your enemy. I—"

The arms dealer happened to glance up at the fire escape on the building beside him. He gasped. "He's here!"

Rueben flicked his gaze upward and caught only a blur as the arms dealer crashed into him and shoved him to the side. Rueben knocked over a garbage can as the arms dealer sprinted past and tried a door handle on a back entrance door. The door opened, and the warm turmeric-y smells of an Indian restaurant rushed out.

The dealer threw himself inside.

Z appeared beside Rueben, breathing hard. He extended a hand and helped Rueben up. "What happened?"

Rueben pointed up at the fire escape landing, but he didn't see anyone or anything up there. "Something spooked him."

"Then let's go after him!"

Rueben darted into a sweltering kitchen. He nearly collided with an angry chef shouting in a language he didn't understand. Through the steam wafting throughout the room, Rueben glimpsed the arms dealer's back.

As he picked his way through the busy area, a large woman in an apron shook a cast iron pan at him. Rueben ducked while Z chuckled behind him, apologizing in a foreign language that placated the woman. Maneuvering around the cook, Rueben barely saw the metal server's cart rolling his way, courtesy of the arms dealer. He blocked it with one palm and sidled around it.

Up ahead, the dealer whipped around with his pistol fully extended.

"Get down," Z shouted, and he and Rueben fell to either side.

The pistol coughed, and metal whined as several bullets struck around the kitchen. The receding sound of frantic footsteps signaled that the man had started running again. The Ruebens rose to their feet and continued their pursuit. Rueben vaulted over a metal prep table and pushed onward out into a small dining area.

"I do like your plan." Z smirked. "Lots of action. And your favorite: running."

"Shut up," Rueben huffed as he spotted his target beelining for the restaurant's front door. The man had gone wide to skirt most of the tables. Rueben cut straight through the restaurant's center, using his swift dance moves to navigate the tight quarters, chairs, and patrons. Some of the customers looked amazed. Others cried out about the lead man having a gun.

The arms dealer threw his shoulder against the front door and pushed it open. As he slid through the doorway, Rueben tackled the man to the sidewalk.

"Aghh!" The man's gun clattered out into the street and honking traffic.

Rueben raised a hand to punch the man across the face, but something hard and heavy smashed over his head. *The metal briefcase,* he realized as he tried to get to his feet. The arms dealer was already sprinting down the sidewalk toward a crowd of people waiting for the light to turn.

"Stop!" Rueben cried.

Disregarding him, the arms dealer pushed his way through the crowd and sprinted out into the traffic.

Rueben pulled to a stop amid the crowd. Z braked right behind him. "Why'd you stop? He ain't roadkill yet."

Out in the street, the arms dealer had nearly made it to the sidewalk on the other side when a taxi struck his trailing foot. The dealer spun to his hands and knees on the sidewalk.

Rueben decided to trust his gut again, and sprinted out into the traffic.

He was halfway across when a horn blared. He threw his hands to the side as brakes squealed and his palms brushed the front of an SUV.

"Watch where ya goin'!"

Disregarding the yelling driver, Rueben waited for a car to pass and sprinted the rest of the way to safety on the other side. Directly up ahead of him, the arms dealer risked a glance behind him. Sweat flew off his face as he whipped back to face the front. He yelped and turned to face Rueben with wide eyes.

A tall man with form-fitting black body armor wrapped around his torso and limbs stepped forward from the crowd. He wore a black ski mask as well as a pair of red-tinted goggles. He looked sort of like a ninja, and he meant business. He leveled a submachine gun at the arms dealer's back.

The dealer shouted, "It's him—"

The submachine gun fired rapidly, and the dealer was thrown forward into Rueben, who caught him. The metal briefcase attached to the man's hand banged against Rueben's knee as they both spun to the ground. As Rueben tried to regain his footing, a shadow loomed over him.

He glanced up in time to see the man in black bend over him. He held a sword in one hand, and with one swift chop, he severed the arms dealer's hand clean off. The handcuff clattered to the sidewalk in a puddle of blood, and the man in black scooped up the briefcase. He made eye contact with Rueben as if daring him to make a move. When Rueben didn't, the assassin turned and disappeared into the crowd.

Footsteps approached. Z.

"Where the hell were you?" Rueben asked. Maybe he was seeing things, but Z's face looked a little pale.

"We've got to get the hell out of here."

"Huh? What's going on? Who was that…guy?"

"A supersoldier. Believe me. We do not want to mess with one of them."

Rueben picked himself up. "A supersoldier? What's that?"

"We need to get away from here." Z tried to tug Rueben's jacket, but he resisted.

"Young Z will wake up and find the arms dealer's body, minus a hand, and wonder what happened to the briefcase."

Z's face tightened. He walked away from the murder scene. "He won't mess with a supersoldier."

Rueben hurried to catch up. "Why? Can they warp?"

"No," Z said soberly. "But they're an enemy you don't want to have. With their weapons and technology, they're nearly invincible. I've never been able to kill one myself, even with warping. Best to leave them alone."

"Shit. I didn't know. How many are there? Armies of them?"

Z rolled his shoulder. "Buzz thinks there's only one."

"Who does it work for? The government?"

Z scoffed, some humor draining back into his face. "No one knows for sure. It rarely appears in public. It doesn't usually openly break the law, and even mainstream media knows not to give it any attention."

"So, what is he? A masked superhero who kills bad guys?"

Z didn't know. Rueben thought that was a bad thing since Z was a badass, and this supersoldier could beat him in his sleep without having warping powers.

"Besides," Z finally said. "You said yourself that the virus detector isn't registering the virus. It isn't in the case. This is a dead end."

"Fine," Rueben said, irritated. "Then let's head to Earth-Z's version of *Paper Warriors*. It would probably be a good idea to communicate with the team back on Earth-A."

"Okay. Okay, yeah, let's do that." Z rubbed behind his neck and discreetly checked over his shoulders to see if anyone was following them. Whoever this supersoldier was, he had Z on edge.

That wasn't good.

CHAPTER THIRTEEN

Earth-A

Marshall took another sip of the green smoothie. "You know, this organic shit ain't half bad." He was standing next to the intergalactic printing press, waiting to receive word from the Ruebens on Earth-Z.

Carolyn grinned sexily beside him. "You know, a green smoothie might go good with your daily hash brown breakfast."

Marshall raised his eyebrows. "Woman, don't even joke about that. Although…I do feel oddly energized after drinking it."

Behind Marshall and Carolyn, one of the three stooges was playing a video game on a tablet. The video game's upbeat music had been giving Marshall a headache while they waited by the printing press. He took another sip of the green smoothie. Another wave of energy flooded into him. Turning mistrustfully to the video game nerd, Marshall said, "You fuckers put drugs in this drink? Uppers? Cranks? Amphetamines?"

The newsman looked up from his handheld game. "N-no sir." He gave Marshall an awkward but serious salute.

"Man, I feel good. I feel like I could run a marathon, figuratively speaking. Carolyn, how about you?"

"It is pretty good stuff," she said with a smile. "That's what clean eating and exercise can do for you."

Marshall leaned in and kissed her. When he pulled back, he said, "I'm vowing right now to get back in shape."

Carolyn raised her eyebrows. "For me?"

Marshall chuckled. "Nah, for me. Believe it or not, I used to love training back when I started on the force. It gave me purpose. After this is over, I think I'll start a running regimen. Hell, maybe I can rope my son into running with me. God knows his endurance could use some improvement."

He met Carolyn's grin with his. He loved this woman so much and couldn't express in words how glad he was to have her back in his life. When her smile faltered, he said, "You're worried about them too, aren't you?"

She nodded, and Marshall put an arm around her shoulders. He wasn't the best with words, and he knew there wasn't anything he could do for her except to be there for her. With her being a battle-worn time warper, she was out of his league, but he could still love her.

"We'll get through this," he said. "We'll weather the storm."

Carolyn smiled weakly. "Thanks."

Marshall gestured with his free hand. "I'm sure they're having a grand ol' time. Adventures and such. Tracking down leads."

He doubted Carolyn's main worry concerned the two Ruebens. She was probably still shaken by Martha's phone call earlier and the dire message he'd typed out on the cabinet computer and they'd sent out to all the worlds. They couldn't be sure of the time on Earth-Z so they'd spammed the message out at one-hour intervals throughout the multiverse around the time the Ruebens were supposed to be on Earth-Z.

Marshall was scared too. Not just spooked but frightened in his bones for the fate of their Earth. The fact that the time virus was now free on Earth-A and rampaging through upstate New York in all directions…

But they didn't talk about that.

"You're right," Carolyn said at last. "I'm sure they're fine. They'll send word or show up at Buzz's lab a few hours earlier from now, and they'll find a way to defeat the virus."

"Yep." Marshall softly patted Carolyn's shoulder. "They're smart kids. They'll find a way to fix things."

"They will," Carolyn agreed.

"They will," Marshall repeated as if merely saying the words would make them come true. He tried to shake the negative thoughts from his head, and when that didn't work, he took a sip of his green smoothie. "Hey, you know what this fancy-shmancy drink reminds me of?"

Carolyn wiped her wet eyes. "What?"

"It reminds me of when I first met you when I was at that café on the college campus."

She giggled. "You mean when you spilled a cup of coffee on me?"

Now Marshall chuckled.

"Marshall Peet. You didn't spill it on me on purpose, did you?"

He hunched his shoulders and raised both hands. "What can I say? I guess it worked."

She playfully smacked his chest and looked up into his eyes. "I think I would fall for you in any world I went to."

Marshall wrapped an arm around her lower back and tenderly pulled her close to him. "Well, I wouldn't want you leaving again anytime soon. I better hold onto you, then."

She placed a hand under his chin. "I'm not going anywhere. I love you."

"I love you too, darling."

The newsman with the tablet suddenly exclaimed, "Woo-hoo! I won!" and the video game music chimed happily.

Marshall shook his head. With Carolyn in his arms, he felt like he'd already won. He hoped their story had a happy ending.

CHAPTER FOURTEEN

Earth-Z

"You sure this is the place?" Rueben asked the taxi driver.

The crusty old driver nodded from the front seat. "That's what the GPS says." The driver paused. "You want me to tell you the story of the first GPS too—"

"That won't be necessary," Rueben said. Their driver had spent most of the trip explaining how a few years back, Uber had changed their name to Taxi and started buying out all the taxi companies throughout the country. He hadn't sold out and had kept his taxi company even though he could barely make ends meet. "Principles," he'd said.

Z paid the man in digital currency, and he and Rueben climbed out of the vehicle. Unbeknownst to Rueben, Jim had slipped Z a digi-card loaded with funds while they were eating. After leaving the scene of the arms dealer's murder, they hailed a taxi to the newspaper office.

The taxi had parked on the curb outside a lavish two-story brick building with brightly colored shutters on the windows and a neon orange door. Several pink flamingo statues and yard gnomes littered the pristinely kept lawn, and there was a bubbling fountain out front.

Back on Earth-A, the place had looked like a real shithole, and there was a decrepit basketball court next door. Here on Earth-Z, there was a Caleb's Ice Cream Emporium fast-food restaurant. People were lined up out the door to get ice cream.

"That place any good?" Rueben asked.

Z shrugged. "I hear it's decent, but the owner is a real dick. Guy's a crook, connected to terrorists and shit but there's never been any evidence to link him to anything. Police have been after his ass for years."

"Geez," Rueben said. "This Earth sure has a lot of terrorists."

"Keeps me and my team in business." Z smirked. "That and the Russians. They're always up to something nefarious."

"I guess." Rueben led the way to the *Paper Warriors* entrance, admiring the sheen on the glazed sidewalk. There were neither cracks nor any weeds to be seen on the whole property. Directly up ahead was the front door. Rueben stopped and turned to Z.

"There's probably no threat inside there, but I think this might be a good time for you to teach me the two-finger knockout technique."

Z regarded him for a moment. "Okay. In my experience, danger often lurks in the most unlikely of places." He stepped up beside Rueben and grabbed his wrist. Then he instructed Rueben to form two of his fingers together.

He gently pressed Rueben's two fingers against his neck at the right spot. Stepping back, he met Rueben's eyes. "Now. You've got to be careful not to jab too hard. You want to incapacitate, not kill, okay?"

Rueben nodded, and Z pressed his fingers on Rueben's neck to emphasize the spot to jab.

"Okay. I think I got it. Can I practice on you?"

Z smirked. "You'd like that, wouldn't you? Well, hell no. Save it for the bad guys."

They walked the remaining steps to the front door. When Rueben reached it and tried the knob, he found it locked. He knocked on the door.

It was opened a few moments later by an attractive girl wearing thick dark sunglasses. She was lithe with long eyelashes. "Hello?" she said helpfully.

Rueben's mouth dropped open in stunned surprise. "Uhhh."

Z stepped up and clapped a hand on Rueben's shoulder. "Ma'am, excuse my associate. He's new on the job." He chuckled. "We were off-duty, but we received a call and decided to stop by to see how big the infestation was."

The girl's eyes widened. "Did you say infestation?" She turned and peeked back inside the office as if looking for someone, but she must not have seen anyone. She faced the Ruebens. "Who are you again?"

Z grinned. "We're the bug guys." He turned to Rueben. "Right, buddy?"

"Oh. Yep. 'See bugs. Kill bugs.' That's our motto."

"Oh." The girl scratched her head. She was a bit uneasy, and twirled her hair around her finger. "What...company are you from?"

"Mr. Buggs," Rueben answered professionally. "You've probably never heard of us before. We're a small family company."

The girl dropped her hand from her hair. "Not many of

those left anymore. Come on in and take a look. I hate bugs. Kill 'em all, I say."

Z flashed Rueben a satisfied look, and they stepped into the *Paper Warriors* office.

"Holy shit," Rueben said when he saw the polished marble floor and the chic tables and chairs in the office. The owner must be a real neat freak—it was spotless.

Z nudged him to keep moving. "The owner is good with money. Also sort of a playboy."

Rueben recalled how the *Paper Warriors* office on Earth-A didn't even have a boss. Three scrawny news guys who didn't know a potato from a tomato managed it.

"I'm going to go check for bugs this way," Z said.

Rueben nodded. "All right. I'll go this—"

A conference room door opened, and two more girls similar in age to the one who'd opened the door came into the main floor with surprised grins.

"Who's this cutie?" the short one asked.

"I don't know," the other one said cautiously. "Nice clothes though."

The girl who'd opened the door turned to Rueben. "We're the three news writers here. Just let us know if you need anything." She batted her eyes and the three girls took their seats at their desks and began to click and type.

Rueben rubbed his forehead. The differences between parallel Earths could be so fascinating. The important similarity here was the printing press sitting in the back against the wall. Since Z was busy "inspecting" the wall on the opposite side, Rueben headed toward the printing press.

It looked identical to the one back on Earth-A, which was good, and he quickly found the green button Buzz had mentioned. He searched for any papers containing messages from Marshall and Carolyn on Earth-A. He didn't see anything.

Walking around the printing press, Rueben stooped to examine a thick power cord that ran down one corner of the machine and disappeared beneath the floor. He turned to survey the rest of the office and saw a tall cabinet against the wall. It seemed oddly positioned back there but he didn't think anything of it.

When he turned back to inspect the printing press again, one of the news girls caught his eye from her desk as she nibbled on the end of a pen. Rueben nodded and turned back to the printing press. He could get used to the workers in this world's *Paper Warriors*.

He didn't see any newspapers anywhere and worried that the press might not even be plugged into a power source or connected to the Internet or multiverse or whatever. Standing up and bending over the press, he saw a curious-looking knob next to the green button. He reached out to fiddle with it.

"Whoa, hey!" the tall girl said and came running up to him. "You can't mess with the printing press."

Rueben cleared his throat. "I think I see a nest in there."

"A nest?"

"I, uh, don't think you've got a bug problem—I think you've got a mouse problem."

"Mice?"

One of the girls back at the desks squealed.

"Afraid so," Rueben said. He started to reach for the knob again. Maybe it was an on or off switch, and the machine was off.

She reached out and caught his wrist. "You can't."

He studied her. "Why not?"

Scratching her head, she said, "It's our boss. He doesn't

allow anyone to touch his precious printing press. Not even we can, and we work here."

"Your boss?"

"Jake Caleb. He owns the ice cream chain next door."

Rueben cocked an eyebrow, impressed. He reached out to turn the knob on the printing press. "I need to turn the machine on. To confirm the nest is inside."

She bit her fingernails. "Caleb won't like that."

He wasn't scared of an ice cream shop owner. He smiled and turned the knob. Nothing happened. Then there was a succession of *clicks* and *whirs*. Red lights began to flash along the printing press.

"It's printing!" one of the news girls exclaimed, rising from her desk and running toward Rueben. The third news girl followed.

Rueben was squinting at the internal mechanisms of the printing press as it primed and warmed itself up. He'd never seen a printing press in person before, but it didn't look anything like what he'd thought it would. It resembled a giant laser-jet printer rather than an old-fashioned printing press. As the machine started to rumble, the tall news girl grabbed his hand and pulled him back a step.

The two halves of the printing press closed like the jaws of a monster. A moment later, paper fed into the mouth, and print began to fill its surface.

Z ambled up to him then and smacked him on the back. "Looks like you found something. Good job, newbie."

The first of the papers had spat out, and Rueben was leaning forward to read its headline story when the news office's front door burst open.

"Oh no!" the tall news girl cried. "He's here."

CHAPTER FIFTEEN

Earth-Z

The man standing in the doorway didn't look all that intimidating. He wore aviator glasses, a Hawaiian shirt, cargo shorts, and loafers. He held a giant ice cream cone topped with vanilla ice cream in one hand. With the other hand, he removed his sunglasses.

"What the hell's going on in here? Who messed with my printing press? Girls?"

The tall news girl stammered. "I told them not to touch it. But they said there's an infestation—"

"They? Who's they?" The ice cream man turned his frosty gaze upon Rueben and Z. "Who are you two?"

"Bug guys," Rueben said. "Mr. Buggs. Small-time family comp—"

"We don't have a bug problem, and I didn't order any bug guys. So who are you and what's your real game?"

Rueben glanced over at Z, who shrugged. Behind them, the printing press continued to print papers. It hadn't stopped ever since it started.

"Sir, you're probably not going to believe this, but your printing press somehow connects with all the parallel worlds of the multiverse. We need to send a message to our friends on another Earth…"

One of the news girls sighed. "Why are the cute ones always so crazy?"

"Anyway," Rueben continued. "I realized the machine was off so I turned it on. Is that a problem?"

Caleb twitched his nose. Then he took a long lick of the ice cream piled on top of his cone. Then he took five steps forward until he was standing directly in front of Rueben.

"Yes. It. Is." The ice cream man raised his cone, tilted it downward, and smashed it onto Rueben's face, accentuating each word. "Yes. It. Is. A. Problem. You. Lying. Son. Of. A. Bitch."

"Okay, okay." Rueben stumbled back a step and tried to fend off the man with his hands, but he couldn't see due to the ice cream dripping into his eyes.

"No. It's. Not. Okay." Caleb smashed the remaining ice cream against Rueben's chest.

After blinking some of the frozen treat out of his eyes, Rueben knocked the man's hand away. "Don't make me hurt you. I'm combat-trained—"

Caleb smashed the ice cream onto Rueben's cheek, and Rueben started to see red. He was used to only using force against bad guys. This wasn't a bad guy. It was some eccentric business owner. He glanced at Z for support, but he only stood there with his arms folded, smirking.

"Getting your ass handed to you by the ice cream man." He chuckled.

What remained of the ice cream in the cone fell out and plopped on the floor. Now Caleb flipped the cone around so that he was gripping it with the point facing toward Rueben as if it were an ice pick.

Rueben grunted. "Am not—oww!"

"Oh fuck!" Z cringed at the ice cream cone jutting from Rueben's eye.

"Holy shit!" Rueben screamed, clutching his face.

"Holy shit," Caleb muttered in agreement. "Shit, man. I didn't mean to—"

Rueben found Z with his remaining eye. "Get me to the printing press. Now!"

Z snapped into action, grabbing Rueben by one shoulder and guiding him to the printing press. As Rueben turned so they could see him, the three news girls screamed. One of them raised her phone and snapped some pictures of him.

Shouting all the way and flailing his hands, Rueben finally reached the printing press still hungrily printing papers.

"Open it," Rueben said. "Open it!"

Understanding full well what Rueben was saying, Z grabbed the printing press' metal upper maw and strained as he raised it. It made an angry spitting and clicking sound that grew in intensity the higher he lifted it.

Rueben wasted no time shoving his head and upper chest onto the lower part of the printing press. It was hot against his cheek. "Do it. Drop the press."

"You sure about warping—"

"I said do it!"

Z didn't need him to repeat it. He let go, and the heavy press crushed Rueben's body.

"Shit," Z muttered as Rueben twitched. "What's black and white and red all over…"

Rueben died.

<u>Earth-Z</u>
(Two Minutes Earlier)

The man standing in the doorway still didn't look all that intimidating. He was still wearing his aviators, Hawaiian shirt, cargo shorts, and loafers. He still held the ice cream cone in one hand. As he reached up to remove his sunglasses with his free hand, Rueben marched up to him and kicked him in the balls.

The ice cream man dropped to his knees, and the ice cream cone fell to the floor with a satisfying *plop*.

Rueben realized that now was his chance to try out his new knockout technique. He raised his hand, held two fingers together, and jabbed Caleb in the neck at the spot Z had instructed him. The man's eyes bulged, he gasped, and he tipped over to the floor, motionless.

"The fuck was that for?" Z roared.

Rueben smirked. "Trust me. He deserved it."

"Deserved it? You fucking killed him…"

The three news girls ran up to their fallen boss. One of them checked his pulse and then shook her head. The second one snapped a photo of him. The third turned to Rueben and said sincerely, "Thank you. That man was such a sexist. See this polished floor? Caleb's a sanitation freak. He makes us clean it in French maid uniforms."

Rueben wasn't listening to the girl. He had other thoughts rushing through his mind. *Holy shit, what have I done…* He turned to Z. "The hell, man? You said that would instantly KO a person—not kill them."

"I warned that it *could* kill a person. Shit. You gotta learn finesse. Self-restraint."

"Fuck," Rueben muttered, grabbing his head between his hands.

"I'll go get a trash bag for the body," one of the news girls was saying.

The second one chimed in. "Good idea. We can probably hide him in the basement until after dark."

"Fuck this," Rueben said and turned seriously to Z. "You've got to kill me." He was already standing in front of the raging printing press when his words finally made sense to Z.

"You sure?"

Rueben gestured at the man lying dead next to the melting ice cream. "I killed a man. I have to warp back and undo it."

Z turned and studied the crime scene. He shrugged. "Sounds like you did this Earth a favor. You ask me; more assholes ought to die. Those three girls seem more than willing to cover it up for you—"

Rueben lanced him with angry eyes. "Do it. Lift the damn thing."

"If you say so."

The printing press made a horrible stuttering sound.

Rueben died.

Earth-Z
(Five Minutes Earlier)

Rueben pulled his hand back from the knob on the printing press. The machine started to click and whirl. As it rumbled, he turned and yelled at Z.

"There's a man about to step through that door. I need you to grab him when he comes in so I can interrogate him. Then I need you to knock him out with the two-finger trick."

Z stared at him. "Let me guess. You already tried that, accidentally killed him, and warped back in time?"

Rueben's face flushed red.

With a shit-eating grin, Z said, "I might not be a trained monkey, but I do love interrogating and using the two-finger trick." He dashed to the front door and waited to one side of it.

A moment later, the door opened, and Caleb stepped into the open doorway.

"Oh no," one of the girls said. "He's here."

Before the ice cream man could say a word, Z grabbed his arm and ripped him inside, closing the door behind him with his foot. Caleb yelped as his ice cream cone plopped sadly to the floor. Meanwhile, Z bound the man's wrists behind his back with a pair of zip ties from his pocket.

"From your body armor?" Rueben asked, to which Z smirked.

Then Z lifted the ice cream man to his feet and shoved his back against the wall.

"Yeah!" one of the news girls cheered.

"Kill him!" said another.

"We have trash bags," said the other one.

Rueben shook his head dismissively at them. Why did the sophisticated girls always turn out to be so crazy?

Without taking his eyes off the man in front of him, Z said, "You said you wanted to interrogate this punk, right?"

"Yes. I think he knows something about whoever owns the printing press."

Grinning, Z plucked the man's aviators off his face with his free hand and crushed the cheap frames in his fist.

The ice cream man whimpered. "Don't hurt me."

Z growled, "Then answer his questions."

Rueben stepped forward and pulled up his jacket sleeves to look more intimidating. Z shook his head. "Who do you work for?"

The ice cream man's eyes crossed briefly. "Huh?"

"Who do you work for?"

"N-no one. I run this business."

Rueben shook his head and tried to pop his knuckles, but they wouldn't pop.

"Man, I don't know who the hell you freaks are, but I'm only a businessman."

Rueben pointed back at the printing press. "Why do you have the printing press turned off?"

"I...I don't have to answer you—eegh!"

Z cut off the man's air supply with a forearm across his throat, then eased up a bit so he could talk.

"Okay, okay. Shit, your pitbull is gonna kill me here."

Z smirked at the comment and Rueben motioned for him to ease up a bit more. Z looked disappointed but removed his forearm from Caleb's neck. Caleb gingerly swallowed while Z bent and picked up the dropped ice cream cone. He licked remaining traces from inside the cone, grinning with appreciation as he monitored the man before him.

"Go on," Rueben said. "I don't have all day."

The ice cream man sighed. "I keep the printing press shut off at all times except for when I get a call to turn it on. That's all I know."

Rueben scratched his chin. Did this man not know anything about the printing press? "When you get a call? A call from who?"

Caleb swallowed again and drew a deep breath. "Man, I don't know anything except ice cream and sanitation and what they tell me to do...oh shit. I'm not saying anything more."

"What?" Rueben said. "Who's 'they?'"

"Not saying anyth—"

Z reapplied pressure to the man's throat with his free hand.

"—the people. The people who own the printing press. I don't know who they are, but they pay me to keep it safe and to keep it turned off unless they need to use it. It's where most of my money comes from. They pay me. Okay?"

Z leaned in toward the man's face and took a bite out of the cone. "What about your ice cream place?"

Caleb whined. "The emporium? It's hemorrhaging money like crazy. But it's my true passion. Who doesn't love good ice cream?"

"I don't," one of the news girls said. "I'm lactose intolerant."

Rueben considered this new information. "You don't know who pays you?"

The ice cream man shook his head. "I don't want to know. Shit, they'll probably kill me for telling you."

"Yes," one of the girls said.

"Serves you right," said another.

Caleb scoffed. "Am I that bad?"

The third news girl put her hands on her hips. "Dude. You make us clean the office in French maid uniforms."

"And I pay you double time for that."

"It's degrading," the tall one said with murder in her eyes.

Caleb turned his attention from his three employees back to Rueben. "I don't know anything else. Can you please let me go now?"

Rueben couldn't think of anything else he could ask. He nodded at Z, who removed his hand from the man's chest.

"Thanks. For a minute there, I thought you guys were gonna—"

Z thrust out with a two-fingered jab to the man's neck, and he collapsed unconscious to the polished floor. When the girls saw that he was still breathing, they looked disappointed. "So… you're not going to kill him?" one of them said.

Rueben groaned. "What? No, you psychos. You can't go around murdering people."

"Says the murderer," Z smirked.

"Doesn't count. I warped back afterward."

Z chuckled. "Fine. Fine. It's only natural for us warpers to abuse our power now and then." He kicked Caleb's foot for the hell of it and locked the front door. When he turned, Rueben was already poring over the papers that the press was still furiously printing. "What do all those papers say?"

Rueben tossed a paper aside and checked the front of the next one. "They're all from different worlds, I think. The font type is all different."

Stepping up beside Rueben, Z pointed at the top corner of the newspaper in Rueben's hand. Above the publication date was written *Earth 193.30418.*

"What's that?" Rueben asked.

"Per Buzz-Z, it's the standardized official designation of the Earth that printed this paper. Think of the number as a unique radio frequency that each parallel Earth has. Instead of calling them Earth-A and Earth-Z etcetera like you guys do, whoever runs the *Paper Warriors* press uses the Earths' proper frequencies."

Rueben shook his head. "Whoever owns this printing press knows about the multiverse. If we knew who it was, maybe they could help us."

Z raised an eyebrow. "Help with a super-mutated time virus?"

"It was an idea." Rueben tossed another paper down and picked up a new one. He read the headlining story: *Man Killed by Lemur at Beijing Zoo.*

"Oh, I've got an idea," Z said. "Actually, a question. Since when are you gung-ho about warping with the virus in me? How many times did you warp already in this office? I have a feeling I killed you more than once with that printing press, with the confident way you told me to kill you."

Rueben disregarded him. "Shut up and help me look."

Z started rummaging through the disjointed stack of papers piling up at the end of the printing press. "Maybe Earth-A doesn't have anything to report back to us."

"Or maybe this press is so logged up with papers that it hasn't printed yet." Rueben tossed another paper aside.

"Maybe we should focus on sending a message back to Earth-A and get back to the task at hand of tracking down the virus—"

"Got it!" Rueben unfolded the paper he was looking at. The top story read: *Rueben-A, Safe to Warp on Earth-Z.* "Oh, thank God," he muttered, then cursed.

"What is it?" Z growled, snatching the paper out of Rueben's hands. "Oh hell, the time virus is free on Earth-A..."

CHAPTER SIXTEEN

<u>**Earth-A**</u>

Buzz lifted his flying goggles and twisted around in the cockpit to better look at Aki and Rosa. "Girls, hold on. This might get a little bumpy."

Aki and Rosa gripped the harnesses holding them in their seats as the dual-rotor jet-copter rose higher into the air.

"Do you see it yet?" Aki called, the wind whipping her hair from the open copter door.

"Just dead trees and dust," Buzz answered as he turned back to face the windshield and controls. The virus was spreading outward from the mountain hideout, and they were following its devastation toward its ever-expanding perimeter. They couldn't see the virus' outer edge yet.

The jet-copter bounced through a rough patch of air current, and Buzz pretended not to hear the *clanking* of a loose bolt shearing off the fuselage and skittering along the outer hull.

Aki scrunched up her eyes. "What was that?"

Buzz shouted back, "Oh, just normal flying sounds. Everything is fine."

In the ceiling-mounted mirror above the cockpit, Buzz saw Rosa lean confidingly toward Aki and whisper something. Aki's face grew angry.

"If you get us killed," she said.

Buzz slapped his forehead. "This thing is perfectly safe."

"Rosa says it's a death trap."

"Rosa!" Buzz's eyes locked on the larger woman, still dressed in her maid outfit.

"Sorry, Mr. Buzz."

"I'll deduct your wage for that."

"You pay your robot?" Aki said. Both Rosa and Buzz turned to stare at her.

"Who ever said that Rosa's a robot?"

Aki held her tongue. She looked at Rosa strapped in next to her. "You are, aren't you?"

Rosa's usually neutral face grew stern. Then her face morphed into a grin. So did Buzz's.

Shaking her head, Aki said, "I should have stayed back in the compound with Martha."

Buzz eased up on the throttle. "Martha doesn't have the experience you do with experimental weapons." Aki sighed, and he peered through the windshield at the expanse of dust where previously lush trees and green growth had covered the mountains. It was a shame. And it had all been because he'd decided to vent the time virus that he converted to an active state.

They'd learned a lot from the experiment, but it was the costliest mistake he'd ever made in his life. If something happened to Rueben on Earth-Z and he was unable to return to Earth-A before this happened, that meant Buzz had single-handedly condemned and exterminated Earth-A's entire population aside from those he'd inoculated: himself, Aki, Martha, Marshall, and Carolyn.

The thought of that sent his heart racing. Marshall was older so it would be up to Buzz to repopulate the Earth. That was an uncomfortable thought so he turned his focus back to the task at hand. Sex was for sexbots. That's what he always said. At least, it was for him. It was usually a joke. It wasn't so funny now though.

He narrowed his eyes. "I see it," he called to Aki and Rosa. Finally, they were nearing the perimeter of the expanding circle of viral death. It was odd because by his estimates, it should've been another minute or so until they reached it. Reaching over with his free hand, he put Martha on speaker.

"Buzz?" she practically had to yell so he could hear her.

"Who else would it be? Of course, it's me."

"You're an idiot, Buzz. That's how you answer the phone. Don't you know anything about human interaction—"

"We geniuses aren't perfect, you know. Are you watching the satellite view now?" He corrected the steering. He wished he had an autopilot built into his jet-copter, but it was a passion project. He never expected to have to use it in an actual combat situation like this. The flight from his mansion out to his underground hideout in the Catskill Mountains had stressed it more than he'd liked, and he hadn't made time to make any repairs to it, hence the loose bolts shearing off—

He winced as another bolt skittered along the outside. In the mirror, he saw Aki glare at him. He didn't blame her. There was a real chance of them dying here. However, if they succeeded, it would be the thing of legends.

"Yeah," Martha said. "I'm watching it right now. I see you approaching the virus' perimeter."

The jet-copter jounced through some turbulence and Aki cursed loudly.

"Uh Buzz, are things okay there?"

"Eh, as good as they can be, given the current variables. Why are we already approaching the perimeter? My calculations said we were farther away."

He envisioned Martha rolling her eyes. "Are you complaining about making better time in your rickety death contraption?"

"It's not a death contraption! Now focus. I'm not complaining—I had this all planned out in my mind." He banked the machine to follow the curve of the virus' outer edge. "We reached it quicker than anticipated, but I accounted for the jet-copter's max speed, which I've been maintaining ever since it was attainable. So that means the virus' growth rate has slowed. Have you noticed?"

"Buzz, I'm watching a satellite view, not in an airplane. The circle gets bigger by about a millimeter every few minutes. I'm not calculating the average rate of growth. It's growing. What more do you want me to say?"

Buzz sighed. Why couldn't the common person be more like him? Why didn't they pay attention to the important details in life instead of binge-watching reruns of *American Idol* and *Big Brother*?

"Why?" Martha asked. "What does it mean if the virus is slowing down?"

Finally. A thoughtful question. Maybe there was hope for her yet. "I don't know," he said simply.

"Then why the hell did you ask me?"

Okay, maybe he was wrong about her.

"I'll call you back if I need you." Buzz terminated the call.

Aki called. "The virus is spreading slower?"

"Yeah. I'm not sure what to make of it. But it's in our favor. Are you about ready?" He saw her nod in the mirror. "Good. Then carefully—I repeat, carefully—unbuckle yourself and Rosa will hand you the weapon."

Aki started to undo her harness. "Okay. Just make sure you keep this death plane steady."

Yet another bolt sheared off, tumbling along the outer skin. "You're upsetting my jet-copter."

Aki climbed out from under her harness and kept a hand on the cargo netting lining both walls of the jet-copter's interior. "Next, you're going to say it has a name."

"Of course. It's Shirley."

"Whatever." Aki edged up to the open doorway. As soon as the wind started whipping her bangs into her eyes, she knew she should've pinned her hair back.

"Allow me, Ms. Aki." Rosa slid a clear hairnet over Aki's head.

"Um, thanks?"

Next, Rosa handed Aki a futuristic weapon that looked like a cross between a sniper rifle and a rocket launcher. It was heavy, and as she leaned against the open doorway on one knee, the weight helped to anchor her. Pressing the butt to her shoulder, she bent her head to peer through the orange-tinted scope.

"Do you need me to zoom in for you?" Rosa said helpfully.

Aki squinted through the scope. "Yes."

Rosa twisted a knob on the scope's side until Aki said it was good.

"You all set?" Buzz called.

"Tell me when to fire."

Buzz flexed his fingers and returned his hands to the yoke. He would have to keep the jet-copter flying at a constant angle to follow the curve of the perimeter. After a deep inhale, Buzz said, "You're good to fire."

Aki peered through the weapon's scope. She had the crosshairs on the edge of the expanding death circle. Aiming just outside it, she pulled the trigger.

The weapon made an electrical sound as the recoil hit her shoulder, then a projectile screamed toward the mountain below. She watched its streaking trail, adrenaline now shooting through her body. The missile impacted inside the trees on the safe side of the perimeter and exploded upward in a rush of smoke and sparks.

Already she was firing farther down the line watching the streaking blur from her peripheral vision as she lined up her next shot.

The jet-copter rocked right before her third shot, and she yelled, "Keep it steady!"

Buzz called, "Sorry!"

Another bolt sheared off and *tinked* along the outer hull. *Sorry, my ass,* Aki thought. If this aircraft fell apart in midair, Buzz would be sorry, all right.

She adjusted her aim and fired when she'd recovered from the aircraft's jouncing. Ordinarily, being in the air didn't faze her. Of course, Buzz wasn't usually behind the controls.

This crazy life of mine... She'd done some covert stuff for the CIA, but her boss had never tasked her with something like this. Her aim with Buzz's prototype weapon was literally saving the world.

She paused long enough to wipe her forehead with her upper arm. Spending time with Rueben's friends was always interesting. She wished Rueben would get back soon. She missed him, and even though he was a time warper—how badass was that?—she did worry about him. He wasn't as experienced as Rueben-Z. Hopefully, things were going all right on Earth-Z.

The jet-copter suddenly hit another patch of rough air, and Aki nearly tumbled from the aircraft. She was halfway through the door when Rosa caught her by the shoulder and pulled her back in.

With her heart in her throat and now nearly dizzy from the adrenaline coursing through her veins, she nodded her thanks.

"You're welcome, Ms. Aki. You're a good shot. Keep it up."

Buzz was fighting the aircraft now. The controls were about to give out, and he feared if he tried to force it any harder, the whole copter might snap apart in multiple places. Glancing up at Aki in the rearview mirror, he could see that she sensed it too. She was strapping herself back into her seat.

"How'd you like my anti-viral railgun?"

Aki clicked the last belt buckle into place. "Fired like a dream. I'm more worried about your flying skills."

Buzz scoffed. "Are you kidding? My flying is just fine, thank you very much. You might not know, but I was flying drones before 'drone' was even a household name. I flew my first ultralight at age eight—with a booster seat—and am the youngest person to achieve their pilot's license in the state. If anyone can pull this off, it's me."

"He is right," Rosa called with a hand on Aki's shoulder. "If anyone can bring this to a safe landing, it's him."

Now the engines were making some rough coughing sounds. Aki cupped her hands over her mouth. "Did the railgun work? Is the virus contained?"

Buzz had to admit, between trying to keep the plane both on course and in the air, he hadn't been able to analyze the results of their efforts. Now he was heading back to the mountain hideout at the center of the circle of death. He called Martha and put her on speakerphone. "Did the virus stop?"

"I…I think so?"

"Maybe we should turn back and fire a few more?" Aki said.

Buzz shook his head. "Can't do. We're uh…running on fumes."

As if in response, the jet-copter sputtered.

Aki cursed.

"You guys going to make it?" Martha asked over the phone line.

"Of course," Buzz said—and hoped—at the same time Aki said, "No."

Suddenly, the copter's nose tilted forward into a dive.

"What the hell, Buzz!"

Buzz didn't look at Aki. He had to focus. He had to find the landing strip outside his mountain hideout. It was the only place he'd be able to land the jet-copter safely.

"Aha!" He found it.

"We're still falling!" Aki said.

Buzz's mind rattled through all their possible options. "That might work…" He began a hypothetical move he'd only read about stunt pilots trying to pull off. "Hold on, ladies."

"Oh shit," Aki said when she realized what he was about to do.

Martha came back over the line. "Yes. It worked. The virus has stopped spreading. Good job, you three!"

The aircraft groaned as Buzz tested its construction to the max.

When they finally touched down upon the landing pad outside the hideout, the engine was aflame, and one of the rotors was coughing heavy smoke.

"Mission success," Buzz breathed.

Aki vomited her lunch.

CHAPTER SEVENTEEN

Earth-Z

Back in the Earth-Z *Paper Warriors* office, Rueben and Z were studying the opened computer cabinet at the back of the room. It housed what appeared to be a template for sending messages to other worlds. They'd found it after Z started tearing up the floor around where the cable ran down the back corner of the printing press. It didn't take long for them to infer that it led to the mysterious cabinet at the back of the room.

When they turned to the three news girls for guidance, they shrugged. Z had broken the cabinet lock, and Rueben had started to type out a response to Marshall's and Carolyn's Earth-A paper.

That's when a knock sounded on the door.

"Don't open that door," Z growled.

One of the news girls looked through the door's peephole. "It's the police."

Rueben groaned. "Police? Shit. Where's Caleb's body?"

"Don't worry about it," said one of the news girls. In

response to Rueben narrowing his eyes at her, she added, "We didn't kill him. He's in an office. We're gonna dress him in a French maid's outfit and see how he likes it."

Shaking his head, Rueben said, "This newspaper office is so messed up."

The tall news girl walked up. "You should see this place on Taco Tuesday."

"I don't think I want to. Is the policeman leaving?"

Another knock sounded on the door.

"It's a police*woman*," the news girl at the peephole said. "Want me to let her in?"

Z grunted. "Do you understand what 'don't open that door' means?"

Rueben turned to Z. "She'll leave, right?"

"How should I know?"

"This is your Earth."

"I already told you the cops want to nail Caleb's ass for his shady dealings. They're probably trying to apply some pressure to him."

"So she'll leave?"

Z considered it. "If they don't have probable cause, yeah, she'll probably leave."

Suddenly, the third news girl screamed.

"What is it?" the tall news girl said.

"I just saw a cockroach. Are those guys really bug guys—"

At that moment, the front door kicked inward.

Rueben and Z rose and spun to face the new silhouette standing in the doorway. "You've got to be kidding me," Rueben said as Martha-Z stepped into the room and raised her gun, pointing it at his chest.

"Police!"

"This isn't what you think," Rueben said.

Martha-Z wore her work blues. Why was she here? Shouldn't she still be at Chuck E. Cheese?

She quickly sized him up. "What should I think this is?" The printing press continued to spit out newspapers.

Rueben grabbed a paper off the disjointed growing stack. "We're newspaper delivery guys."

Z nudged him and whispered, "Don't incriminate us any further."

"We didn't do anything—"

"They tried to kill me!" Caleb's muffled voice shouted from one of the conference rooms. A loud *smack* followed it.

Rueben took a step toward Martha-Z. She looked a bit tougher and fiercer than Martha-A.

"Stay where you are."

Rueben took another confident step forward. It couldn't be a coincidence she was here. "Why are you here?"

"I said stop." She gestured with her handgun.

"Dude, what are you doing?" Z asked from behind him.

Rueben smirked. "It's not like I have anything to lose—"

Martha-Z fired, her shot taking Rueben in the leg.

"Son of a bitch," he cried as he fell over, clutching at the entry wound.

Z chuckled. "Damn rookie mistake. You want me to kill you?"

Martha-Z jerked the gun in Z's direction. "There will be no killing here. Now. Hands in the air."

Rueben took his hands off his bleeding leg and started to crawl toward Martha-Z.

"What the fuck kind of drugs are you people hyped up on? I said, 'Stay where you are.'"

"Can't do that." Rueben forced himself into a half-crouch. He couldn't continue this mission with a leg injury. He'd have to die. Again.

"You got a death wish?" Martha-Z asked.

He looked her in the eyes and nodded. Then he lunged for her. He anticipated her stepping off to the side and compensated so he fell right on her. She had no choice but to shoot.

Rueben grunted and rolled off to the side.

Then he died.

<u>Earth-Z</u>
(Four Minutes Earlier)

"Get ready." Rueben stood by the front door.

Z nodded.

Rueben ripped open the door. Martha-Z was standing there with her hand raised, about to knock.

"Officer Dragone," Rueben said politely. "So nice to see you today. Come in."

Martha-Z studied Rueben. "Um…do I know you? You look familiar."

Rueben chuckled nervously and motioned her in. As she cautiously stepped past him, he unclipped her pistol and tossed it to Z, who deftly caught it.

"Bastard—" Martha-Z ripped a small device from her other hip and tried to aim it at Rueben. He knocked it to the side with a swift chop. It clattered to the floor. It was a taser.

Rueben already had the door closed and locked behind them, and Z was zip-tying Martha's hands.

"You don't know what you're doing," Martha grunted. "You don't want to do this."

Rueben calmly met her eyes. "We're on the same side."

She lashed out with a kick to his groin, and he barely deflected it.

Z nodded approvingly. "Nice reflexes."

Now Martha-Z got her first good look at Z. "You…Rueben?"

Z grinned. "In the flesh."

She turned her gaze back to the younger Rueben. "Two of you! But how? The hell is going on? Am I tripping? What kind of trick is this?"

"No trick." Z held up a hand to Rueben, signaling to allow him to explain. "Short story: there are parallel Earths out there. My accomplice here is me from one of those Earths, one where he's younger."

"But you…"

Z scooped up a newspaper and pointed at the headline: *Creeping Death Continues Spread Through Earth*. "I'm from this Earth, but I somehow get infected by a deadly, world-ending virus. Once this Earth died a few times and I warped back each time, I decided to go to other Earths to search for a cure." He sighed. "I think I found it. We need one more sample of the virus from this Earth. Since I went back in time in a space and time capsule, I am technically a duplicate of the younger Rueben currently inhabiting this Earth."

"Shit," Martha-Z said. "That's a hell of a lot to take in. How do I know this isn't some con game?" She wriggled against her bindings. "You did tie me up."

"Would you have listened to us any other way?" Z asked.

Martha-Z narrowed her eyes. "Who says I'm listening to you now?"

"What led you here?" Rueben asked.

"Huh?"

"Why aren't you still at Emma's birthday party?"

"How do you know about that?"

Rueben knew he had to be careful. Martha-Z's angry voice kinda scared him even though her wrists were bound.

"We know," Rueben said, "because what he said is true. We're trying to stop a deadly virus on this Earth, and you happen to be involved in it. So what led you here? Why did you choose this exact time to knock on the ice cream man's door?"

Martha-Z bit her lip as she studied him.

"We're not going to hurt you," Rueben said.

"Prove it. Cut my bindings."

Rueben nodded at Z, and the man did as she said. Surprisingly, Martha-Z didn't try anything. As she felt her wrists, she said, "I didn't expect you to do that. You're both either really dumb or…"

Rueben tilted his head. "Telling the truth?"

"This is crazy," Martha-Z said. "Absolutely bat shit crazy."

"Your childhood friend can time warp, mind you," Rueben said. "And you have some form of déjà vu powers."

"Okay. Okay." Martha-Z threw up her hands. "Rueben—my Rueben—found an arms dealer in the street. Dead. With his hand missing along with the metal briefcase attached to it." She gave both of them a long hard look. "There were two men reportedly with him when someone killed him. You were there, weren't you?"

Z raised a hand. "Guilty."

Martha-Z dropped her head into her hands. "This is so messed up."

"So…what?" Rueben pressed. "How'd you connect the dots to here?"

Martha-Z shook her head. "Since there's a supersoldier in the equation, Rueben decided to let this one alone." She glanced at Z. "From experience, we know better than to engage with one of them. Besides, a rival arms dealer probably hired the supersoldier."

Now, this was the Martha that Rueben knew. He grinned. "So instead of letting things go, you decided to shake up the hornet's nest? Do some investigating of your own?"

Martha-Z nodded. "This Caleb creep reputedly has dealings with that dead arms dealer. Thought I'd come check it out to see if he knew anything. I do like scaring criminals."

One of the news girls stepped into the office with a clear plastic bag in her hands. "My boss is a criminal," she said with a cheerful smile. Martha-Z stared at her.

Z turned to Rueben. "What are we going to do now? Sit around and twiddle our thumbs like a couple of schmucks? Buzz-A isn't responding. For all we know, something bad happened back on Earth-A."

Rueben shook his head, deep in thought.

"Then what? Something tells me you have an idea."

"I do." Rueben angled his head toward Martha-Z. "We need help. I think it's time we introduce ourselves to the rest of Team Z."

CHAPTER EIGHTEEN

<u>Earth-Z</u>

"I like this ballsier version of you," Z said with a soft chuckle.

Rueben rubbed his jaw as they watched Buzz's mansion from the tree line. "Well, let's hope our little gambit pays off. If Martha double-crosses us and Young Z decides to warp back to when we first arrived here to get the jump on us..."

Z nudged Rueben's arm. "I trust your gut. It was a good call."

They were going against what Buzz had told them to do for the second time now. First with him warping when they didn't know if it was safe or not, and now by directly interacting with Earth-Z's version of themselves.

Working with the team would be the quickest way to track down the origin of the time virus. They wouldn't have to keep tracking down possible leads and find ways to circumvent Team Z. Besides; they didn't want Young Z to get infected. If the man knew about the true threat, he could be more cautious on whichever mission would lead to his infection.

Rueben raised his monocular at the mansion's front door and focused on Martha-Z. Rosa-Z opened the door for her, and she stepped inside. A few minutes later, a dark SUV pulled up to the mansion, and Aki-Z and Emma got out. After glancing over both shoulders, Aki-Z and Emma proceeded to the door and Rosa-Z let them in.

"Now we wait," Z said and sat in a half-crouch against a tree.

As they waited, Rueben felt in his pockets. He nearly cut his finger on something sharp. "What the hell…" He pulled out the broken fragments of the special glass vial that Buzz had given him. "This isn't good," Rueben said. "Please tell me that your vial is still intact…"

Z grimaced and shook his head. "Nah. Must've broke mine too back at the *Paper Warriors* office."

"Shit, how are we going to get a sample of the ground zero virus now? Why didn't you tell me when you realized?"

With a shrug, Z said, "You're the responsible one out of the two of us. Why weren't you more careful with your vial?"

"Don't try to put this on me. We're a team."

"Relax. Buzz-Z is a genius like Buzz-A. He'll be able to hook us up with another special vial that can contain a super virus. Probably."

Rueben sighed. "I hope you're right."

They passed the next few minutes in silence. Eventually, Martha opened the mansion's front door and waved with both hands. Rueben hadn't told her where they would be watching from, only that she should wave when they reached a consensus that it was safe for them to come in and talk.

Rueben and Z exchanged glances.

"Go time," Z said.

Rosa-Z opened the door for Rueben and Z. "Hello, fellow Ruebens. We have been expecting you."

Z frowned, but Rueben tried not to read into the words.

Rosa closed the door behind them. "Follow me." She led them down corridors eerily familiar to those in Buzz-A's recently destroyed mansion. For a moment, Rueben felt like he was back on Earth-A. Then Rosa deposited them in Buzz's expansive living room. Rueben was ready to sit on one of Buzz's super comfortable couches and recliners and was surprised to see that instead, futuristic treadmills dotted the room.

Rueben scratched the back of his head. "At least I know how you stay in such good shape on Earth-Z."

Z smirked. "Aki's suggestion. She keeps Buzz and me in good shape."

"Buzz goes on missions too?"

"Nah. But ever since he gave up alcohol, he became a big health nut. He lives and dies for this kale and lemon green juice he takes every morning. He says it helps him look more attractive for the ladies, but between you and me, I think he realized that the alcohol was killing his brain cells." Z grunted. "The man still has more brain cells than everyone combined in a fifty-mile radius."

Rosa swooped into the room with a silver platter. "Organic Twinkie?"

Rueben raised a hand. "I'm good." Footsteps sounded from the hallway outside, and he turned to see Aki-Z and Martha-Z striding into the living room.

Aki-Z stopped short and sized them up. "A younger and an older version of my husband, how strange."

Z looked about to say something, but he held his tongue. There was a poignant sadness to his face that made Rueben re-evaluate the man. He didn't blame Z. This was technically his wife, but he couldn't be with her.

Rueben thought of something then. What was Z's end game on Earth-Z? With a Young Z already in this world, how would Z resume his old life on Earth-Z? Surely he had a plan. Rueben made a mental note to ask him later.

Aki-Z propped her hands on her hips. "Where the hell is Buzz?"

Rosa raised a hand. "I've already paged him three times. He should be here any time."

"I'm here, I'm here," Buzz-Z called from the hallway. "People, calm down…" He strode into the room in a pair of tight jogging pants and an unbuttoned lab coat. His bare chest beneath the white lab coat was scrawny, but it was extraordinarily tan. It was near as orange as a carrot.

Rueben's eyes passed disbelievingly up his parallel Earth best friend until he reached his face. Then he did a doubletake.

"Keep calm, keep calm, people." Buzz-Z leveled a futuristic-looking rifle at Rueben and Z. "Except for you two."

Rueben wasn't even looking at the weapon though—his eyes remained glued to Buzz-Z's face. It was shiny and taut and frozen into a sort of arrogant, fake smile.

Z grunted and thrust up both hands. "Buzz? What's the meaning of this?"

"I'm not your Buzz," Buzz-Z said with a shake of his head. "I don't know who you are and I won't until I have a chance to run some tests on your DNA."

Z stared at Buzz-Z. "All you have to do is ask. You don't have to go Rambo on my ass."

Chuckling, Buzz said, "You think this is going Rambo on your ass? Check out my best friend."

At the sound of approaching boot steps, Z turned to face Young Z entering the room with a futuristic-looking bazooka in his hands, leveled at Rueben and Z.

"Yo! Other guy," Buzz-Z called, and Rueben realized he was talking to him. "You all right?"

Rueben blinked and rubbed his hands over his eyes. "Yeah?"

"Then what the hell are you staring at? You on drugs or something?"

Rueben glanced over his shoulder and saw Young Z and his futuristic bazooka. "Shit." He turned toward Rosa and saw that she had a futuristic-looking pistol beneath her silver Twinkie platter trained on them. "You too, Rosa?"

"Face it, assholes," Young Z said. "You're outgunned."

Silence settled upon the expansive living room, then Z started to laugh. It was a deep belly laugh, and it was so unexpected, Rueben partly felt like laughing himself despite the grim situation.

Young Z took a step toward Z while fingering his weapon.

"Outgunned? Ha." Z smirked, then turned to Aki. "I taught you well, babe."

Aki frowned, and Young Z gritted his teeth. "Watch it, or I'll blast you away."

"I'm a Repeater," Z said goadingly. "You kill me; I show back up and kick your ass before you even know I'm here." It was a bluff, but Team Z didn't know that.

Now it was Young Z's turn to laugh. He patted his futuristic bazooka. "Oh, this won't kill you. But it'll paralyze you instantly, and with the pain you'll feel...you'll wish you were dead."

Z laughed louder. "Pain? That thing doesn't cause any pain. I made you take that feature out in case you ever decided to use it against me. Remember?"

The smirk on Young Z's face shifted to an angry frown. "I…" He whipped his head around to face Buzz-Z. "How'd he know that?"

"Because I'm you from the future, asshole," Z said.

Buzz-Z waved dismissively at Z. "Probably has the lab bugged somehow."

"You wish," Z said. "I know all about you guys, and it's not due to a bug. For example, Martha, I know your favorite animal is a toucan—you have a plastic toucan on your keychain. Buzz, you had a lumberjack phase when you were a child. Aki, your favorite flower is cherry blossom."

Aki's eye twitched. "The blossom I found in that warehouse…"

Z nodded.

Young Z didn't like what he saw. He prepared to fire. "Don't bullshit a bullshitter."

Z smiled sadly. "I'm not. And you. You feel like shit for missing out on your child's birthday party and childhood. But at the same time, you get off on what you do. You love your job—"

"Shut up!" Young Z turned his weapon on Rueben now.

Jerking at him with his bazooka, Young Z said, "Open your mouth one more time, I shoot. If you know about this weapon, the results are instant. And my trigger finger is well-trained."

Z raised his palms upward in surrender, but only after pressing a button on the listening device in his pocket.

"Well," Z said, turning to Rueben. "What say you?"

Rueben didn't know what to say. They were standing in

Buzz's living room, a space that on Earth-A had been the scene of countless good times and relaxing with his best bud. This place, though…it looked like a gym with a high ceiling.

Finally, he said, "You don't have to believe who we are. All you need to understand is that we're from the future. And in the future, there's a massive threat to the entire multiverse that we're here to try to prevent."

"Enough of these lies," Young Z said.

"You should hear them out."

The voice was soft and girlish and belonged to Emma, standing in the doorway.

CHAPTER NINETEEN

Earth-Z

"What?" Young Z said as Aki-Z rushed over to Emma and hugged her against her legs.

Emma pressed one cheek up against Aki-Z's legs. "They're telling the truth. They're from the future."

"How do you know?" Young Z said.

"Because they told me."

At this, Young Z's eyes bulged. "You talked with my daughter?"

"When you missed her birthday party," Z clarified.

"That's it. I'm shooting you both—"

"Maybe," Aki-Z said, "we should hear what they have to say." She whispered to Emma to go back to the pool room. Emma nodded and dashed out in the way that little kids do. Then Aki-Z turned to Martha. "Innocent until proven guilty, right?"

Martha nodded slowly. In all the suspense, Rueben only then noticed that she had her service pistol trained on them.

At the sight of Emma now, she lowered the gun. However, Buzz-Z and Young Z still had their weapons up.

Martha chewed her lip. "Why don't you tell us your story. Why you're here."

Rueben and Z exchanged glances. Then Z nodded at Rueben to explain.

"Sometime in the next day to few days, this Earth's Rueben is infected by a time virus which develops into a time disease that destroys this Earth." He paused, a bit surprised that Team Z was listening to him and also that they hadn't shot him yet.

Buzz-Z stared at Rueben. "Time disease? Interesting. Who named it? And why? Explain."

Rueben continued. "I named it on my Earth. You said you liked the name. Because it turns all organic life into dust, withering them in a matter of seconds as if an entire lifespan has passed in a blink of an eye."

"That's disconcerting," Aki-Z said with a look at Martha-Z, who nodded.

"If it's true," Young Z countered.

Rueben turned his attention to the man. "You get infected. Then…" Rueben glanced at Z to make sure it was okay to continue.

"This is your decision to tell them," Z said. "You're the one who's gotta own up to your mistakes if that's what they turn out to be."

Rueben quickly thought it over and decided to tell Team Z what had happened to Z when he inadvertently infected Earth-Z and the other parallel Earths. "Better to ask for forgiveness than permission, right?"

Z grinned. "I've taught you everything I know now."

Young Z fidgeted, showing his impatience. "You're saying I let some…time pandemic destroy this Earth?"

"No—" Rueben began.

"And if you're me…" Young Z jabbed a finger at Z. "How did I get to another world? A parallel Earth?" He turned to Buzz-Z. "Is this even possible?"

Buzz-Z shuffled his feet.

"I mean, tell me, if you're not making this up. How would one travel between worlds?"

Z nodded at Buzz-Z. "A space and time capsule. I took your capsule, the one you've been working on in secret."

Young Z roared with laughter. When he realized Buzz-Z wasn't laughing, his face paled. "Wait. You're saying you really do have a time capsule? You know about other Earths? Shit, man, why wouldn't you tell me? Tell us?" With a sweep of his arms, he indicated Buzz-Z, Aki-Z, and Martha-Z.

"Well, buddy. I wasn't a hundred percent certain it would work. The only way to verify the existence of other parallel Earths would be to send a person in the space and time capsule once I complete it. Which I haven't. But it's close." Buzz-Z squinted at Z. "You're saying that I succeeded? That you're the same person as him?" He jerked his head sideways at Young Z.

Z nodded.

Buzz-Z grabbed his head. "Egads. This changes…everything." The genius' eyes darted to the ceiling and down at the futuristic rifle in his hands. "You telling us about this now. What if this changes things? Changes the future on this Earth?"

Z reached out and leaned against a treadmill. "That's what we're banking on. If we don't change things—mainly me getting infected by the time virus—this Earth doesn't have a future."

Buzz-Z stroked his chin. "Time virus. Time virus…you

must have some idea of its origins." It wasn't a question but a statement.

"Most likely," Z said. "I—he—gets infected on one of our upcoming missions."

"You don't know which one?" Young Z said incredulously. "If you're me, you should have a nanobot in your blood system that Buzz can access and see the world from your eyes."

Z lifted one foot and stretched it on the side of a treadmill. "We've gone through my nanobot footage on another Earth with another Buzz. It's spotty in places. It shorts out."

While Young Z shook his head disbelievingly, Buzz-Z said, "What's the first memory where your nanobot vision fades?"

"On a tanker mission that occurs in a day or two," Z said.

"Tanker mission?" Martha-Z asked.

Rueben nodded. "A seemingly unmanned tanker heads toward the coastline. It maybe has a weapon on board."

"I sink it," Z added. "But I don't recall the mission too clearly. It's like the virus has messed with my mind and doesn't want me to remember the details of what happened aboard it."

Young Z laughed harshly. "This has to be the dumbest sci-fi movie premise ever."

Rueben turned to Aki-Z. She was the leader of Team Z, wasn't she? Calmly, he asked her if she knew of any suspicious tankers in the Atlantic Ocean.

"Let me check." She scooped up a tablet sitting on a side table and swiped a few times. Then she scrolled through a data feed. "A tanker was flagged upon leaving Europe. But...a few hours after, the report came down." She did some mental calculations. "If it was at those coordinates fifteen hours ago, that would put it about here. If it maintained its projected course," she glanced up and swept her gaze over them all. "Then it could possibly reach the eastern US coast in about twenty-four hours."

"Babe, you don't believe them do you?" Young Z was standing with his hands still wrapped around the futuristic bazooka.

She looked at him tenderly. "If this threat is as grave as they say it is, I don't think we should take any chances."

Young Z passed his eyes over Rueben and Z. "I say these are a couple of con men."

Rueben sighed. "Look, we need to get on the same page. What can we do that will prove that we're the good guys? That we're on the same side and want to help you and your Earth."

Young Z considered it. "There is one way you could prove to me that what you're saying is true. A test, you could say."

"A blood sample from each of them?" Buzz-Z suggested with a glint in his scientist's eyes.

"No."

When Young Z told them what he had in mind, Rueben dropped his head. "Are you serious?"

"Deadly," Young Z said.

"Shit," Rueben said.

With a smirk, Z patted Rueben on the shoulder. "You've got this."

CHAPTER TWENTY

<u>Earth-Z</u>

"This is not a test," Rueben said.

Young Z flexed his arms outward and popped his knuckles before him. "A duel is a sort of test."

"This isn't a duel—it's a fight to the death."

Rubbing his hands together, Young Z said, "If you're a Repeater, what are you so scared about?"

"I'm not scared. It's just that this isn't necessary."

"Eh, you'll be all right." Z leaned over Rueben's shoulder. "Go in with a left hook—he'll never see that coming."

Rueben frowned. "I was thinking about going for his hip. You said it's injured, right?"

"Won't work." Z studied Young Z on the other side of the ring. "It's an indestructible hip replacement. You'd only hurt your hand."

"Enough talk." Young Z stepped away from Aki-Z after pecking her on the cheek. "Let's do this."

Z grabbed Rueben by the shoulder and shoved him forward into the makeshift arena. Not for the first time since being thrown into this situation, Rueben studied the space. It was an expansive garden shed located behind the mansion. On the walls were the typical weed-eaters, shovels, garden spades, some sickles. There were also a couple of machetes, a chainsaw, and a fencing saber. There was no lack of ways to kill or be killed.

Suddenly, Young Z shot forward like a mongoose. Rueben sidestepped, but his opponent was already lashing out with a long fat blade he'd had concealed behind his back. The knife passed through Rueben's ribs and penetrated his heart.

Rueben fell to his knees and died.

Earth-Z
(One Minute Earlier)

Young Z shot forward like a mongoose. Rueben sidestepped, but his opponent was already lashing out with a long fat blade he'd had concealed behind his back. Anticipating the attack, Rueben caught Young Z's wrist, ducked in, and dealt the man an unexpected blow to the gut.

Young Z cursed, then kicked the toe of his boot against the floor. A blade snicked out, and Rueben watched in frustration as the man kicked upward, the boot blade impaling Rueben through the temple.

"Shit," Rueben muttered, then died.

Earth-Z
(Two Minutes Earlier)

Young Z shot forward like a mongoose. Rueben sidestepped, but his opponent was already lashing out with a long fat blade he'd had concealed behind his back. Anticipating the attack, Rueben caught Young Z's wrist, and ducked in, and dealt the man an unexpected blow to the gut.

Young Z cursed, then kicked the toe of his boot against the floor. A blade snicked out, and Rueben dodged the man's vicious upward kick. Rueben rushed forward again, catching Young Z beneath the knee and shoving him back against the tool shed's wall.

Rueben was already reaching for the needle nose pliers as Young Z grunted with the impact. Rueben managed to get the pliers off the wall, but before he could use it, Young Z back-handed him across the jaw, and he staggered backward.

"Nice moves," Young Z said. "I wonder how many times I've killed you already for you to get the jump on me like that."

Rueben wiped his mouth on his sleeve. "Maybe I haven't died yet."

Young Z nodded appraisingly. "Maybe you haven't." He glanced over Rueben's shoulder, momentarily distracting him. Then the man rushed forward and slammed a pair of hedge-trimming shears into Rueben's gut. "But now you have."

Rueben died.

Earth-Z
(Two Minutes Earlier)

Young Z nodded appraisingly. "Maybe you haven't." He glanced over Rueben's shoulder, but Rueben didn't fall for it. With a grunt, the man rushed forward and tried to slam a pair of hedge-trimming shears into Rueben's gut.

Rueben sidestepped the thrusting attack and delivered a kick to Young Z's crotch from behind.

"You bastard," the man moaned, clutching himself as he spun and eyed Rueben with rage in his eyes. He backed up until he reached the shed's wall and selected a machete.

"Nice one." Z grabbed a machete and tossed it to Rueben, who barely managed to catch it.

Rueben was adjusting his grip on the hilt when Young Z charged forward, his blade falling on its downswing. Rueben lifted his blade and blocked it, but the blow forced him back a step. Young Z followed up with a slash across Rueben's shins, and Rueben fell to his knees. His eyes crossed as his opponent's machete embedded itself in the top of his skull.

Rueben died.

Earth-Z
(One Minute Earlier)

Young Z rushed forward. Instead of trying to block the machete's downward swing, Rueben darted back out of reach. As a result, Young Z missed with his attack, leaving him wide open for Rueben to bury his machete into the side of Young Z's neck.

He didn't. Sure, killing Young Z would let the man know that Rueben had bested him once, but Rueben didn't want to have to contend with how far back Young Z would warp. The man could very well go back to right before the fight had started, and Rueben thought that might wipe his mind of the knowledge he had learned so far in the fight.

He knew how masochistic Z could be. What if Young Z kept Rueben trapped in a fight that never ended until the man said it ended? That was why Rueben had thought it was best to roll with the punches and not kill Young Z but let the man kill him—over and over again—so he could learn the man's weaknesses and get the edge on him. If he could beat Young Z badly enough, he would probably give in and listen to Rueben's and Z's request for help in stopping the time virus.

With a start, Young Z lunged with his machete. Rueben parried and backed away. His opponent reclosed the gap, attacking with sideways swipes and a vertical hack. Rueben knocked them all aside and got in a kick to Young Z's hip, staggering him against a work table.

Seeing a chance to get another blow in, Rueben quick-stepped forward and raised the machete to slam the butt into Young Z's back. Instead, he received a kick to the gut that sent him sprawling. As Rueben skidded along the floor on his back, Young Z loomed menacingly over him, a chainsaw in his hands. As it rumbled to life, Rueben's head struck a generator, and he groaned. The world started to fade out, and that's when Young Z bent forward, and the chainsaw bit into him.

He died.

Earth-Z
(One Minute Earlier)

Enough with this dying bullshit.

Young Z raised a boot to kick out at Rueben, but Rueben avoided it. Giving in to his pissed-off rage, he slammed the machete down at Young Z. It cut into the man's wrist, striking bone, and Young Z screamed in pain.

"First blood, bitch," Rueben said.

"Nice," Z called from the sideline.

As he turned to look at the older man, Rosa stepped inside the shed with a silver platter containing a carafe and some glasses filled with ice. "Lemonade?"

Buzz-Z grinned. "Turmeric ginseng lemonade?"

"Of course," Rosa said.

Buzz-Z nodded emphatically. "Oh, yes please."

Rueben saw Z shake his head no. Then he caught the movement from Young Z. He turned in time to see the man run his neck through with a sickle.

He died.

Earth-Z
(Five Minutes Earlier)

It was time to finish this fight. With a calm, focused mind, Rueben warped back to right before the fight started. Z was about to shove him into the arena, but Rueben pushed the hands aside and stepped toward Young Z.

Young Z shot forward like a mongoose. Rueben sidestepped, but his opponent was already lashing out with a long fat blade he'd had concealed behind his back. Anticipating the attack, Rueben caught Young Z's wrist, ducked in, and dealt the man an unexpected blow to the gut.

Young Z cursed, then kicked the toe of his boot against the floor. A blade snicked out, and Rueben dodged the man's vicious upward kick. Rueben rushed forward again, catching Young Z beneath the knee and shoving him back against the tool shed's wall.

They separated.

Young Z caught his breath and rushed forward with a pair of hedge-trimming shears. Rueben sidestepped the thrusting attack and delivered a kick to Young Z's crotch from behind.

"You bastard," the man moaned, clutching himself as he spun and eyed Rueben with rage in his eyes. He backed up until he reached the shed's wall and selected a machete.

"Nice one." Z grabbed a machete and tossed it to Rueben, who caught it and darted forward at his opponent like a professional fencer. He struck swiftly, knocking Young Z's blade from his grip. Young Z reached for a chainsaw, and Rueben smashed the machete's pommel over his head. His opponent sank to one knee. Rueben flashed forward and kicked him in the hip. It made a popping sound. The man grabbed it and collapsed onto the floor.

Just then, Rosa stepped inside the shed with a silver platter. "Lemonade?"

Rueben leaned against a wall and wiped the sweat from his forehead. Z trudged up to him and clapped a hand on his shoulder. "Guess that hip wasn't indestructible after all. Man, that was vicious. You did good. You did real good."

CHAPTER TWENTY-ONE

Earth-A

"They ought to be replying," Marshall said. He shook his head as he passed his gaze over the *Paper Warriors* news office. "I think something is wrong on their end."

Marshall and Carolyn had been waiting for a response from Rueben and Z for a few hours now.

Carolyn smiled weakly. "Maybe there's another way to get hold of them. I'll call Buzz and see if he has any ideas."

While she did that, Marshall turned back to the printing press. It hadn't printed a paper since they got there, aside from a proof of the one they'd sent to Earth-Z. Oh well, if the press wasn't publishing anything, he'd put his investigation skills to use and try to figure out anything he could on the machine.

He ran his hands over the metal struts and inspected the ink lines, but he couldn't find markings of any kind. There wasn't even the name of a manufacturer to be found anywhere on it. In his mind, it made sense that the manufacturer of an intergalactic printing press would know something important when it came to parallel Earths and such.

Meanwhile, although Buzz wouldn't pick up his phone, Carolyn managed to get hold of Martha. Marshall half-listened as he continued to search the printing press and was glad to hear it when Martha said Buzz and Aki had stopped the time virus' progress at least for the time being.

"We wanted to ask Buzz if he had any ideas for how to contact the Ruebens on Earth-Z. They're not responding to our paper we sent to Earth-Z."

Carolyn and Martha continued to talk while Marshall, frustrated at finding nothing, crossed his arms and turned to face the back of the office. The cabinet caught his eye. He shuffled over to it and briefly inspected the housing and the computer itself. Its only identifying information was the label on the front of the door, but someone had purposely worn it down to the point where it was undefinable. He mentally reviewed all the tricks he'd learned while on the police force for trying to read clues. He'd already taken a piece of paper and did a pencil rub across the label, but the company name was inconclusive. It started with a V was all he could tell.

Suddenly, he had an idea. During his college days, he had started as a computer information systems major. So he knew a thing or two about computer hardware. Retrieving a pocketknife from his pocket, he began to pry off the computer's panels. While the computer's innards looked more updated and different from what he was used to back in the day, he knew what he was looking at.

Once he started to inspect the circuit boards and other paraphernalia inside the computer housing, he realized someone had filed the manufacturer names off these too.

Who the hell built this and what are they trying to hide?

Careful not to disturb any computer parts, Marshall inspected the various components, but he couldn't see anything.

"Be nice to get some damn lighting in here," he muttered and retrieved a penlight from his pocket. He shined it over the computer and whistled. "Hot damn." He stared at the partially hidden company name for a moment longer to make sure he hadn't read it wrong. Then he got up and walked over to Carolyn.

"Oh," Martha said from the other line, "Buzz just walked in."

Before Carolyn could ask him about how to communicate with Earth-A beside the *Paper Warriors* press, Marshall said, "Buzz, I need you to run down a company name with your computer genius."

"Umm, okay," Buzz said in an irritated manner. It sounded like he was tapping on a keyboard.

"Valence Systems Corp."

Rapid keystrokes came over the phone line. When he spoke, Buzz seemed even more irritated. "That's a computer hardware manufacturer." A chair or stool scraped against a floor. "Now, if you'll excuse me, I'm going to take a warm, relaxing shower—"

"Now just one second, buckaroo," Marshall said. "This computer company. Who owns it?"

More keystrokes followed an irritated sigh. "It looks like... oh uh, it's owned by a parent company called Neutron Fix Consolidated."

Marshall spun his hand for Buzz to hurry up even though Buzz couldn't see him. "Who owns that?"

More keystrokes. "Another parent company."

"And who owns it?"

"Holy shit."

"Holy shit owns it?"

"Ugh. No," Buzz said, his irritation replaced by tempered excitement.

Marshall smirked at Carolyn, who giggled. He could still make his wife laugh. That made him feel good. He turned back to Carolyn's phone. "The suspense is killing me. Who owns the company that owns them all?"

When Buzz didn't answer, Marshall growled, "Well, come on. Your genius brain have a damn stroke or something?"

"Um," Buzz said. "No. No, I didn't. It's just..."

"For crying out loud, who owns it?"

Buzz swallowed. "Nunez Corporation."

Earth-Z

"So? How was it?" Z asked Rueben as he stepped into Buzz-Z's computer lab. He'd thought that Buzz-A's mansion lab had been impressive but this one...it was quadruple the size. And instead of monitors, there were holographic screens everywhere.

Rueben finished toweling his hair dry. "That bath was like heaven." He was wearing his futuristic pants and jacket, which Rosa had somehow washed and dried while he'd been in the bathhouse. He wiped a trickle of water off his forehead. "All those water jets. And the complimentary massage..."

Z nodded knowingly. "I see Buzz treated you to the VIP treatment."

Rueben fluffed his jacket collar. "That and then some."

"That means he trusts us. That's good. Now, your bath 'massage'... Did you prefer Binnie's or Biddie's hands?"

Blushing, Rueben gave Z a sideways glance. Aki was

already in the room. "I'll tell you as long as you don't tell Aki when we get back."

Z snickered. "I won't as long as you don't tell my babe."

"Deal." He leaned in and whispered to Z.

"Good choice." Z straightened and quickly showed Rueben around Buzz's computer lab. He stopped behind Aki's workstation and peered over her shoulders. "What do we have?"

She turned and regarded Z interestedly. "Buzz's computers have been searching for patterns and anomalies. We've got something."

Young Z strode into the room and didn't like how close Z was standing next to Aki. Z acted like he didn't care, and Young Z approached and peered over Aki-Z's other shoulder at the holographic computer screen.

"What is it, babe?" Young Z said.

Aki-Z glanced up at him. "That arms dealer you found in the street with his hand cut off. Buzz's AI traced a money payment to him from a dead-end Caymans account."

Criminals always had ways of hiding their money. *Some things stay the same in all the worlds,* Rueben mused.

"I was able to trace it back to a Valence Systems Corp."

Z's eyes narrowed. "What kind of company is that?"

"Computer parts manufacturer. Well, that's what they started as. These days they work intensively with state-of-the-art robotic sentries. That's not the most interesting thing about them. They're owned by several parent companies, with Nunez Corp. at the top."

"Doesn't ring a bell," Young Z said.

Z, meanwhile, thumbed his lip. "Nunez…for some reason, that name rings a bell. Can you search for him?"

"Sure," Aki-Z said. "I can't find anything out about Nunez

Corp. aside from they're in the scientific applications field. Probably tied with the government."

Aki-Z clacked at the keyboard. "Here's a news article on a Dr. Eduardo Nunez. It's over twenty years old, though. 'Dr. Nunez was involved in theoretical physics for much of his professional career. There has still been no trace of Nunez after he disappeared during the testing of an experimental black hole device that shut down shortly after—'" Aki-Z stopped short. "Wait, I think I remember this guy from back in my CIA days. If memory serves, he was into time travel."

Rueben nodded. "Same on my Earth. There was something about how he managed to transport a banana back in time or something."

Z scratched his chin. "Something tells me the man didn't just disappear. I think he's beyond transporting bananas in a lab. This time virus has a scientist's fingerprints all over it."

Young Z turned and eyed him intensely. "You think so?"

Z raised his fist against his heart. "I'd bet my life on it."

"But why?" Rueben said. "What's in this for Nunez if he's behind it?"

Buzz-Z appeared through the lab's doorway. "Power. Prestige. Privilege. Have your pick."

"Have you ever heard of this Nunez guy?" Young Z asked.

Buzz-Z nodded. "Of course. Every fledgling scientist back in the day had heard of Nunez. Of course, he was kinda known as a crackpot, even around the most fringe scientists among us."

"So," Rueben said. "Where does that leave us? This Eduardo Nunez crazy scientist guy paid an arms dealer, then had him killed?"

Everyone's eyes narrowed.

"You think so?" Z asked.

Rueben shrugged. "What I want to know is what was in that metal briefcase."

"Doesn't really matter, does it?" Z said. "It wasn't the time virus or the virus detector would've been going crazy.

"We need to figure out what Nunez's plan is. Maybe it involves the time virus. Where is the headquarters for Nunez Corp?" Rueben asked.

Aki-Z did some more typing. "It's a place in northern Maine."

"Maine?" Martha-Z said. "Isn't that where all Stephen King's creepy stories take place?"

"Only a couple hours' flight by jet-copter," Buzz said proudly.

Rueben eyed Team Z. "I know I'm not from this Earth, but I say we check it out."

"Fine," Young Z said. "You earned that from beating me in the tool shed." His eyes wandered to Emma sitting on a stool off to the side. "Buzz, can you get everyone prepared?"

Buzz nodded as Young Z stepped over to Emma. "Baby, Mom and I gotta go again. I'm sorry."

Emma smiled. "Dad, it's okay that you missed my birthday party. I understand what you do is important."

Young Z kissed Emma on the forehead and Rueben thought he saw the man's eyes start to blur with tears. Then the man was back to his normal self and barking orders.

As they headed toward Buzz's hangar, Rueben asked if there was a way for them to communicate with their friends on Earth-A.

Buzz-Z grinned. "I've developed a way for Organic Jim to be able to talk to other versions of himself on the other worlds. I'll have someone round him up for us."

"Good," Rueben said. "Because I need to speak with my team."

"Got you covered, buddy," Buzz-Z said.

Rueben stared at this older version of his friend with his plastic surgery-altered face and cheery persona. "Great."

CHAPTER TWENTY-TWO

Earth-A

The ratchet clattered to the hangar floor yet again. "Damn," Buzz muttered as he picked up the tool and resumed tightening the bolts on the jet-copter.

On the other side of the hull, Rosa paused her work to call, "Mr. Buzz? Are you okay?"

"I'm fine. I'm fine. My hands aren't built to do this kind of work."

"Sorry to hear that, Mr. Buzz. The good news is that we're almost finished."

Buzz wiped the sweat off his forehead. Saving the world was so tiring. He needed a beer.

A few minutes later, he raised his tool and tightened the last bolt on the aircraft's hull. He wobbled to his feet. "I'm going to go grab a cold one and pass out."

Rosa waved. "I will finish up the repairs and sand off all the rust. Then I'll apply the new paint job we discussed. It will be like brand new."

"You're the best," Buzz muttered as he wandered through

the hangar toward the fridge. It was an outdated box-style model, one of the first electrical appliances he fixed before the age of ten. He stood in front of it for a moment, admiring the round contours and the dents it had acquired over the years.

Sighing, he opened the fridge and gazed zombie-like at the shelves of beer and wine. He selected a beer can and closed the door.

"Egads!" He started at the wiry figure standing beside the fridge. "Who-who, what…" Buzz reached inside his lab coat for his taser, but he was starting to see that wouldn't be necessary. "Organic Jim?"

Standing before him was the homeless man, Jim, dressed in tattered trousers and a white t-shirt with a jean jacket over it. Thorns and brambles decorated his pants and jacket, and his clothing bore several holes and tears. Layers of dust coated his shoulders and soaked his unruly hair.

Jim muttered something incomprehensible.

"Holy shit," Buzz said. "How'd you get here?"

"Cows go moo, and the moon stays blue."

"Huh?"

"The world goes round; the time to quest is now."

Snapping out of his weary funk, Buzz set his beer down and snatched Jim by both shoulders. Dust puffed up into the air. "Jim. What the hell? How…how did you get here? This compound is in the middle of the mountains. And you live in NYC."

"The buzz buzz buzz," Jim answered.

Buzz scratched his head. "The buzz?"

Jim shut both eyes and began to pound his palms against each ear. "In my ears. It's in my ears."

"What is in your ears?"

"The buzz that tells me where to go."

"You hear voices in your head?" Of course. That made sense. Jim was slightly crazy, driven mad by the déjà vu-like ability he had in being able to see the timelines that didn't happen when Rueben or Rueben-Z warped back in time.

Jim shook his head emphatically. "Yes. The voice. The voice told me where to go. And also how to detox." His eyes widened. "With kale and lemon juice."

"Ugh." Buzz placed a hand to his head. "You make little sense." Reaching out, he swiped a finger in the dust lining Jim's clothes and hair. When he rubbed it between two fingers, he saw that it wasn't normal dust. "If you had come a bit sooner, the time virus would have turned you to dust. You got lucky."

"Not lucky. Quest. Important. The buzz tells me so. I wander up mountain and down vale, but I am not lost. The buzz tells me so."

"Right. Right." Buzz picked up his beer and popped the tab. "Does this 'buzz' tell you to do anything else?"

Jim nodded emphatically. "It says to tell you... 'Binnie Protocol 69 was the worst idea ever.'"

The beer can slipped from Buzz's hands. When it struck the hangar floor, beer sloshed up through the hole and the can tipped over, leaking.

"Mr. Buzz, is everything all right?" Rosa asked as she approached the two men, hefting a heavy torque wrench menacingly in her hands.

Buzz's face was pale as he faced her. "Y-yes. But I need to ask you to gather the team."

"What should I tell them?"

Buzz swallowed. "I'm not yet sure how my counterpart figured it out. But tell them that we've made contact with Buzz-Z on Earth-Z. Via a conduit named Organic Jim."

CHAPTER TWENTY-THREE

Earth-Z

Buzz-Z's jet-copter touched down in the meadow of northern Maine, its twin rotors spraying the tall grass out to the sides like a rippling sea. It was nighttime, and the moon gleamed brightly down upon the meadow.

"Here we are, people," Buzz-Z said as he powered down the aircraft's engine and removed his pilot's helmet. He kept his aviators on and turned back to face the occupant, Rueben, Z, Young Z, and Aki-Z.

Rueben unbuckled his seat harness and picked up a tablet beside him. "You said this is a corporate warehouse?"

All of their futuristic earpieces crackled in unison. Aki-Z's voice said, "Nunez Corp.'s global headquarters and testing center."

"Looks like a warehouse." Rueben stared at the satellite image on the tablet in his hands.

Z smacked his shoulder. "Don't judge a book by its cover. Like me."

"I still think you're a horrible person," Rueben muttered.

"Whatever, thief. We make a good team. Like Sonny and Cher."

"As long as I'm Sonny," Rueben said.

"Hah. You wish."

Buzz-Z messed with the aircraft's controls. "Would you two quit flirting? We're on a mission."

Rueben and Z fist-bumped.

Aki-Z's voice came back over their earpieces. "Heat view doesn't show anything so either there's no one home, or the building has shielding against satellites."

Rueben said, "So we could be walking into a trap…"

"Get used to it," Z said. "Even with the best intel, some-times shit goes wrong."

Rueben nodded. "I'm not used to going on 'official missions.' My team is more…grassroots, I guess?" He laughed and glanced down at the futuristic body vest and padded clothes he wore and touched the visored helmet on his head. "But I could get used to this."

"You haven't seen anything yet." Z nudged the weapon in Rueben's hands. It resembled a submachine gun, but it had a scope, and they'd assured him that it was as accurate as a rifle with minimal recoil.

Young Z finished checking his gun and turned to Rueben and Z. "You two ready?"

They were. Rueben hopped out of the jet-copter and planted his feet in the grassy meadow.

Aki-Z spoke up again. "Plotting the safest course for you all now."

Suddenly, Rueben's helmet visor flashed green, and a green arrow appeared at the bottom of his vision. It formed a path through the grassy field and up a hill. The Nunez Corp. building was on the other side. He also noticed indicators for several other things, among them the direction he was facing, his weapon's ammo count, and his general health.

"This is like a friggin' video game," Rueben said.

Z hopped out of the jet-copter and smirked. "Welcome to the future."

The trek up the hill was uneventful. Once at the crest, they kept low in the tall grass and peered down at the Nunez Corp. building. It was a drab-looking warehouse-type structure. There was no signage visible anywhere on it.

Aki-Z's voice announced, "Still no sentries."

"This might be an easy mission," Z said.

Young Z scoffed. "There's no such thing. On me."

The three Ruebens followed the flashing green holographic pathway on their heads-up display on their visors.

"I don't see any video cameras," Buzz-Z said. He was monitoring the situation from a portable tech station aboard the jet-copter. "Or sensors of any kind. Odd..."

Moving in a brisk half-crouch, they followed the path to the back of the building to some loading docks. Rueben kept up. He was breathing hard, but at least he wasn't as out of breath as usual.

"Still no sign of any activity," Buzz-Z said. "Go, go, go."

Young Z was in the lead as they approached the building's loading docks.

"It may look abandoned, but check out these tracks. There's been activity recently." Z indicated the pavement.

Rueben narrowed his eyes from behind the gun as he held it to his shoulder. "Then where are the guards and security?"

"Maybe they went home for the night," Buzz-Z chided over the earpiece.

"I have a bad feeling about this," Rueben said as he climbed onto the loading dock.

Z reached down and helped him up. "Oh, that was probably your stomach catching up to Buzz's piloting."

"Hey!"

Z slapped Rueben on the back. "Buck up. You can warp, don't you forget."

They edged up to a side door. Young Z pressed a circular device to the door, and a lock *clicked*.

The door silently slid open to the side.

Young Z motioned for Rueben and Z to follow. Then he ducked inside, keeping a low profile with his weapon raised.

They found themselves in a sterile-looking corridor. There were no longer any direction arrows on his visor screen so Rueben followed Young Z while keeping his eyes peeled for any movement off to either side.

They came into a large spacious warehouse room with tall ceilings. Metal racks upon metal racks stood throughout the open space. The room was dark. There was no one around.

"Doing a scan," Young Z said with a hand to his helmet.

Z edged up to Rueben. "Do a quick search. See if you can find anything."

"Like what?"

Z shrugged and pressed on into the room.

The one thing Rueben noticed right away was that the warehouse was clean. He couldn't see any dust anywhere, and the shelves were all neatly organized. Mostly they contained mechanical parts: clamps, O-rings, metal ball bearings. There were tons of futuristic circuit boards too.

It was dark so Rueben switched on his visor's green-tinted

night vision feature, allowing him to see better. This was the coolest experience ever. He felt like the hero of some action spy thriller minus all the action, which was fine—for the moment. He was on a different Earth, years into the future. Who only knew what threats might lie here… At least he had good backup and a badass-looking weapon. He was itching to fire it.

"Found something." It was Z.

Rueben and Young Z quickly formed up around him. "You sure?" Young Z said.

Z slapped the flat vertical side of a seven-foot-tall metal box with fat wires and cables protruding from its backside. Inside was a keyboard and holographic screen as well as several mechanical arms, some clutching syringes. It sort of looked like some mad scientist's version of an old-fashioned telephone booth.

A futuristic barrier that resembled a thick layer of impenetrable glass encased the metal booth.

Rueben rubbed at his jaw. "What—"

"You have company," Aki-Z's voice called over their earpieces.

Z and Young Z snapped to attention. "What are we up against?" Z asked. Young Z glared at him for taking charge.

Now Buzz-Z's voice came over the line. "I see all kinds of electronic signatures. Coming from the north, west, and south walls. Can you head east?"

Turning that direction, as indicated on their heads-up displays, they saw a pair of closed double doors. They started in that direction.

Suddenly, doors opened along the north, west, and south walls.

"Hurry," Aki-Z warned.

They reached the double doors as metal footsteps *clopped* into the warehouse. The doors wouldn't open. They were metal and reinforced from the other side.

"What kind of security does the future have?" Rueben threw his back against the wall, aiming his weapon toward the building's interior.

Z sidled close to him and whispered. "You know what Cylons look like from *Battlestar Galactica*? Big. Metal. Slow…"

Rueben nodded.

"Well, these are a lot scarier."

"That's nice," Rueben said. "I thought robots would be more human on this Earth."

Z shrugged.

The sound of trudging metallic stomps approached from around the metal racks to either side of them. At the doors, Young Z fumbled with his door-opening device. "It's not working," he mumbled.

"Get ready," Z said from behind his gun. "We're about to see some action."

CHAPTER TWENTY-FOUR

<u>Earth-Z</u>

The robot sentries came from several directions at once.

"Take 'em before they get a lock on us!" Z said.

A robot with two legs like metal tree trunks, a short wide torso, and metal arms with futuristic cannons on each stepped into the light where Rueben could see it. It raised one metal arm, and a red circular glow emitted from the weapon fused to its arm.

Rueben squinted through his scope and squeezed his weapon's trigger a few times. Several bursts of rounds fired from his gun and plowed into the robot sentry, dotting its metal chest with holes. There was hardly any recoil at all. The robot faltered and toppled over.

Another red glow from the other side grew, and Rueben heard Z fire a single burst that dropped the imposing robot. A third robot appeared. Before it could even lift its arm cannon, Rueben peppered it with a single burst. He felt like such a massive robot would require more than one, but the sentry tipped to the side, the holes in its chest smoking.

"What the hell are our guns firing?"

Z shot at another robot guard. He grinned at Rueben. "Pretty nice, huh?"

"Basically," Buzz-Z began to intone in Rueben's ears, "supersonically propelled molten lead with some nanobot enhancements to shred through tough inorganic matter—"

"For the love of God, just shoot!" Z said as three robot guards raised their arm cannons.

Things were too easy. *Finally, a challenge...*

Rueben pulled the trigger, dropping the first guard while Z took the second. Rueben was firing on the third robot guard when its red glowing weapon barrel shifted to a green glow.

"Fuck, get down!" Z shouted as he pivoted and threw a shoulder against Young Z and caught Rueben with his arm.

Rueben had already fired though, and his bullets—were they bullets?—had already penetrated the metal robot, effectively killing it. However, the green glow had disappeared, and as the three Ruebens fell to the warehouse floor, a green laser shot out of the dead robot's weapon, incinerating the reinforced double doors.

The Ruebens lay in a heap upon the floor next to the smoking, now wide-open entrance. Young Z glared at Rueben. "You are the worst—"

"Hey." Rueben chuckled as he reloaded. "I opened the door, didn't I?"

Z was already helping Rueben and Young Z up by gripping their shoulders. "Nice tactic. Almost convincing that it was your plan all along..."

Rueben caught the sly grin that Z was throwing him. He nodded. "Oh yeah. That was definitely planned. Yep—"

"Move!" Z called behind the scope of his raised weapon as he fired at the newest robot guards closing on their position.

Rueben and Young Z wasted no time. They barreled through the door, careful not to brush against the outward spreading metal of the molten doors. The way the laser continued to burn through the metal, widening the hole, reminded Rueben of how the time virus spread.

The time virus. Right. *Stay on mission...*

He followed on Young Z's heels as Aki-Z cried out over their earpieces. "I heard a laser discharge. Are you guys okay?"

Young Z and Rueben moved down a metal corridor with closed doors off to each side. With a serious glance at Rueben, Young Z answered. "We're fine, babe. It was a 'calculated' discharge."

"You need to get out of there."

"Looking for the way out, babe." They came to an intersection of corridors, and after stopping for a moment, Young Z selected a branch.

Before taking the turn and following Young Z, Rueben glanced over his shoulder. He saw no sign of Z. "We should wait," Rueben said.

Young Z neither stopped nor looked back over his shoulder. "He's fine. Come on."

Rueben gritted his teeth. "We're a team. I'm going back for him."

Now Young Z turned. "Are you crazy?"

"What?" Rueben said. "We're Repeaters. What's there to be afraid of?"

Young Z swallowed. "If there's one way of dying that I can't stand, it's death by laser melting."

Rueben shrugged. "I've been killed by a microwave bomb. More than once. Can't be worse than that."

As Young Z started to say something, Rueben rushed back the way they had come.

He was about halfway down the hallway when Z appeared through the gaping hole in the wall. His eyes bulged. "What the hell are you doing? Run!"

"I've got this," Rueben said as he lowered himself to a one-knee crouch and leveled his gun at the ruined doors.

Z tried to grab Rueben's shoulder as he passed him to pull him after him.

"I'll hold them off. Go!"

Five robot guards appeared through the doorway. Rueben managed to take down three of them before the other two struck him with their green lasers.

Rueben felt a hot cooking sensation in his body. Then his skin started to melt from his body. With his scream trapped in his melting throat, his eyes caught sight of bone beneath his skin where his arm was a moment ago. Then his eyes caught fire and melted with twin *pops*, and he was vaguely aware of his body dropping to the floor.

He died.

Earth-Z
(One Minute Earlier)

Rueben was about halfway down the hallway. As he fingered the gun in his hands, Z appeared through the gaping hole in the wall. His eyes bulged. "What the hell are you doing? Run!"

Rueben didn't run. Instead, he raised his gun and started firing at the doorway.

Z sprinted past him in a half-crouch with his hands over his head. "Shit!"

From the doorway, five robot guards toppled over the threshold, effectively sealing off the door from the rest of the robot guards for the moment.

Z stopped and turned, eyeing the heaped-up metal carnage. "Nice shooting. Their lasers don't work on their kind. That rubble pile will take them some time to clear."

Z gave Rueben a stern look as the two of them started down the hallway again the way Young Z had gone. "It's a good thing you didn't get lasered. Hurts like a…" He let his words trail off as Rueben's face tightened. "Well, you son of a bitch, you did get lasered." He slapped Rueben on the back as they continued. "My condolences. Thanks for watching my back."

Rueben grimly nodded as they came to an intersection. He called into his mic, "Hey, where'd you go?"

There was no response.

"Buzz?" Rueben called. "Aki?"

Z smirked. "Bastard somehow turned off yours and my earpieces."

"But why?"

"Isn't it obvious? Young Z doesn't trust us."

Rueben grunted and reloaded his gun. "We'll deal with him when we catch up to him. Since you're an older version of him, which way do you think Young Z would've gone?"

Z only considered it for a moment. "Follow me." He took the left corridor, and Rueben followed.

"Any particular reason why this way?"

Z grinned. "Because I have a rule when coming to forks in the road. Or tunnel. Or maze. Always go left. That way, you can easily retrace your steps if you get lost."

They followed the left-branching hallway but soon realized it was a dead end. There were a few doors, but they were locked and constructed of reinforced metal. Young Z hadn't come this way…

From around the corner came the sound of metal robots tearing back the dead robots in the doorway. By the sound of it, they were trying to crawl over the top of the downed robots.

Rueben and Z broke out in a sprint back to the intersection of the corridors, stopping just before the confluence. Rueben elbowed Z. "Try the right passageway. I'll cover you."

Z huffed. "Why don't I cover you?"

Rueben peeked around the corner. "Because you can't warp. I can. Better only one of us has to feel the pain of that death again."

"Aw shucks. I'm growing on you, aren't I?"

"Like a fungus. Now get ready." Rueben rested his finger on the trigger as the sound of robots drew closer.

He was about to peek around the corner and fire at the seven robot guards trudging toward their position when the sound of steel slicing through metal echoed down the hall. It came again and again. Then there was the loud *crash* of three robots going down in a heap.

With the gunstock pressed firmly against his shoulder, Rueben crouched and stole another peek into the hallway at the approaching robot guards. There was another slicing *snick,* and a fourth robot guard tumbled to the floor. Rueben felt a hand on his shoulder as Z peered around the corner above him.

"Oh fuck. This ain't good."

Rueben watched in disbelief as a fifth robot went down. "What—oh."

The sixth and seventh robots pivoted and fired up their lasers, but it was too late for them. A sturdy, razor-edged wide blade had already severed the laser cannons from their arms. As their arm weapons dropped to the floor, the sword blade *swished* toward their metal necks, and a moment later, their heads clattered on the floor.

The blade's wielder finished in a pose with the sword held dramatically out to the side after he finished his seven-robot slaughter. Then he rose from his practiced victorious stance and craned his head in Rueben's and Z's direction.

It was the supersoldier who'd assassinated the arms dealer in the street.

CHAPTER TWENTY-FIVE

<u>Earth Z</u>

Dressed all in black ninja garb, their new opponent exuded silent menace as he positioned the blade in Rueben and Z's direction.

"I think we better run," Rueben said.

Z bit his lip. "I think you're right."

Rueben shot out into the corridor, making it safely across the intersection. He heard Z sprinting behind him, then a solid *thunk*. He turned in time to see Z collapse to the floor, the supersoldier's blade embedded in his side.

"Damnit," Rueben muttered, knowing that he had to die again for this jerk. *Might as well test out this ninja's strengths.* He darted out into the intersection.

The ninja had silently darted in and was in the process of crouching to retrieve his blade from Z's corpse. Rueben lashed out with his foot, expecting to catch the supersoldier across the shoulder and thus spin him facedown onto the floor. What happened instead was the supersoldier evaded, and Rueben's foot soared through empty space, leaving him in an awkward, vulnerable position.

Seeing this, the ninja rose from his side crouch and with fingers curled like cat claws, jammed his black leather-clad fist first against Rueben's side, then into Rueben's lower back with a sickening *crack*.

Oh, fuck!

Rueben lost all feeling beneath his waist, and before he knew it, he was face-first on the floor.

He managed to push himself up with his palms. Still, his legs didn't work. Was he paralyzed? If this asshole left him like this, he'd have to find a way to kill himself to warp back. He'd expected a quick, merciful death, not this.

Above him, the supersoldier bent and grabbed a handful of Rueben's hair. Then he pried Rueben's head up as if to get a better look at him. The ninja's cunning eyes behind his red goggles bored into Rueben's.

Just cut my throat and be done with it.

The supersoldier instead released his grip and Rueben again collapsed to the floor. The ninja started walking away.

Rude.

"Hey, you asshole! You're just going to leave me here?"

For a moment, Rueben didn't think the supersoldier had heard him. Then, stopping on a dime, the ninja spun and launched his blade at Rueben, and it impaled his head.

He died.

Earth-Z

(Four Minutes Earlier)

Z slapped Rueben on the back as they ran down the corridor. "Thanks for watching my back."

If you only knew...

They came to the intersection. "Let's go right," Rueben said.

Z shook his head. "That's not what I'd do. I'd go left. I always go left when I come to an intersection so that—"

"—you don't get lost. Yeah, I know. But Young Z didn't go left."

Z looked unconvinced. "Why would he do that?"

Rueben grunted. "I don't know. How 'bout we make it out of here, and we go ask him?" He started down the right corridor, but Z wouldn't follow him. Instead, he dashed back to the left hall.

Rueben muttered, "Are you serious?"

The fallen robot guards got hauled out of the doorway, and seven additional robot guards clambered into the corridor.

"We can take them," Z called from the other side of the intersection.

Rueben thought about that. They each had badass guns. Why was he even worried about the supersoldier? As far as Rueben could tell, the ninja had no firearms—only that fat deadly blade that could seemingly cut through anything.

Rueben and Z took up defensive positions at both sides of the corridor. Rueben drew deep breaths as he waited for the supersoldier to make his appearance. When he did, he held his breath at each vicious slice of the warrior's blade.

"Why didn't you tell me there was a supersoldier in here?" Z asked.

Rueben mental face palmed. "I'll tell you on the next go around if it comes to that."

"Shit, how many times have you Repeated this corridor?"

"Fire on three," Rueben said. "One, two, three."

They each swiveled out into the main corridor and fired burst after burst at the supersoldier. Rueben expected the ninja to go down like a bullet-ridden sock puppet. Instead, their guns' projectiles deflected harmlessly away from the ninja as if a forcefield protected him.

"This," Z called, "is why we don't fight supersoldiers." He paused. "However, there is one thing I've always wanted to try against them…"

The supersoldier began to slink silently toward them, his blade held out and downward at his side. When he was near their position, Z broke from cover and dashed up to the ninja. Then he gave the supersoldier a vicious kick to the crotch. In return, Z received the neat horizontal slash of the blade that sent his head tumbling to the floor, a smirk plastered on his lips.

Rueben, already committed to dying, thought he'd try a different tactic against the supersoldier before it killed him. As the ninja strode his way, Rueben clutched his gun. Maybe the forcefield or whatever didn't protect the supersoldier if someone fired a gun point-blank.

Rueben charged the ninja, feinting and managing to press the gun's muzzle against the ninja's abdomen. He pulled the trigger.

In a blaze of white-hot light, Rueben's gun exploded, taking his hand and part of his wrist with it. As he screamed in agony, the supersoldier swept his blade across Rueben's gut in a quick zigzag motion. Then the assassin strode past him down the hall.

Soon, Rueben went into shock. Then he died.

Earth-Z
(Five Minutes Earlier)

"Thanks for watching my back," Z said right before he and Rueben came to the intersection.

Rueben promptly turned and socked Z across the jaw. "Listen here, motherfucker, we're turning right."

Z spat out a mouthful of blood and rubbed his stubbled jaw. He regarded Rueben like a wary caged wolf. "Are we now?"

Rueben didn't back down. He thrust a hand back down the corridor at the doorway heaped with robot guards. "Supersoldier. Coming."

Z dropped his hostile guard. "Why didn't you say so? Go ahead and take lead."

Clearing his throat, Rueben led Z to the right. Now that there wasn't anyone or anything trying to kill them, they wound their way through another corridor and to another dead end. There were plenty of doors in this corridor like the west one, and one of them had been forced open. Rueben peered at the stenciled word on it. *Laboratory*. They stepped inside.

It was a lab of some sort, but judging from all the dust, it hadn't been in use for years, maybe a decade. Multiple workstations lined the room, complete with water faucets and countertops and expensive microscopes.

The good thing about the dust was that it was all too easy to track Z's footprints across the darkened lab to an emergency side door at the back of the room. Rueben briskly followed the trail, hearing the sounds of the seven robot guards farther back in the main corridor. Soon the supersoldier would reduce them to scrap metal and shortly after that the ninja warrior would come after them.

Before exiting, Z caught Rueben by the shoulder and angled his head at a tiny LED on a laptop sitting on a desk. Z fished a futuristic flash drive from his pocket.

"How about we see if there's any intel in here first? With Buzz's little gadget here, all I have to do is insert and wait two seconds..." Z plugged the flash drive into the laptop's port. Two seconds later, the USB drive flashed green. "Good to go."

Z retrieved the flash drive, and Rueben pushed open the door and stepped out. A chilly night breeze met his face. They were outside.

Suddenly Rueben's and Z's earpieces spat to life.

"We've got to go," Young Z was saying.

Aki-Z sighed. "We can't just leave them."

"I don't trust them. For all I know, this was all a big setup, a trap, and they were in on it."

"Buddy," Buzz-Z said. "I know you've been under a lot of stress here lately but—"

"Listen up, you asshole," Z called over the communication line while he and Rueben started across the tall grass toward the hill and the jet-copter waiting on the other side. "I didn't set this trap, and I'm not out to get you. I'm you from the future, and my partner is from another planet. Buzz can confirm this with blood samples when we get back to the mansion."

A terse silence followed over the line.

Rueben joined in. "Yeah, that was pretty shitty of you to leave us in the building with a horde of laser-toting robot guards and a supersoldier."

Buzz-Z gasped. "Egads. A supersoldier? Here? Why?"

Rueben and Z were now cresting the hill at a trot. Down at the bottom in the overgrown meadow sat the jet-copter.

"Does it matter—" Z said but a slicing *swish* cut him off. He cursed as he stumbled forward a step. Even in the darkness, Rueben could see the small dagger projecting from Z's back and shoulder.

Turning back at the way they'd come, Rueben saw the supersoldier frozen in a post-throw motion. They were nearly fifty yards away. Throwing a dagger that far was impossible. It must've been technologically assisted or something.

It didn't matter. With a quick repositioning of his body, the ninja prepared to sprint right at them.

Rueben threw an arm around Z's shoulder. "Come on, you big lughead, let's get to the chopper."

Already there was a glaze to Z's eyes. "Huh? Ahmm mmph…" The man passed out, slumping over face-first onto the dirt. Behind them, the supersoldier charged their way.

Bastard must have poisoned Z with the dagger...

Rueben considered pulling the dagger out from Z's shoulder, but he didn't want to cause further damage. They were so close to the chopper, to their escape, that he didn't want to die if he didn't have to. Not again. Not by the masochistic hands of the supersoldier.

Making up his mind, Rueben gripped Z under both arms and dragged him down the hill.

He succeeded in making it nearly halfway down when the supersoldier appeared at the top, brandishing his blade at his side. The moon reflected off it in a sick twilight gleam.

Just keep going, Rueben told himself. *Just keep going.*

He had only a quarter of the distance to go, but a brief backward glance showed that he wasn't going to make it. The supersoldier was almost right on top of him.

CHAPTER TWENTY-SIX

Earth-Z

"You owe me big time!" Rueben shouted as one of his hands went to his gun and shoved it back behind him. He blind-fired behind him while continuing to drag Z after him down the hill.

As he fired, he heard the sound of the bullets deflecting to the sides, embedding in the grassy earth. When he expended the gun's magazine, he let go of his weapon. It snapped to his hip holster, and he stole a desperate peek past his shoulder. The supersoldier had stopped and was raising an arm to throw a dagger at him.

Rueben dodged to the side, hoping for the best. The dagger sliced through the side of his outer thigh and thunked into the earth. In a mad scramble, Rueben shot to his feet and grabbed Z again to try to drag him the rest of the way to the jet-chopper. It was only twenty yards away now. Throwing his balance forward and downward, he felt Z's body give way, but then Rueben started to feel woozy.

Right. It carries poisoned daggers.

Rueben knew then that a Repeat death was in order, but then something unexpected happened. The jet-copter's twin rotors activated, throwing down a violent spray of wind.

Behind him, the supersoldier silently stalked toward him, sword raised with lethal intent, his red goggles eerily reflecting the moon. The violent draft of air forced the ninja to pause a moment and raise a forearm to defend against it.

That bought Rueben a few seconds to trudge forward toward the jet-copter at the hill's base. Buzz-Z was firing up the engine. They were going to wait for him and Z. They could help them. Maybe he wouldn't have to die and Repeat after all.

The jet-copter rose into the night air.

Oh goddamn it...

Rueben couldn't see it, but he felt the menace in the ninja's satisfied grin, hidden beneath the dark layers of his facemask and goggles.

The supersoldier was now looming right over Rueben. With the flat of his blade, he struck Rueben over the head. Already feeling woozy from the dagger poison coursing through his veins, Rueben tottered sideways as if in slow motion, crashing numbly to the grassy earth.

He was vaguely aware of the dark shadow looming above him like a tower. Z was next to him, unconscious and still breathing, Rueben guessed.

As his would-be assassin prepared to strike with his blade, Rueben's hands reflexively sought his gun and a spare ammo magazine. With fingers growing numb and his mind succumbing to fog, he managed to snap the magazine upward. He let loose a barrage of rounds that curved supernaturally around the descending supersoldier's invisible forcefield.

Brrrr...

The sound was deafening and came from somewhere directly above Rueben.

Brrrr... Brrrr...

The ground exploded all around Rueben as heavy gunfire decimated the earth where the supersoldier had stood only moments before. Dirt and shreds of grass sprinkled upon Rueben as his vision started to fade.

One of the last things he remembered before passing out was arms under his armpits and hands strapping him into a seat harness. He caught a glimpse of Young Z crouching in front of him and fastening a buckle.

"You..." Rueben tried to say, but all that came out was a mumble.

Then he slept.

CHAPTER TWENTY-SEVEN

Earth-A

Buzz had assembled everyone in the hangar outside his underground mountain hideout. The camouflaged roof naturally blended in with the surrounding trees but since there were no longer any trees for a mile in all directions, it most definitely stood out.

"Jim," Buzz said. "How about we take this from the top again?"

Jim was sitting on an upturned bucket at the center of the ring of people. The new clothing he wore made him look more presentable and less crazy and aloof. Rosa had purchased it from the nearest town. The khaki slacks and button-up polyester shirt looked good on him, respectful even. He wore a cream fedora on his head, which didn't tame his wild hairdo but at least hid it. Most of it.

The people sitting around him on buckets of their own included Buzz, Martha, Aki, Marshall, and Carolyn.

Buzz waved impatiently for Jim to restart his tale.

Jim made an exaggerated gesture with his finger at his ears

and made a face, taking the time to stare blankly into the faces of all those gathered around him. "The buzz. In my ear."

Aki wrinkled her nose. "Like a bee? You've got a bee in your ear?"

Jim erratically shook his hands in the air. "Not a buzz. A *Buzz.*"

Buzz rolled his eyes. "People. It's simple. He's communicating with another Buzz in his head."

The excited nodding of Jim's head elicited smiles from all gathered, even Marshall. It felt like they were finally getting somewhere now. When Jim arrived in Buzz's hangar, he had been a babbling mess until they'd soothed him with some warm milk.

Martha prodded him with a wave. "This other Buzz. What is he saying to you?"

Jim crossed his arms. "Buzz no speak now. Left for mission."

Marshall stirred on his bucket. "Mission?" He let out a long yawn, fatigued by his and Carolyn's long return trip from the *Paper Warriors* office in NYC.

"Factory. Not a factory. Building set upon a hill of grass. Not on it, beside it. Satellite view. No sentries."

Martha brushed a bang out of her eyes. "Huh?"

"No sentries. Unless the roof. Blocks heat view. The Buzz goes on and on. He did. Then they went on important mission."

Buzz nodded slowly. "Uh-huh. And have they returned from the mission yet?"

Jim cocked his head as if he was trying to straighten a TV antenna and his head was it. For a long time, he remained still as a statue, tuning into a frequency only he could hear.

"Is he…" Aki pressed on the front of her pants… "you know, okay?"

Suddenly, Jim's eyes shot wide. He gasped, out of breath. "They return from the mission."

Leaning forward, Marshall asked, "Was it a successful mission?"

"Jim is asking," Jim said, which seemed odd to Buzz but it made sense. Then Jim vigorously shook his head no. "Two men. Wounded during the mission."

Now it was Aki's turn to lean forward. "Two men? What men?" She turned to Buzz and the rest of the group while Jim mentally communicated with his Earth-Z counterpart. "Surely Rueben and Rueben-Z didn't interact with their versions on Earth-Z…"

Buzz pursed his lips. "I sincerely hope not. I told them like ten times. It could mess things up on both Earth-Z and this Earth. And not even a brain trust of intergalactic Buzzes could fix that mess…" Blinking, Buzz said, "Heh. A brain trust of Buzzes. Now that's a stellar idea. *Inter*stellar, you might say."

They all groaned at the pun. Marshall shook his head. "Son, you've got to have kids before you can make dad jokes that bad."

Buzz smirked. "How do you know that I don't have a kid or two somewhere out in the world—"

Martha and Aki both interjected at the same time. "You don't."

Buzz's grin faltered. People could be so mean. They were right, of course. Sexbots couldn't have human babies. That was somewhere science wasn't supposed to go. Or was it?

He snapped back to attention as Jim started gesturing

before him as if fingerpainting on an invisible pane of glass or washing a window.

"Jim?" Aki asked softly.

"Two men. Wounded in the fight. On the mission."

Martha nodded. "And…"

"One man," Jim continued. "One Rueben wounded. The bad one. But he isn't so bad anymore. Asshole he is called by many. The asshole is wounded."

Buzz let out a chuckle. Martha flashed him a dirty look, then snickered herself.

Aki remained serious though. "Jim. Jim, who was the second man?"

"Yes, besides the injured 'asshole,'" Buzz clarified.

Jim's eyes rolled up in their sockets as if he was trying to see his hairline. Then his eyes lowered back to face Aki. "The good Rueben."

"Shit." The word escaped Aki's lips like a release of stale air. Then, "How badly is he hurt?"

Aki wasn't the only one with a grave look on her face. Marshall was leaning forward with his elbows digging into his knees. Beside him, Carolyn patted his arm comfortingly. Marshall shared a look with her and stifled a yawn that overtook him. He looked annoyed by the tiredness seeping into his older bones.

Jim, too, yawned. "Can't tell. They are both gone now." The man stretched his arms tall over his head, then out wide to the sides. He climbed off the bucket and lay down on the hangar floor, nestling his head on top of his hands folded together like a pillow.

"Gone?" Marshall demanded, "Are they okay or not?"

Jim's eyes fluttered closed. "The Buzz. In my ears. Tires

me." He gave another great yawn. "Feed. Me. Chicken." Jim's whole body relaxed then, and he began to snore softly.

Agitated, Marshall jumped up, but Carolyn gripped his arm. "We'll find out soon," she said. "Look at him. He needs some rest."

Marshall looked at his wife. His words were insistent, but he kept them kind. "I need rest. But my boy is trapped on a parallel Earth, and there's nothing we can do here to help him. We need to wake this man up and ask him to reconnect to his psychic déjà vu connection or whatever the hell it is…" He paused as he noticed Aki standing before him, a worried look lining her face as well.

"Rueben's a Repeater. And he's got a lot of training. He'll be fine. I think the best thing we can do for him right now is to be strong."

Marshall took in the weight of her words, then nodded. "You're right. That doesn't mean we can't still work the problem. We can get this man some fried chicken."

"You're right," Carolyn said. "But we're not exactly within Hurley's Chicken's delivery distance."

Marshall smirked. "And if they had drone delivery, I doubt it would be able to find us out here in the middle of nowhere up in the mountains."

Buzz, for his part, wasn't exactly devoting his resources to the problem. He'd cracked open another beer and was savoring the refreshing sting of the carbonation going down his throat.

"I got it," Marshall said, throwing up his hand. "We don't have to get the fried chicken from Hurley's…we can make it here."

"Make it here?" Martha said.

"Yeah. That female chef robot that kinda looks like a

Jetsons robot. In Buzz's hideout. She can cook restaurant-quality food based on recipes she finds on the Internet." Marshall beamed with pride.

Carolyn patted his shoulder. "Great idea, honey."

Buzz, who had heard the last part, absentmindedly said, "Emma? I'll summon her." He retrieved a tablet from a side table and tapped on its screen. A few moments later he reported, "Emma says the Hurley's recipe chicken will be ready within twenty minutes."

Marshall passed a relieved hand over his sweating forehead. "That's not bad. I'm going to grab a quick power nap."

"Want me to wake you in twenty?" Martha asked.

Marshall patted his bulging belly. "Nah. The smell of fried chicken will wake me." He flicked a glance at Carolyn who was smiling knowingly.

CHAPTER TWENTY-EIGHT

"Just because you're future me doesn't mean you know what's best for me," Young Z said.

Rueben opened his eyes. He was lying on his back in Buzz-Z's futuristic computer lab. Glancing down, he saw that it was a floating zero-gravity chair. Also, none of his body parts were bound or tied down. He sat up, expecting his slashed hip to ache, but it didn't. It didn't even feel numb. He slid his hand down and felt the wound with his fingers and was surprised to find it neither sewed up nor patched up. There was a slightly raised line but no sign of a prior injury. From what he could recall, he had been sliced up pretty bad by the supersoldier's dagger.

He blinked. His head was fine—no mental fog. There was no sign of unsteadiness or disorientation. He rotated his shoulders, wrists, and ankles and flexed his knees. He felt in tip-top shape. Extracting himself from the hovering zero gravity chair, he noticed Young Z's, Aki-Z's, Buzz-Z's, and Z's eyes on him.

Z clapped. "The princess awakes."

"Asshole," Rueben muttered and popped his neck. He felt good. He felt refreshed. Turning back to Team Z, he said, "I have two questions. One, why do I feel like a million dollars after being cut and poisoned? And two, what are you arguing about?"

Twirling a tablet stylus around, Buzz-Z stepped forth and opened his mouth.

"Keep it short, will ya?" Young Z chided.

Buzz-Z grinned. "Of course, of course." He pointed the stylus at Rueben's leg, and a green laser light pinpointed the place the dagger had sliced. "A top-of-the-line medical application, the Buzz Patch, was applied to your wound."

"A Buzz Patch?" Rueben said.

"Think of it as a liquid bandage that dissolves over a wound with a ton of nutrients that stimulate your body's healing factor tenfold. Also, once it absorbed into your bloodstream, it took care of the poison on that dagger too."

Rueben was impressed. "Wow. Sounds expensive."

"Not when you know someone," Buzz-Z said. "This is the luckiest special operations team in the world." He sharpened his words. "Not that the technology is appreciated." He directed his gaze at Young Z, who threw up his hands.

"What? I can warp back in time to prevent an injury. Why get a giant liquid bandage when I could avoid the wound altogether?"

"For the sake of science," Buzz-Z said as if it was obvious. "For the sake of science."

Rueben quipped, "Wait. So you could say that bleeding-edge technology healed me? Get it? Bleeding edge. I was bleeding."

Z slowly slapped his forehead. Aki-Z shook her head.

Buzz-Z conceded. "Well, when we got you onto the jet-copter, you were bleeding quite profusely."

Rueben rubbed the fully healed injury under his pants. "Which brings up another question. Why did you rescue us when you'd intended to leave us behind?" He directed the question at Young Z, who bore the gaze as if it didn't faze him. Rueben angled his eyes over to Z. "Is that what you two were arguing over?"

Z crossed his arms and nodded smugly. "Bastard double-crossed us. He claims he did it to look out for his family and friends." He took a step toward Young Z. "Let me tell you, I'm not one to be crossed."

Young Z matched Z's step forward. Now they were standing nose to nose. "I know. We're the same person, different times. Buzz already ran blood samples for the two of you."

"Then why'd you try to leave us?" Z said, unpacified.

"Didn't know it at the time, did I?"

Intervening before someone got killed, Rueben grabbed Z by the collar and yanked him back half a step. Z looked perturbed by the action. "Chill, okay?" Rueben said. "What's wrong with you? The time virus starting to turn you back into an even bigger asshole again?"

At that idea, Rueben pulled out the virus detector. It registered as no virus activity.

"Your warping doesn't affect me, remember?" Z said.

Rueben shrugged. "There are a lot of rules to Repeating. Maybe we discovered a new one."

Buzz-Z chuckled. "Oh, my Rules to Repeating? So far, I'm up to thirty-seven rules and twelve and a half exceptions. Are we all good now?"

From a glance at Z and Young Z, Rueben could tell that

things were not all good. For some reason, the fact that Young Z had betrayed him was digging into Z. Rueben thought again about how there could only be one Rueben-Z on this Earth. Was Z's plan to get Young Z out of the picture so he could take his place and live life with his family again? The look in Z's eyes seemed to say that he thought Young Z was unworthy.

Rueben caught Z's attention. "How about we have a private chat."

Z shrugged. "Okay."

"Meanwhile," Aki said. "That tanker we were keeping tabs on…it's still on a course for NYC, like you said. I'm monitoring it closely, but it's strange. There doesn't appear to be anyone on board. Like you said. Even stranger, Buzz's algorithms have picked up chatter from the Russians. There's mention of a 'valuable item' on a tanker in the Atlantic. It looks like a Russian special ops team might be en route to the tanker for recovery. I'll keep monitoring the situation."

Rueben and Z nodded at her and stepped outside the lab to talk.

"What?" Z said. "You think I'm losing it?"

Rueben shook his head. "No. You were right to give Young Z hell for leaving us. But now we have to work with them, and I think they finally trust us. You good with that?"

After a few moments, Z nodded. "I miss my wife. You know what I mean?"

"Yeah. I do." At that moment, Rueben wished he could communicate with Aki back on Earth-A to let her know that he was okay. He wanted to check to make sure she was okay too. Operating on a different parallel Earth was stressing the concept of a "long-distance" relationship. How Z was keeping it together now, being so close to Aki-Z and yet so far, Rueben couldn't begin to fathom.

"You asked about my hip injury," Z said softly.

"Huh?"

Z solemnly met Rueben's eyes. "We were climbing a mountain to celebrate our wedding anniversary. Just me and Aki. We got caught in a small avalanche. I threw myself over Aki, but I took a big hit to the hip and leg." He sighed. "My leg healed but my hip…by the time I finally went to Buzz about it, he said it was too late to rehabilitate with a Buzz Patch. He hooked me up with an implant—the best alternative he had."

Rueben regarded Z. "This has already happened on this Earth?"

Z shook his head. "No. In the future. It bonded Aki and me together even stronger. Sure, at the time, I could've warped back and avoided the avalanche. I was arrogant and didn't think the injury was that bad. For two days, we had to take care of each other while we waited for Buzz to find and extricate us. Those were two glorious days and nights. I can still recall how we holed up in a cave with nothing but love and a fire between us. Man, I love that woman."

Z patted his hip, a longing gaze crossing over his eyes. "Believe me when I say it was worth it." He met Rueben's eyes. "You know the worst part? She and I will never get to experience that now because Young Z has already taken my place on this Earth."

Rueben bit his lip. About that… Surely there was a way to fix that. "We can figure something out. Buzz is a genius. Both of them."

Z shrugged off the notion. "Let's get back to the lab. I'm tired."

Rueben caught Z's shoulder. "Thanks. For telling me. I know that's not something you've probably ever told anyone."

A shimmer came over Z's eyes. Then he blinked it away. "You know something else I've never told anyone?"

"What?"

"How on a mission in Mexico I once clogged a toilet after eating nothing but tacos for three days straight—"

"Okay, okay," Rueben said, shoving his hand raised in Z's face. "I don't need to know that kind of shit."

"Oh. It was shit all right…"

As they made their way back to Buzz-Z's lab, they heard Jim-Z's voice.

When they passed into the lab, Jim-Z smiled at Rueben. "Ah, here he is. Yes. He appears quite fine." To Rueben, Jim-Z said, "It's Aki. On Earth-A."

Buzz-Z piped up and explained, "We've finally figured out how to communicate with our counterparts on Earth-A. Pretty snazzy, huh?"

Z smirked. "More efficient than waiting for the paper to come."

Rueben had to admit, communicating via the *Paper Warriors* intergalactic printing press hadn't been the best idea, but it had been the best idea they'd had at the time.

Rueben stepped up to Jim-Z. "Can I speak with her?"

Jim-Z nodded. "Through me, yes. What would you like to say?"

Swallowing, Rueben said, "That I love her and I can't wait to get back to her."

Jim-Z conveyed the message and after a pause, relayed Aki's heartfelt message back to Rueben.

A sense of calm came over Rueben. Communicating through Jim was a far cry from seeing Aki in person, but it only gave him more incentive to recover the ground zero virus sample and get back home to her.

Off to the side of him, Z sauntered up to Young Z and extended his hand. "We good?"

After a glance at Z's hand, Young Z accepted it, and they shook. "We're good."

"What did we miss since we stepped out? Jim say anything else of worth?"

Nodding, Young Z said, "Something about the mountain hideout where 'Team A' is right now. There was a strange incident with a bunch of trees. The time virus got loose from the hideout and started to wither a few trees but stopped, all on its own. Later, it started back up and devoured everything in a growing circle around the hideout. Buzz-A was barely able to contain it."

Z considered this news with some thought while Rueben was relieved that Buzz had solved the problem, even if it was only for the moment. The time virus probably hadn't been stopped for good on Earth-A. This was only a reprieve.

Aki-Z suddenly spoke up from a computer terminal. "I just ran diagnostics on the flash drive you two recovered from the Nunez lab. You wouldn't believe what I found out about the experiments he was conducting. There's a lot of redactions, but for decades he was experimenting with a virus that could warp time." She paused. "According to what I've found, it looks like whatever is on that tanker is the final piece to his puzzle."

"And that Russian special ops team you mentioned?" Rueben asked.

Aki frowned. "If we leave now, I think we'll be able to beat them there."

"Shit," Young Z said. "We have to intercept that tanker. Now."

CHAPTER TWENTY-NINE

Earth-A

What Jim had told them shook them to the core. A mad doctor named Nunez had been tinkering with a virus that could potentially manipulate time. He had a warehouse or testing facility of some sort in Maine. Team Z had already infiltrated the building on Earth-Z and was gearing up to stop it by intercepting an item transported on a tanker in the Atlantic Ocean.

At long length, they'd agreed that they needed to get to Nunez's warehouse on Earth-A to see if they could recover more non-redacted information. With the time virus temporarily halted, it seemed like the best idea at the moment. If anything went wrong, they had Carolyn, a Repeater, in their crew.

At least they were all gathered in the kitchen of Buzz's mountain hideout as Jim explained the situation. Food helped one think.

Marshall stifled a belch as he set the remains of his fried chicken bones on his plate. He wiped his greasy fingers on a

195

napkin that Buzz's kitchen robot had neatly placed at each seat around the table.

He sighed, glancing up from his napkin at the rest of the team gathered around the table. Everyone at the table was finishing up as well. Jim however, sat cross-legged on the floor beside them, happily munching on a chicken leg. A bowl of organic salad sat on his lap, drenched by green goddess salad dressing.

"And," Jim said between mouthfuls. "Team Z. Going to tanker. Atlantic Ocean. Virus ground zero. Possible." He'd already said this but kept repeating Team Z's verbal transmissions as he ate.

Amazing how good that robot can cook, Marshall mused as he wiped his mouth again. He grinned at Carolyn sitting beside him, who returned the gesture.

"Dr. Eduardo Nunez connection. Warehouse. Or is it a testing facility? Maine. Northern. Device. Shielded. Earth-Z."

It had taken some time and much back and forth through the mental conduit comprised between Jim-A and Jim-Z as well as both respective Buzzes. Finally, the representatives from both Earths had agreed upon the nomenclature of Earth-A and Earth-Z for the benefit of everyone understanding who or what was under discussion and where.

Jim gnawed the crispy breading off a chicken thigh, crumbs sprinkling the floor. Emma swiftly stepped in with an extended broom and dustpan and swept them up. Now Jim repeated back to Earth-Z what Team A had decided to do. "Team A. Going to Testing Facility. On Earth-A. Uncover additional information. Monitor. Time virus." He paused as he relayed what Team Z had replied. "Nunez has security. Caution required."

Marshall and the rest of them didn't mind Jim rehashing

everything. They wanted to make sure that both parties understood each other's missions. Now they were on the same page and would continue to stay synced as long as...

"Two teams. Two missions. Stay in contact. Bring Jim. Feed Jim. More chicken..." At this, Jim-A grinned mischievously.

Aki cocked her head toward Emma. "We're going to need an order to go."

"My pleasure," Emma said with a *beep* and she headed back into the kitchen to prepare it.

Now Jim burped. He set the chicken down and started shoving handfuls of salad into his mouth. He resembled a happy toddler.

When it was apparent Jim was done speaking, Buzz pushed his chair out and stood. "I'll finish the last-minute preparations. Rosa should have the jet-copter repair job complete."

"Good," Aki said. "So we won't have to worry about it falling apart in midair?"

Buzz frowned. "All faulty bolts have been replaced. And, there's an additional surprise that I can't wait for you all to see in the hangar."

Martha wiped her mouth on a napkin. "Gee. Can't wait."

Buzz stared dully at her. "Your anticipation is contagious," he said flatly.

Shrugging, Martha said, "So is yours." She rose from the table as well and nodded at Aki. "How about we go over our guns and ammo?"

Aki washed down her last bite of food with her water. "Sounds good to me." She turned to Marshall. "Wanna help?"

Marshall studied Aki for a few moments. Rueben was a lucky man. He'd landed a fine woman. For a brief moment,

Marshall recalled when he'd first laid eyes on Carolyn back when they were younger. He was happy for Rueben and Aki. They'd be good for each other, assuming they succeeded in fixing this time virus mess that was threatening the multiverse.

Marshall lifted a hand dismissively. "Nah. Go on ahead, girls. I trust your gun evaluating."

Beside him at the table, Carolyn blinked. "Marshall Peet. I've never known you to pass up an opportunity involving looking at guns. Especially when it's women handling them." Carolyn and Marshall exchanged an inside smile. "Are you sure you're okay?"

Marshall again waved Aki and Martha onward before turning back to his wife. Buzz also left the room. "Never been better," Marshall said. He scooted his chair back and slowly pushed himself up to a standing position.

He ignored the slight pain in his hip. After this was over, he would get in shape again, and he was going to drag his son into the plan too if he could manage to get Rueben away from Aki long enough. He inwardly chuckled at the idea.

"Honey," he addressed Carolyn, waving her to stand beside him. He wrapped an arm around her waist and grinned slyly at her. "How about we go get some fresh air topside?"

Buzz peeked his head around the corner. "Oh, I can assure you the air down here is triple-HEPA filtered, and each room equipped with a negative ion generator for fresher—" He stopped abruptly at the looks Carolyn and Marshall were giving him. Backing toward the doorway, he said, "I'll go do the last check."

Carolyn smiled at him, and Buzz blushed as he exited the room. Now it was only Marshall, Carolyn, and Emma making cooking sounds in the kitchen.

Giving Carolyn's hip a quick squeeze, Marshall guided his wife around, and together they walked up the stairwell leading to the trap door that led up to the small patio at the cavern's entrance. The petite patio furniture was their little "secret spot" they'd claimed for themselves when they first arrived here. An involuntary grin came over Marshall's face as he spotted the empty wine bottle they'd shared the night before.

He stopped and turned toward Carolyn, their faces inches apart. Then, very carefully, he went down on one knee, took her left hand, and kissed it. He creakily rose back to his feet. "I know I don't say this nearly enough, but I love you. I love you with my whole heart and I always will. I want you to know it."

"Oh, Marshall. I am so, so sorry I ever left you. I'm so grateful you've welcomed me back with such open arms."

With eyes starting to shimmer, he said, "I'm the grateful one. After you left, I became something I hated. Now I've come to terms with everything, and I'm better for it."

For a few minutes, they stood there, holding each other on the patio.

"This mission. Could be dangerous," Carolyn whispered at last.

Marshall gripped her closer. "It's a good thing I'm married to a Repeater."

They both chuckled.

Carolyn batted her eyelashes at him. "You're not exactly helpless yourself."

"That I am not—" he started, then his hip popped. "Uh-huh, but my body isn't in as good a shape as yours. It will be though. Hell, maybe one day we can both fight crime together with Rueben and Aki and Buzz and Martha..." He trailed off at her weary glance. He brushed some of her bangs away. "Or we could retire to the islands."

Carolyn tipped her lips up and kissed him. Then she pulled back. "We've done enough fighting and running. I like that idea a lot."

Marshall grinned. "They say that hot sand between the toes and a cold beer in one hand can cure anything."

Carolyn giggled. "I guess we'll find out."

Twenty minutes later, they all gathered outside the hangar door. When Buzz led them inside, they smiled and cheered.

"Well, I'll be damned," Marshall said as he stared in awe at Buzz's jet-copter. Aside from making repairs, Rosa had painted some big, bold letters on the side in bright paint.

"The A-TEAM," Marshall read aloud. "Now we're talking. I don't care what they say about you. You're all right, Buzz."

Buzz looked puzzled. "What do they say about me?" he muttered.

Martha placed a hand on Buzz's shoulder and directed him toward the jet-copter. "Any more last-minute touches?" she asked.

Buzz's eyes returned to focus. "Yes, as a matter of fact. New and improved seat harnesses. Rotor tweaks to reduce choppiness. And an autopilot program."

"Autopilot?" Martha said with a grin back at Marshall, and she and Buzz headed up to the jet-copter.

Marshall stood back and observed the aircraft with Carolyn pressed up against his side. *This is good. We'll get the mission done, and the Ruebens will complete theirs, and everything will be good.*

Jim shuffled past him clutching a partially eaten chicken leg he'd retrieved from the giant insulated backpack cooler strapped to his back. From the way the man walked, the cooler was full of chicken.

Marshall chuckled and pulled Carolyn closer.

They were all good and for the moment, the time virus was still good. What could go wrong?

The figure observed Buzz's hangar silently, his black-clad body hidden among the ashes of the withered mountain forest like a ghillie suit.

Dr. Nunez's security system had alerted him the moment that they'd gone snooping on the Internet about Valence Systems Corp. and Neutron Fix Consolidated, which had, in turn, led them to Nunez Corp.

The supersoldier shook his head. Dr. Nunez had been so careful not to leave a trail back to him. These people were intelligent adversaries—their underground hideout proved it. Once the automated security protocol had traced their IP signal back to somewhere in the Catskill Mountains, it had immediately dispatched him. He'd traveled as far as he could by motorbike until going on foot was the only option.

The signal triangulation had been a rough estimate, and it might have taken him days to find the underground hideout had it not been for the withered trees in a mile-wide radius. He reckoned that the tree cover would've kept the hangar perfectly concealed under ordinary conditions. Now that all was dust on the mountainside, the green-painted hangar roof stood out rather gaudily.

It made things rather too easy.

Behind his red-tinted goggles, the supersoldier watched motionless as the twin-rotor aircraft lifted from the hangar.

It appeared that he had arrived only a few minutes too late to eliminate the threat to the good doctor's plans.

He remained still, lying prone in the ash until the aircraft was turned away from him and starting to shrink with the distance. When he had judged that it was safe for him to do so, he raised a monocular device to his eye and tagged the departing aircraft with a homing laser.

Oh well.

Their last-minute escape would only make the chase more satisfying when he caught them.

And eliminated them.

CHAPTER THIRTY

<u>Earth-Z</u>

Team Z was once again riding in Buzz-Z's jet-copter. Everyone had safely harnessed themselves inside, even Jim-Z, who was munching on a bag of Organic Fried Chicken-Flavored Vegetable Straws.

Rueben turned to the side as Z reached over and grabbed a handful of the snack food, nodding his thanks. "Want some?" Z asked Rueben.

Rueben shook his head. He didn't have a good track record of keeping his food down when in Buzz's jet-copter although he had to admit, the ride was very smooth. Glancing down at the tablet in his hands, he saw that they were about twenty minutes out from the tanker. Outside, the darkness of night would help conceal their approach.

All in all, their plan was going well. They had not one but two functional Repeaters in their group if things went wrong. This was it. Buzz-Z had supplied them with additional glass vials that could contain the virus sample. After this mission, they'd be able to go back to Earth-A and figure out how best to stop the virus. *Virus ground zero. Bring it on...*

Rueben closed his eyes and was starting to doze off when Jim-Z made a sudden choking sound. At first, it seemed that the man had choked on a veggie straw. But he wasn't clutching his throat or doubling over against his restraints. Instead, he was wide-eyed, and his hair was on end.

"There is a disturbance," he gasped.

Buzz-Z leaned back in his pilot's chair. "You mean, in the Force?" Then he saw the grave look on Jim's face, and he grew serious. "What's wrong? What's happening?"

Young Z had already unclipped his harness and was starting to unbuckle Jim-Z's when Jim's fingers latched onto his arms. "The multiverse is in grave danger. There is a dark cloud coming for us."

"Dark cloud?" Young Z rubbed his chin.

"It is coming..."

Earth-A

"It swarms. It forms. The dark cloud. It comes!"

Buzz glanced back at Jim going crazy in the jet-copter's cargo space. Carolyn unbuckled herself in an instant and was trying to calm him down.

"To devour! It comes. It tears through the frequencies. Burrowing. Like a worm. But more like a panther..."

Buzz's mind froze in terror. "What did you say? Panther?"

"Like a storm cloud. It comes. To devour all that grows."

"Oh shit," Buzz muttered.

"What the hell is going on?" Marshall roared, trying to extract himself from his seat, but Carolyn motioned him to stay seated.

Buzz made sure that the jet-copter's autopilot was still functioning before turning back to his team. "Jim is somehow connected to the multiverse. I think he just had a vision or communication or something."

"Communication?" Marshall massaged his forehead. "Communication with what? Jim-Z?"

"No," Buzz said. "With the time monster. It's mutated again."

"And?" Martha prodded.

"It's found a way to travel through space and time."

Marshall crossed his arms. "Layman's terms?"

Buzz gulped. "It can hop from Earth to Earth and warp back in time."

"Goodbye, Earth." Jim slumped back in his seat, exhausted and snoring.

Earth-Z

Jim-Z was leaning forward in his seat, gently snoring. Young Z turned to Buzz-Z, insistent. "Is what he said true? That time monster from the future is heading backward in time to our location?"

The paleness of Buzz-Z's face stunned Rueben, not that he was surprised. Sure, Buzz-A had speculated that the time monster AKA mutated time virus might eventually be able to warp through time but that had seemed like a long way away. It couldn't possibly mutate that quickly, could it?

"Buzz!" Young Z called from his position squatted in front of Jim-Z. "Snap out of it."

"Huh, uh…yes. Yes, it's possible. I have to run some tests…" Buzz-Z made sure the autopilot was still functioning and made his way to the back of the jet-copter to the mobile tech station. He rapidly began pulling up holographic screens in the air.

Young Z was in the process of standing to take his seat when a violent tremor shook the jet-copter. It rocked sideways, then righted, and started to tip again.

"Buzz, what the hell is going on?" Aki-Z yelled.

Rueben was leaned forward against his harness, his eyes trained on the spot where Young Z had been standing. "Guys, where's Young Z?"

"Who?" Aki-Z started, then her face was terrified. "Rueben! Rueben, where are you?"

The jet-copter had righted itself. The only sound inside the aircraft was the wind rushing by the open side door.

Buzz-Z picked himself up off the floor. Already he had a nasty bump rising on his forehead, which clashed with his shiny Botox face.

"Autopilot malfunction?" Z asked.

Shaking his head, Buzz-Z said, "That was no malfunction. Someone hacked us."

"Hacked?" Z said.

Just then, Young Z's voice shouted over the roar of the outside wind. "A little help? I'm losing my grip."

CHAPTER THIRTY-ONE

<u>Earth-Z</u>

Rueben and Z both shared coordinated looks, able to sense what the other was thinking by the look of their eyes. Rueben unbuckled and sprinted to Buzz's side while Z threw off his harness and dashed to Aki-Z, now holding on to the vertical rails on the wall beside the open side door.

From his position bending over beside the computer genius, Rueben could see the open side door.

"Pull me in, will ya?" Young Z called. Aki-Z leaned outward and got thrown off balance.

"Watch out!" Z caught Aki-Z's arm as she nearly got sucked out of the aircraft. Aki-Z met Z's eyes, and for a moment, Z's resolve to help Young Z seemed to falter.

"Help me in, dammit! Falling to your death sucks!"

Rueben was starting to wonder if Z was going to help Young Z back inside or if Young Z would have to die and Repeat back inside the aircraft. Rueben had to admit that there was some part of the notion he liked. Young Z had abandoned them, after all, back in the testing facility.

207

Then Z carefully leaned out and helped Aki-Z pull Young Z back inside the aircraft.

Rueben turned back to Buzz-Z. The man rubbed the bump on his head and groaned. "I'm due for a magazine photoshoot tomorrow afternoon."

"Can't you heal it super quick?" Rueben asked.

"Yeah, but—"

The jet-copter tilted again.

"Are we still being hacked?" Rueben reached out to grasp something and steady himself as Buzz-Z, and the rest of the team did the same.

"The jet-copter isn't being hacked. Its autopilot program is."

Young Z called, "Semantics, buddy. Can you fix it or not?"

"I can try. I can try."

Rueben helped Buzz-Z up, bracing both of them when the jet-copter rocked hard again. Rueben felt food coming up from all the rough riding, but he managed to keep it in his stomach. Jim still sat harnessed in his seat, his arms and legs flopping with the continuous changes to the aircraft's direction.

Once Buzz-Z reached his mobile tech center again at the back of the aircraft, he frantically keyed in some commands. The good thing about the holographic screens was that they didn't fall with all the jerky movements.

About half a minute passed with sweat rolling off Buzz-Z's artificial-looking face when Buzz-Z turned to the rest of his team, his tone grave. "Got it."

The aircraft straightened out and corrected course.

"What happened? Who hacked it?" Young Z asked.

Buzz wiped a palm over his sweaty cheek. "I think it was the Russians. Their tech sector has boomed over the past decade. We have to hurry up to get to the tanker before their Special Ops team gets there. Also, before the time monster gets us."

"What more could go wrong?" Aki-Z said.

Young Z pulled her close. "Doesn't matter, babe. We have each other."

Z winced at the gesture of affection. Steadying himself against the railing beside the open door, Rueben steeled himself. "There's the tanker. Are we all ready to end this?"

It was a few minutes until sunrise when Buzz-Z dropped the three Ruebens off on the deck of the moving tanker. It had been tricky, but Buzz-Z had hovered over the deck, and they slid down a rope. Once they were on the deck, Buzz-Z took off. He'd return to exfiltrate them when the mission was complete. Aki-Z was staying on board to help Buzz-Z.

On the deck, as they quickly examined their surroundings in the early morning, Rueben wondered aloud, "How come we aren't wearing our high-tech battle suits?"

"All the salt in the air interferes with the electronics," Z said.

Rueben sarcastically added, "But our earpieces still work? It's amazing that future tech can heal a wound super-fast but can't protect electronics from sea salt in the air. I'm pretty sure that's not even an issue on Earth-A."

Young Z smacked Rueben over the head. "Head focused on the mission."

Z smacked Rueben over the head as well. "Yeah. We're running against the clock here. Got to beat that Russian Spec Ops team before they find the Nunez machine part."

Rubbing the back of his head, Rueben said, "From the nanobot footage from…" Rueben didn't know whether or not to point to Z or Young Z. "Anyway, the footage didn't show any machine part. All I remember is a metal box in the control room. Then the footage went out. Maybe we should start looking there?"

"No." Young Z shook his head. "We need to clear the rest of the tanker first."

Whistling, Z said, "It's an awfully big ship. Besides, we might not have time."

The tension between Z and Young Z was as palpable as the salt in the air. Young Z finally relented. "Fine. You happen to know the way down to this control room?"

Rueben had an idea: the virus detector. If it registered the time virus, it would confirm that it was onboard. Also, it might lead them right to it.

As soon as he pulled the device from his pocket, he saw the virus reading start to rise. "It's here," he said with a grin. He stepped around the deck and was relieved to see the reading spike the nearer he moved to a ladderway leading belowdecks. He was about to wave them forward when there came a sound on the deck below them.

Young Z turned a mistrustful glance at Rueben and Z. "This tanker is abandoned, right?"

Z cursed. "The Russian team must have beaten us here. They're already down below."

The humming of a speedboat approaching over the sea grabbed their attention. "And I think they have got extra buddies coming. We need to be quick about this."

At least we've got guns, Rueben thought. Hopefully, they didn't need to use them.

Before they headed below deck, Young Z handed them

each a set of compact goggles. "They'll help us detect heat and movement. So we can avoid the patrols below deck."

"How do you know…" Rueben started.

"Look," Young Z said. "I ran ahead and tried it my way. Those commandos down there are packing. Let's avoid them altogether. Like you said."

Rueben smirked. He wouldn't have even known Young Z had Repeated if the man hadn't told him. Now he knew what his friends must feel like when he did the same thing. "Sounds good to me. Let's get the virus sample and go."

On the next floor down, they nearly confronted the Russian Spec Ops team twice. Both times, the Ruebens were able to duck silently out of view with the help of Young Z's special goggles. It was apparent that these guys were pros. The Russians must have wanted this Nunez machine part.

There was no way that Rueben was going to let Nunez or the Russians get it.

They were creeping down a ladderway to the next lowest deck when the Russians ambushed them.

The Ruebens had amazing firepower, but so did the Russians. A stream of bullets took off Young Z's hand and nearly blew Z's leg off at the kneecap. Rueben turned his gun on himself and fired.

He died.

Earth-Z

"This way. Quick," Rueben whispered, leading Z and Young Z away from the ladderway and the ambush waiting at the bottom. They found another route and descended farther into the ship.

They continued in this fashion through the tanker. There

were plenty of locked doors, but Rueben disregarded them. They pushed onward until they reached the metal door leading to the control room. Rueben stepped up to it, placed his hands on the metal wheel, and turned.

It didn't budge.

Z joined him and assisted with the turning. The metal wheel screeched as it moved, releasing the locking mechanism. Together, they opened the door.

CHAPTER THIRTY-TWO

Earth-A

The jet-copter touched down in northern Maine in a well-manicured meadow next to a hill. *This looks like a good place to park it.* Buzz unbuckled himself from the pilot's seat. He hadn't been piloting, though. While his newly completed autopilot program took care of that, he was busy plotting the course of the time monster. If his calculations were correct, the time monster was homing in on Team Z on Earth-Z, probably because it knew that they posed a serious threat to its existence.

Unless I'm overestimating its intelligence.

He thought it better to overestimate than underestimate. He hoped the Ruebens obtained the ground zero virus sample and got back to Earth-A so he could formulate the cure ASAP.

Everyone climbed out of the aircraft and Rosa approached Buzz. "As agreed upon, I will guard the jet-copter."

Buzz nodded, then handed out everyone's badges. They were part of his final preparations, and he'd printed them before leaving the lab. He handed one to Martha, Marshall, Carolyn, and Jim-A.

Next, Buzz distributed the white lab coats to his team. Surprisingly, everyone looked like scientists except for Marshall. He looked embarrassed in his coat which was too short and tight in the waist for him.

Martha, Aki, and Marshall checked their guns then and concealed them under their lab coats. Before they headed up the hill, Buzz cleared his throat and addressed his team. Behind them, the shiny letters "the A-TEAM" gleamed in the sunlight. "We need more information on what kind of machine Nunez is building. It must be in here, or at least some prototype or plans. We get it, and we get out. The fate of the multiverse may depend on it."

They all nodded grimly. Then they marched up the hill.

The Nunez testing facility lay on the other side of a partially filled concrete parking lot.

"Looks like we'll have company inside." Marshall patted his side, and the weapon concealed there. They all wore weapons hidden beneath their lab coats except for Buzz. Unless it was in the name of science, he much preferred others to use weapons.

Buzz's lips tightened. "Need I remind you all, this mission requires stealth—not action heroes."

Marshall motioned at all the parked cars. "You think these are all civilians? They're working on some time travel virus that threatens the existence of the entire multiverse."

Marshall quieted at the touch of Carolyn's hand on his wrist.

The warehouse or testing facility or whatever it was, was now twenty yards away. Walking across the parking lot, they didn't look as strange as if they had come directly from a grassy hill. Straightening his lab coat, Buzz said, "Follow me."

They followed him in through the front entrance's automated sliding doors and stopped just inside. Two burly security guards stood in front of a walk-through metal detector.

"Step through, please," one of the guards said.

Martha and Aki exchanged nervous glances. They all had guns.

Buzz coolly raised a hand to his ear. "Zach, you ready?"

There was no response for a moment, and Buzz feared something had happened to their remote, resident hacker. Then Zach's voice came over their earpieces.

"I think everything should be good now."

"You think?" Martha harshly whispered.

The two security guards were starting to scrutinize them. The first one said, "Step for—"

Buzz dismissively raised a palm to the man. "I know. I know. I've done this hundreds of times before." He stepped into the vertical metal detector, hoping Zach was right.

Green lights flashed from inside the metal detector's frame, and Buzz sighed. He waited on the other side for the rest of his team to come through.

Next, they waited in line for a receptionist to scan their badges. After scanning and then reading the name on Buzz's badge, she glanced curiously at him and said, "Welcome, Dr. D'Awesome." Buzz grinned while his teammates groaned. Luckily, it didn't raise any flags, and they proceeded into the building.

When they had made it around a corner, Buzz pressed a hand to his ear. "Thanks, Zach. You're a real lifesaver."

"Glad to help. Just a reminder though, I do expect a full debrief afterward to use for fodder for my next thriller book."

"You got it, Patterson," Marshall joked, and Carolyn giggled.

They continued down a hallway containing a firehose and fire ax behind glass as well as locked doors on each side. One of them said *Laboratory*. Buzz tried the door, but it was locked. When he waved his badge over the key reader, it didn't work. "Zach, you think you can unlock this?"

There was a pause, then Zach came over the line. "Sorry. Whatever they're working on in that lab, they've got it sealed up good. I don't think even my decryption software can break it."

They passed the door to the lab. Following the corridor, they came around another corner into a sprawling mess of low cubicle walls. Employees frantically typed on their keyboards and stared at their screens.

While it was a wide-open room, Buzz realized there were no exits beside the corridor they'd taken. If something went wrong, it would trap them in here. *What an inefficient building layout.*

The nearest two cubicle workers were chatting amongst themselves. "The newest breakthrough in virus tech," one of them whispered excitedly. "And in our office!"

When Buzz stepped toward them, they hushed up and went back to work, but he knew what he'd heard. Nunez was working on viruses. That probably was what the lab contained. He wished he could get in there and study what they were doing, but they didn't have time.

Suddenly he worried that Jim might do something to blow their cover. Spinning around, Buzz saw that Jim was placidly glancing about the place. It was Marshall's actions that worried him. The man had spotted a manager's office on the wall and was now trudging toward it.

"What are you doing?" Buzz whispered.

Marshall stopped and glanced over his shoulders. "If there's anyone who would have intel we need, it's the person inside that office."

"Huh?"

"Read the nameplate on the door."

Buzz squinted his eyes. "Egads…" The gold nameplate read *Dr. Eduardo Nunez.*

That's when Buzz spotted the plainclothes security guard sitting in a chair outside the manager's office. Marshall must have spotted him too, because he abruptly turned and walked past Buzz and the rest of the team without a word. He continued until he'd left the office room.

Not liking Marshall's suspicious actions, Buzz approached Carolyn. "What is your husband doing?"

"I'm not sure. But whatever it is, it's probably something clever."

Martha stepped up beside Carolyn. "She's right. He has good instincts. Marshall is one of the brightest minds I've ever met."

Buzz flashed her an irritable look.

"Not as bright as yours, though," Martha added. "Your mind is bright enough to light up the whole room—"

Marshall burst into the room. "It's the lab! The biggest goddamn breakthrough of the century!" Standing there in his white lab coat which barely extended to his shins, he looked more than a bit eccentric.

Eyes widened and excited whispers spread through the cubicle workers. One of them got up and trotted for the hallway. Two more followed. Then a stampede of office workers.

After they'd all rushed out, that left Team A and the security guard sitting out front of Nunez's office. The man was on full alert. He rose, reaching for a weapon concealed at his side as Marshall approached in an exaggerated waddle.

"Stop right there."

Marshall guffawed like a mad man and gestured for the guard to follow the cubicle workers.

"I said stop right there." The man was drawing a service pistol when Marshall closed in on him.

"You've got to see it to believe it. It's a miracle—" He grunted as he threw his fist at the guard, his knuckles cracking against the man's thick chin. The guard dropped to the floor, and his pistol clattered beside him. Marshall sucked on his aching knuckles.

"Nice acting." Buzz stepped past the man and up to the door with the gold nameplate. "Zach. If you will?"

The key reader beside the office door flashed green, and Buzz opened the door.

CHAPTER THIRTY-THREE

Earth Z

The tanker's control room looked old. It was full of dark furniture and a cluttered desk as in Z's nanobot footage. For some reason, it gave Rueben the sense that he was in a film noir and he was the detective. Rueben, Z, and Young Z searched the room.

"Found something," Young Z called. He sneered. "Oh wait, it's only a pile of junk. You sure there's something of value in here?"

Rueben stared down at the virus detector in his hand. The reading had been gradually increasing the farther belowdecks they traveled. Now it had leveled off, but it was high. Very high. Z glanced over at him and read the reading. They were so close now.

Their earpieces crackled. Buzz-Z was calling from the jet-copter. "Uh, guys. You find any evidence of the time virus on the tanker?"

"Oh yeah," Rueben said. "It's definitely in here. In this room."

Aki-Z's voice seemed relieved. "Good. That's good to hear. Any confrontation with the Russian team?"

"Nope," Young Z lied.

"Rueben," Aki-Z said. "You know you can't lie to me."

Young Z threw up his hands even though Aki-Z couldn't see him. "It was a minor confrontation. I warped back. Not even a scratch on me now. They haven't reached the control room yet."

"Good," Buzz-Z said. "Now, you better hurry."

Rather cockily, Young Z nodded at Rueben and said, "We're Repeaters. Time is on our side."

Buzz-Z's reply was terse. "Tell that to the time monster coming your way. According to my calculations and Jim's… link to the monster or whatever, it'll be there before you know it. Hurry up and get the sample of the ground zero virus so you can get your ass back here. With help from the Buzz on Earth-A, we should be able to figure out how to destroy the virus…"

In the background, Jim-Z started babbling. "Monster. Monster! MONSTER."

"Calm down," Aki-Z was saying.

Jim-Z sucked in a breath. "Danger ahhhhhh! The chicken is enraged. It wants to eat us all." Suddenly changing up his voice, Jim-Z said, "Uh folks, we interrupt your regular broadcast for an urgent weather forecast: Cloudy. With a chance of intergalactic destruction… Ahhhh! I can't see! My mind!"

As the man's words devolved into incomprehensible warbling, Rueben looked grimly at Z and Young Z. "That's not good. Jim-Z is supposed to be the levelheaded Jim. Now he sounds worse than Jim-A."

Z shook his head forlornly. "I can only imagine how Jim-A is faring."

. . .

Earth-A

"My mind is on fire! It's coming for the tanker on the bad Rueben's Earth!"

Standing in the doorway to Nunez's office, Buzz turned to Jim with a puzzled look. "That's the most coherent thing you've ever said."

Martha punched Buzz in the arm.

Earth-Z

Jim-Z had finally stopped screaming in their ears so Aki-Z or Buzz-Z must have silenced Jim's mic.

"Poor bastard," Z muttered. Then, "Shit. Look what I found."

Rueben left the pile of junk he was searching through and joined Z by his side. "Is that…"

Z nodded.

Propped up against the wall behind an old padded chair was a silver briefcase. A handcuff was attached to the handle along with a bloody chain.

"The arms dealer," Z said.

Rueben approached it, keeping an eye on the virus detector in his hand.

Z rubbed his forehead. "I don't get it. It had the time virus in it the whole time? The detector didn't even register it on the street."

Rueben crouched beside the briefcase. "I guess we're about to find out why." He flipped the latches. After a quick breath, he opened it.

He blinked.

He reached down and retrieved a small silver piston-like object from the velvet-lined interior. "Huh?" Holding it close to the virus detector, he saw no spike in the reading.

"Must be the final part to the Nunez machine," Z said.

Rueben had to admit, that made sense. Kind of. The machine part had been in this briefcase the entire time. The supersoldier had stolen off a street in NYC. Nunez's factory was in northern Maine, a day's drive away. So why was the part in the Atlantic Ocean on a tanker careening toward the coast of New York?

That was the riddle Rueben was trying to figure out when he noticed Young Z standing over a cluttered desk a few yards away. In his hand was a silver box. On the top was the engraved word *Nunez.* Young Z was about to open the latch.

Rueben pocketed the small machine part. "Wait," he called, but it was too late. Young Z had already opened the box, revealing an aged photograph.

When Rueben and Z took a closer look at the picture, they gasped.

Earth-A

"Come on, you damn computer. Open up!" No matter how much Marshall growled at it, Nunez's locked computer screen wouldn't unlock. It was a black screen with a bar to type in a password.

They had been waiting for several minutes as Zach remotely tried to hack the password.

"Zach," Buzz said with a hand to his earpiece. "You think you can hack it or not? We don't have long before everyone realizes there was no breakthrough in the lab."

"I'm trying. I'm trying. This hacking program can work miracles…"

"Except for on that lab door," Martha commented.

"Yeah," Zach said. "That was a crazy complex lock. This is only a computer password…aha! I think I got it."

Buzz watched as asterisks populated in the password box—Zach typing remotely via the USB dongle they had inserted into the laptop.

A giant *Welcome* replaced the password box. Then Buzz was looking at Eduardo Nunez's home screen. It was a photo. Judging by the clothing style of the people in it, it had to be about twenty or twenty-five years old.

It looked like the photo had been taken in a hospital. In it, a young woman was holding a newborn baby. A man wearing surgical gloves and a mask stood over her shoulder. Both beamed down at the baby boy in the woman's arms.

Recognition flashed across Buzz's face. Not for the baby or the doctor, but the woman holding the baby. With utter confusion tugging at the fraying strings of his mind, Buzz twisted his head to look at Carolyn, but her face had already gone white.

"Carolyn?" Marshall asked breathlessly. "Why…how…what…?"

Carolyn began to sob.

Earth-Z

Rueben stared dumbstruck at the photograph in the silver box Young Z held. "Why is there a picture of my mom in that box?"

"It can't be," Z said beside Rueben. "It doesn't make sense. How could…"

Even Young Z was shaking his head. "Is it real? This…this can't be me."

"Or is it me?" Rueben asked. After all, he was from a different Earth than Z and Young Z.

Young Z lifted the photograph from the box and scrutinized it. Rueben was no longer looking at the photo, though. He was staring triumphantly at the glass vial of purplish liquid in the box beneath where the photo had been. Maybe it was only his eyes, but it appeared to have a crack down the glass side.

Lifting the virus detector toward the box, he saw the reading spike. Momentarily forgetting the photo, Rueben turned to Z. "That's it. That's ground zero for the virus—where you initially got infected."

Rueben wasted no time in scooping up a sample in the vial Buzz-Z had provided him.

Then Z took the metal box from Young Z and snapped it closed. "Mission accomplished. Let's go." He tapped his earpiece. "Buzz, we're ready for you to swing back around and pick us up on the deck."

Buzz didn't reply.

Clutching the Carolyn photo in one hand, Young Z touched his earpiece. "Buzz? Buzz, are you still circling the tanker? We're ready for extraction."

Rueben was starting to think that something was wrong. His notion was proven a moment later when a figure stepped out from the shadows of the room.

The figure was tall and wrapped in black cloth and armor. A pair of gleaming red goggles concealed his eyes, and he held a sword in one hand.

The supersoldier's words were breathy and sinister. "No one is coming to extract you."

CHAPTER THIRTY-FOUR

Earth-A

Buzz was so engaged in extracting all the data he could from Nunez's computer that he didn't at first hear the sirens blaring through the office.

Neither did Marshall, Carolyn, and Martha. They were still trying to understand the home screen photo on Nunez's computer. The young woman in the photo was Carolyn, and the doctor they had pretty much confirmed was Dr. Eduardo Nunez himself. His face matched that of a man in another photo resting on the desk in a golden frame. In this second photo, Nunez was clutching a beautiful woman with gold curls to him. It was a much younger photo than the one home screen photo and the couple looked very much in love.

How did it all connect?

As for Jim, he was cowering on the office floor in the fetal position.

It was Aki who brought everyone to their senses. "Hello? Earth to Team A. Hear the siren?"

They all snapped to attention, their ears perking at the loud noise.

"You're right," Marshall said. "We've got to scram. That alarm is loud enough to wake up the next county over." He reached out and grabbed Buzz by the sleeve. "We've got to go."

"Just a minute. Just a minute." Buzz was frantically scrolling through the information on the computer screen. "This…I understand now what this is all about. I know how the time virus came to be. With this data, I'll be able to reverse the effects of the Time Disease for sure. Just got to grab the flash drive."

He plucked the drive from the USB port and shut the laptop. He started to leave, then on second thought, tucked the laptop under his arm and followed the rest of the team out of the office. Marshall was in the lead, carrying Organic Jim over his shoulder.

The security guard still lay unconscious by the door, and the cubicles appeared empty. When they were nearly halfway through the cubicles, Marshall stopped.

"Why are we stopping?" Buzz called from the back of the line as he fumbled with the flash drive and Nunez's laptop. Then he saw the tall ninja-clad warrior blocking their exit.

Marshall didn't look scared. "Just who the hell are you, pal?"

Buzz noticed a patina of dust on the ninja's shoulders.

The ninja's black face mask only muffled his words slightly. "I am your pursuer. I have tracked you for many miles."

Based on the dust, Buzz said, "My mountain hideout. You were there."

The ninja nodded. "I progressed through the forest that turned to ash. I only missed you by a few minutes."

"Serves you right, you creep," Martha said.

Buzz quickly assessed their situation. While they outnumbered the ninja, their opponent looked well trained. Plus, he carried a lot of sharp weapons. Buzz glanced past the ninja to the narrow corridor beyond—the only way out of this office room. They were trapped. Buzz groaned. "You're a real big pain in the ass. You know that?"

"You whine," the ninja said sharply.

"I don't whine—"

"I don't like whining. I shall perform my duty now." The warrior drew his blade from its scabbard with a scraping sound.

Aki threw off her lab coat and grabbed her gun. "What duty would that be?"

The ninja silently popped his neck left and right. "To eliminate all threats posed to Dr. Nunez and his work."

Earth-Z

"What did you say?" Rueben asked the supersoldier on the tanker.

"Your corpses will sink with this ship."

Young Z tucked the photo into his pocket. He sneered. "What did we do to deserve this fate?"

"You pose a threat to Dr. Nunez and his work. I will eliminate you per protocol."

"Protocol?" Rueben mused.

"I have served Dr. Nunez throughout the years. I have protected him. Shielded him. Enabled him to achieve his end goal. He is so close."

"Oh?" Z said. "What is that end goal? Why does he want to go back in time?"

The ninja scoffed. "Like I would tell you."

Rueben grinned. "You're going to kill us. Why not?" From what little Z had told him about the supersoldier, he rarely made mistakes. Even though the supersoldier couldn't warp, Z had never been able to kill him.

If Rueben thought the supersoldier would comply, he was disappointed. Instead of spilling Nunez's end game, he commenced his attack.

Earth-A

The supersoldier dropped to a poised crouch.

Marshall watched as Martha and Aki unloaded their pistols at him. To his astonishment, the bullets arced around the ninja, punching through the cubicle walls around them.

"Who the hell is that?" Marshall stammered as he drew his gun.

The ninja sliced the gun from Marshall's hand. "Shit." Before he could react, a horizontal kick to his shoulder sent him soaring against the office copier with a *crash*.

Carolyn bent to help him up. "Whoever he is, I can warp backward if I need to—"

The ninja crashed into her with a flying kick against her back that launched her airborne. Marshall watched, horrified as her body smashed through a cubicle wall and she struck her head on a desk. She lay limp on the floor.

"I am Nunez's supersoldier," the ninja proclaimed.

"You're a bastard," Marshall growled, lowering to an American football hike stance. Then he leapt forward at the attacker to grab him.

The ninja easily slipped out of his grasp and smacked the

flat of his blade across Marshall's hip and lower back. There was a popping sound, and Marshall fell to the floor.

Aki threw a paperweight at the ninja, but the supersoldier caught it and launched it right back at her with freakishly good reflexes. She barely dove under a desk in time as the heavy object tore a divot in the desktop.

A flat computer monitor flew at the ninja courtesy of Martha, but he sidestepped, slicing the monitor in half with his sword. "This fight bores me," the supersoldier rasped.

From his position on the floor, Marshall slammed a piece of splintered wood against the ninja's shin. It splintered apart with no visible reaction from his target. The ninja stomped a foot down upon Marshall's hand, crippling it with the *crunch* of bone.

"Ow damnit!"

As Marshall rolled to the side in agony, he saw that the supersoldier was leaving him and striding toward Buzz at the back of the room.

Meanwhile, Aki fired at the ninja from the cover of a desk, but the bullets swerved around him. One of the bullets sheared upward, shattering some of the office's fluorescent lighting.

Martha darted in with a metal letter opener. The ninja deftly disarmed her with a chop to her wrist. He gripped her by the collar and swung her up and over a cubicle wall, where she crashed upon a desk and some computer equipment.

Still writhing in agony, Marshall gasped. Martha was like a daughter to him. Always had been and always would be. For all he knew, this man had killed her. *No. Not a man,* he thought. A man wouldn't have been strong enough to toss her over a cubicle like that. This thing had to be…

A robot. A goddamned ninja robot.

The last time he'd confronted a robot, it had been at the police precinct. It had the appearance of a lumberjack, and he'd defeated it by pushing it out the second-floor window. That wouldn't work this time because they were at ground level.

He did know one weakness, though. Robots didn't tend to like water.

"Ah!" Buzz screamed as he ran farther back in the office, trying to find a place to hide from the supersoldier coming his way.

"You're going…the wrong way," Marshall sputtered, but it was no use. Buzz didn't hear him. The scientist had book smarts but not many street smarts. Buzz was running himself into a corner instead of heading for the room's only exit, which was now unguarded.

Marshall tried to stand, but pain shot up his hip and back. Were they broken? He was able to crawl forward on his good hand. Whenever he bumped his crushed hand against the floor, it throbbed so painfully that he thought he might pass out.

If I pass out, I won't be any damn use to anyone.

He crawled up beside Carolyn. She was still breathing.

Beside her lay a giant paperweight, and Marshall hated himself for seeing the most obvious way out. With their only Repeater currently knocked unconscious, it would be only moments before the ninja-supersoldier-whoever butchered them all with that sword.

The man in black hadn't come to talk nicely to them, that was for certain. Since the supersoldier was connected to Nunez and the time virus, what if he knew that Carolyn was a Repeater? What if he knew about Carolyn's warping ability? He might keep her unconscious so she couldn't warp back and undo all their deaths, similar to how a then-psychotic Rueben-Z had once kidnaped Rueben.

The only way to prevent that scenario from happening was if Carolyn died and warped back in time. Since she was unconscious and unable to control the warp, she'd go back a full three days—at least that was his understanding of her powers. Would that mess up the timeline since that was before Rueben had left in the space and time capsule?

He loved both his wife and his son, and he didn't know what to do. If Carolyn warped backward, at least they wouldn't be in this scenario. But the ninja had already destroyed his handgun.

Marshall glanced at the hefty paperweight lying beside Carolyn. And swallowed. Could he kill his wife? In such a brutal manner?

Even though it wasn't killing her—she'd warp back afterward to before it happened—and even though he wouldn't remember it afterward since he didn't have the Repeater gene, it was still murder in his book. He was and always would be a police officer, goddammit. He protected and served.

He couldn't kill his wife so she could warp back and save them all with her superpower. He just couldn't.

Could he?

At the other end of the office, the ninja advanced upon Buzz, who had stumbled backward out of a corner and against a desk. As he scuttled around, he groped with his free hand for anything he could use as a weapon. His fingers enclosed around an ink pen. He thrust it forward.

"Ha! The pen is mightier than the—"

The supersoldier's blade took off half of the pen in Buzz's outstretched hand.

"Nooo!"

Buzz twisted to the side, and the ninja's blade descended on him as he managed to raise Nunez's laptop over his head in his defense. The laptop separated in two, and Buzz awkwardly toppled backward over the desk. Pain shot through him like electricity, but at least he still had the flash drive between his fingers.

With another swift swipe, the ninja's blade sliced into the flash drive. It was there one moment, gone the next.

"Eeeiiiahhh!"

The ninja turned to see Jim racing toward him, pushing a rolling chair before him like a renegade shopping cart. Easily sidestepping the attack, the supersoldier planted a foot onto Jim's back and kicked. Jim blasted through a cubical wall, leaving the wild-armed outline of a hole in the wall like something straight out of a Looney Tunes cartoon.

Buzz couldn't help but suppress a chuckle at the sight as he realized there wasn't much hope for them in surviving this. Where was Carolyn? The fact that she hadn't Repeated meant that she must have been knocked unconscious by the supersoldier.

Made sense. The ninja worked for Nunez. Nunez probably created the time virus. Hence, the supersoldier's priority had probably been to incapacitate her first.

Smart.

The supersoldier loomed up before Buzz and raised his katana.

"Hey!" Martha shouted from a few steps behind the ninja. Scratches and cuts covered her face and neck. The supersoldier craned his head around right as Martha fired her handgun at his face at point-blank range.

Impossibly, Martha's gun exploded in a hot flash, and she stumbled to the floor holding her hand. The supersoldier's face remained unharmed.

There was a blur off to the side as Aki rushed in with a combat knife gripped in her hand. The ninja spun, and Aki ducked under his blade. Then she swung upward, slicing a swatch of the supersoldier's black fabric on his chest as he jumped backward. Recovering superhumanly fast, he unleased a downward diagonal cut upon her.

Luckily, Aki dodged to the side, but the slash shortened her hair. She growled, and the ninja quickstepped up to her and kicked her across the jaw. Like a lapping wave of ocean water, she slumped fluidly to the floor.

The supersoldier turned back to face Buzz. "Prepare to meet your maker," he rasped.

Buzz gulped. His genius mind couldn't find a way out of this situation, but at least he could go out in style. "Maker?" he said bravely. "I don't have a maker. I'm a product of evolution, you damned bible thumper ninja."

The ninja shook his head. "Such silly last words." His black-clothed and armored torso twisted as he prepared to execute Buzz with a vicious horizontal slash.

As Buzz closed his eyes, he bitterly realized that there was no hope for them. Team A had failed its mission.

The only question now was, had Team Z also failed?

CHAPTER THIRTY-FIVE

Earth-Z

The supersoldier crouched, and Rueben fired his gun. Not surprisingly, the bullet curved around the ninja, tearing into the furniture and metal walls of the control room.

Young Z tucked his head and attempted to tackle the ninja, but the assassin evaded and used Young Z's momentum against him, tossing him on top of the cluttered desk. The man disappeared in a crash of splinters and junk.

Z fired a few rounds to grab the ninja's attention.

"This guy have any weaknesses?" Rueben reloaded.

Z cursed. "None that Buzz or I know of."

The ninja readied a dagger to throw at Rueben and Z dove to the side.

Continuing, Z said, "At least we now know why he's such a badass. He serves a madman scientist with who only knows how many resources, considering he's built a time machine…" He dodged another dagger that embedded itself into an overturned chair.

As the supersoldier approached Z, Rueben fired at his

back to draw his attention. The bullets didn't touch the ninja, but he turned regardless.

"Seriously, how do we fight this thing?" Rueben touched his earpiece. "Buzz? Buzz, are you there?"

The supersoldier's red goggles gleamed. "They have already perished. The Russians hacked into the autopilot. As we speak, they are sinking to the ocean floor, much like you and this tanker shortly."

Rueben considered this. "I don't buy that. Buzz is smarter than that. He wouldn't let his jet-copter go down. He regained control—"

"Only because I let him," the supersoldier continued. "During the first hack of the jet-copter, I intervened. The Nunez Protocol dictated that I allow you to come to the tanker so I could ascertain what you knew. Then eliminate you." He took a step toward Rueben.

"Eliminate us like how you eliminated that arms dealer?"

"Dr. Nunez doesn't like loose ends. I am his tool to wield as he wishes."

"Tool?" Rueben asked. "What are you? A brainwashed slave..."

"No," Z said. "I know why it's always one step ahead. Why its reflexes are so good."

The two Ruebens met each others' gaze. "Robot," they said in unison.

Rueben addressed the ninja assassin. "You're a robot?"

Z shook his head confusedly. "But I've lived through this memory before, and I don't recall a ninja robot in it."

The supersoldier sneered at him from behind his red-tinted goggles. He lifted the flap of a black pouch on his side, revealing a neat row of syringes. "Knockout serum for dealing with Repeaters. Also messes with one's memory. Compromises neural function over time."

Z growled. "So you shanghaied me the first time I was on this tanker with some knockout serum? You mean to say that I contracted the time virus here at ground zero *and* started a slow descent into madness on this tanker? I fucking hate this tanker."

Z shared a knowing glance with Rueben. Then he drew a deep breath. They split up and fired at the supersoldier, temporarily confusing it.

"Did Nunez create you?" Rueben asked quickly.

The ninja turned to Rueben.

"So that head of yours is filled with circuit boards instead of brain matter?" Z asked.

Spinning now to face Z, the soldier shook his head. "I am a superior soldier. No man can match my reflexes. My speed. Not even a Repeater."

"So you know about us?" Rueben said.

"Of course. Nunez created both of you the same as he created me."

Rueben's eyes tightened. His gut twisted. "I'm a human. A scientist didn't create me."

The ninja selected another poison-tipped dagger from a hip pouch. He prepared to throw it at Rueben or Z, but when Young Z attempted to sneak up on it from behind, the ninja threw it behind himself, striking Young Z in the chest. He slumped sideways as he fell toward the ninja, reaching out with both hands. The supersoldier simply flicked a foot out at him, striking Young Z in the cheek and sending him sideways, and destroying another cluttered desk.

"See how smart I am? That man also is a Repeater. But he cannot Repeat while he is unconscious."

"I don't care what you say," Rueben said. "I know the truth. I'm not a computer or a clone or anything. My mother was Carolyn."

Z darted forward to attack the ninja and received a kick to the chest that sent him sprawling on his back.

"Yes. Your mother was Carolyn. But she was injected with Nunez's virus."

"Virus?"

"Experimentation with parallel dimensions yielded a virus affected with the ability to warp back in time. Most subjects injected with it couldn't harness it. The virus withered them into a super-aged pile of dust. Carolyn, your biological mother, was the first and only subject to survive the procedure."

Rueben was shocked. He didn't know what to believe. "If that's true, Nunez is a monster."

The ninja shook his head. "No. He is humanity's savior. Their only chance at survival. Humans are ruining this earth. They are greedy animals. They have no restraint. They lack discipline. They want what they can't have. Nunez sought to—"

"To what? Fix humanity?"

"No. To reverse time. To go back to before things were beyond the brink."

"Oh really? Did he know that he unleashed his time virus into the world?"

The ninja looked appalled. "He did no such thing. He took the utmost precaution."

Rueben raised the virus detector. "Then explain why the virus is here."

"A trick," the ninja said. Then he retrieved a second sword

from his back and tossed it to Rueben. Rueben caught it. "Are you scared to face me? Human."

Rueben glanced down at the blade in one hand and the gun in his other. "This blade can't hurt you, can it? Not with your forcefield or whatever."

"It can. Will you be able to get close enough to use it against me?"

Rueben eyed his opponent and let his gun snap back to his hip. "You just robot-splained to me how you're superior to me. Why would you give me a chance to face you like this? Why not 'eliminate' me?"

The supersoldier regarded him silently. "I wish to test you. One of Nunez's creations pitted against the other. We are both one of a kind. We are also similar. A virus created you. A different kind of virus created me."

Rueben drew the Nunez machine part from his pocket. "Is that what this is for? Is that how Nunez's machine works? Some kind of computer virus inside it?"

Instead of answering, the ninja rushed forward, preparing to slice him horizontally at the waist.

Rueben had fought the supersoldier back at the warehouse and knew some of his tricks. He didn't want to die again.

He parried downward. The ninja followed up with a dagger in his other hand. He plunged it into Rueben's temple.

Rueben died.

Earth-Z
(Five Seconds Earlier)

The supersoldier lashed out with a horizontal slice. Rueben parried downward, then ducked as the ninja struck out with the dagger in his other hand. The ninja twisted and brought the sword up. Rueben blocked it, but the supersoldier swept his ankle, and he fell on his back. Then the ninja descended upon him with the dagger through his heart.

He died.

Earth-Z
(Five Seconds Earlier)

The supersoldier lashed out with a horizontal slice. Rueben parried downward, then ducked as the ninja struck out with the dagger in his other hand. The ninja twisted and brought the sword up. Rueben blocked it, and the ninja tried to sweep his ankle. Easily hopping over the attempt, Rueben punched the ninja square in the goggles.

The supersoldier fell back a step, one hand on its goggles as it stood. One of the lenses now had a hairline fracture in it.

"Impressive," the ninja said and appraised Rueben for a time. Without warning, his hand descended to one of his pouches and launched a dagger at Rueben.

He dodged it, but the dagger sliced his jacket it had been so close.

The ninja chortled. "How many times have you already died? Are you ready to admit that I am Nunez's most perfect creation?"

Z clambered up from where he had fallen. "You? Perfect? Underneath that facemask, I bet you don't even have a face."

The ninja fumed. Then, while keeping its red goggles on, it pulled back its facemask.

Both Rueben and Z froze. "I'll admit," Z said, "I didn't see that coming." The ninja's face was the same as Z's. "So Nunez created his robot guard in my image? I'm flattered. Definitely makes *me* more superior."

That enraged the supersoldier even more. It reapplied its face mask. "Dr. Nunez will reward me when I bring him your unconscious bodies."

Rueben twirled his sword. "Where is this almighty Dr. Nunez? If he's so important, how come we haven't ever seen him? How come he hasn't ever tried to reach out to us or even kidnap us so he could experiment on us?"

The supersoldier sneered. "Why do you think? If you knew where he was, you could undo him."

Z hmphed. "Good point. What if Nunez is already dead? What if he's out of the picture and you're following some old 'protocol' of his?"

"That is...not possible. The doctor wouldn't... He would inform me..."

Rueben laughed. "Inform you? Inform you that he died? I know you're a robot, but that's not exactly how death works."

"Yeah," Z said. "His time virus probably killed him, turned him to a pile of dust years ago while robots and scientists continued to try to complete his plan."

The ninja sliced the air with his sword. "That is not true!" It charged at Rueben and Rueben met his blade. Then Rueben lifted back and struck the ninja across the leg. Its padded armor took most of the swipe.

Rueben smirked. "Didn't even have to warp to get that strike in. You're slipping."

"I do not make mistakes." The supersoldier swung around with his blade, cutting into Rueben's back along both shoulder blades.

Rueben grimaced but then smiled. "Nice. But you think you can stop two Repeaters?"

The ninja glared at Rueben and Z. "Oh? What is this development? I have scanned your genetics again. Only one of you can warp." Its red goggles focused on Z. "You are neutered."

"Hey now. I'm not 'neutered—'"

"You are," the robot said.

Rueben darted toward him from the backside. The robot sent a backward thrust at Rueben's chest that felt like it caved in some ribs. Rueben groaned as he struck the floor on his shoulder. For a moment, he was in such pain that he felt like he couldn't move. He watched as Z drove his fist against the supersoldier's chin, staggering him. Then Z raised his gun, preparing to strike the assassin again with the butt.

There was a squishy, liquid sound and Z grunted. Bloody froth dribbled from one side of his mouth. The supersoldier had impaled Z through the gut with his blade.

"You'll…pay," Z managed to say and tried to fall forward upon the ninja, but the robot sidestepped and drew out his blade. Z's body crashed unceremoniously to the control room floor.

No…

Rueben fought to push himself up, but the supersoldier's shadow fell over him, and Rueben gazed up at the descending boot strike that broke his nose and shoved his head back against the floor.

CHAPTER THIRTY-SIX

<u>Earth-Z</u>

Fighting desperately to retain his consciousness, Rueben stared blurrily to the side at Young Z's body lying upon a heap of junk and splinters. Wincing, Rueben realized he'd landed upon some of the debris, and he had a fragment the size of a pencil shoved into his lower leg.

The supersoldier reached a hand down and pushed its thumb into the wound.

Rueben cried out in agony. He felt his gun being ripped away and then a spare knife he had strapped to his leg.

"You won't be Repeating. Not today." The ninja leaned over him, studying a dagger.

So it was going to be a poison-tipped dagger that put him to sleep? Was he going to black out and wake up on Eduardo Nunez's operating table?

With all the pain he was enduring, he was about to pass out anyway without the dagger poison. *Got to stay awake...*

Rueben pressed his index finger into his leg wound. His eyes jolted wide.

The ninja withdrew a hand from Rueben's pocket, holding up the Nunez machine part.

Even though the robot was pinning him down, Rueben struggled, managing to kick the supersoldier in the crotch. It didn't faze him. The ninja carefully slid the part into his pouch and then returned his dagger to its sheath. Then he leaned forward on top of Rueben, straddling him so that he couldn't move and his red goggles were inches from Rueben's. Rueben stared at his pale reflection in the goggles' reflection.

"Why use poison when I can choke you unconscious?"

Unconscious...

Rueben had two options. He could try to fight the ninja. Or he could try to kill himself. He didn't feel much like being able to do anything at the moment, but he did have the two-finger jab trick. But would it work against the robot ninja? It was certainly very lifelike, as lifelike as Buzz's Binnies and other robots. If only Buzz could spend some time with this killer robot supersoldier. He'd probably be ecstatic for the chance.

For that to be a possibility, Rueben first had to incapacitate or kill it.

The ninja brought both of its hands to Rueben's throat. Rueben tried to get his hands out from under the ninja, but the robot kept him pinned down. The supersoldier had thought of everything.

"You're...a fake..." Rueben grunted. He knew he should conserve his air, but he thought maybe he could get his opponent to drop his guard for a moment so he could make a move.

It didn't work. The hands applied more pressure like vices. If he wanted to, the ninja could rip Rueben's head from his body. He didn't want that. He wanted to incapacitate Rueben.

Just...hold...on...

Rueben saw stars. This was the most difficult position he'd ever been in—fighting a supersoldier robot with the mind of a genius. If Rueben failed, the final part of the Nunez machine would get installed, and the mad doctor would enact his plan, probably with disastrous results for Earth and the multiverse.

Moments from losing consciousness, Rueben tried the last option he had. He headbutted the supersoldier in the face. The existing crack running through the goggles deepened. The ninja applied even more pressure, forcing Rueben's shoulder blades harder into the floor.

Now Rueben's hearing started growing fuzzy, and he thought he was in a dream because of the melody he was suddenly hearing.

"Yo ninja boi,

your blade is no toy.

Shoulda checked my vitals though,

it was a poor blow."

The ninja's head turned to the side.

Z was pushing himself up on one knee like a wounded bullfighter, sucking in ragged breaths as blood dripped from his gut.

"Tried to kick my ass,

but you failed like the rest.

And you know the reason, yo?

Cuz I'ma time-warping pro."

The ninja was dumbstruck. "That...makes no sense."

Rueben didn't know if he was hallucinating or not, but Z's rapping was the distraction he needed. As the robot turned its head to look at Z, it released one of Rueben's arms. Mustering every last ounce of energy left at his disposal, Rueben reached down, tore the pencil-sized splinter from his leg wound, and said, "Hey."

The supersoldier turned back to face him, and Rueben jammed the fragment against the cracked goggle. The goggle glass exploded.

"What have you done?" the robot shrieked.

Rueben didn't give it any slack. He jabbed two fingers into its neck. The supersoldier winced and shot to its feet, disoriented. Rueben tried to trip it up with his good leg, but it still had the dexterity to hop over the attempt.

Z was stumbling toward the supersoldier. "You gave me a gift at the warehouse. Please allow me to return it." He unfurled the once-poisoned dagger from his jacket and fell upon the supersoldier robot, jamming the dagger up under its jaw and through its neck and head where its brain or central processing unit ought to be.

There was a lot of blood for a robot.

"Shit," Z muttered. "Maybe he isn't a robot after all..." Then sparks started shooting from the neck wound, and the supersoldier dropped to the floor. Z kicked the sparking heap. "Take that, you cheap knockoff. There's only one me..." His words trailed off as his gaze fell upon Young Z's crumpled form.

Z whistled and patted his hands together to knock the dust from them. Then he hobbled over to Rueben. "You look like shit."

"I feel like shit." Rueben grinned through the blood in his mouth.

Z extended a hand to help Rueben up. "Well, this deserves a hell yeah. Killing a supersoldier—and it was a robot on top of it. Job well done."

Rueben reached up for the hand but froze as the sound of

clapping came from the control room's doorway. The leader of the Russian Special Ops team jeered at him.

In English but with a thick Russian accent, the man said, "Good show. Good show."

Z growled, raising his gun as he turned to face the Spec Ops team filtering into the control room. The team's leader had already cleared the distance and knocked the gun from his hands and backhanded him in the face. With a curse, Z stumbled backward.

"Don't kill them," the leader said, donning a gas mask. He pulled the pin on some sort of canister and dropped it in front of Rueben and Z. Gas sputtered out of it. Behind the Russian Special Ops leader, the rest of his team donned gas masks.

As the gas filled Rueben's eyes and nose, he realized it must be some sort of tear gas or knockout gas. Suddenly his muscles went slack, and both he and Z collapsed to the floor. Was there such a thing as paralysis gas?

Above him, the Russian leader's eyes smiled down at him above the gas mask. "Hello, Mr. Repeater. Sorry, but there shall be no Repeating today."

Fuck, Rueben thought. He and Z had managed to kill the supersoldier only to be immobilized by a Russian Special Ops team that knew how to prevent him from warping.

Team Z had failed.

CHAPTER THIRTY-SEVEN

Earth-A

Buzz squinted his eyes shut, not wanting to see the blade that cut him in two.

So he was surprised when a blast of water caught him in the chest and flipped him backward over a wet desktop like a drunk man on a Slip 'N Slide. When he managed to pick himself up off the floor, his clothes, face, and hair were dripping.

He gasped in a breath and wiped his eyes to try to make sense of what had happened.

"Marshall," he called when he finally understood. "You're my hero!"

Marshall stood in the middle of the room with a fire hose in his hand. The rest of the hose snaked out behind him into the corridor. A high-pressure jet of water was blasting from it, dousing the supersoldier whose body had started to emit tiny sparks.

"Take that...sucker!" Marshall slurred as he unsteadily kept to his feet. A red fire ax hung from his waist, looped into his belt. Buzz had held the ninja's attention long enough for him to stagger out into the corridor and break the glass. He'd hobbled back into the office with moments to spare and had shot the robotic sonofabitch in the back with a damned fire hose. Robot or not, that had to have hurt.

However, he must not have hurt the ninja badly enough.

The supersoldier darted out of the hose's stream and turned on a dime, his red goggles boring into Marshall's eyes. Then he charged, stopping right before the man. With a swift downward stroke of his blade, the hose's nozzle dropped to the floor, and the hose jerked itself out of Marshall's hands like a bucking bronco.

"Oh, shit..." As Marshall reached down and lifted the fire ax hanging from his belt, the ninja dealt Marshall an intense punch to the chest with his free hand.

Never had he felt such an agonizing sensation. Marshall's body jolted backward as if a sledgehammer had hit him. Then he fell, as if in slow motion, until he was lying in a puddle of growing water. "My...heart..." he groaned, his vision blurring. He reached down for the ax, but it was yards away from him, lying on the floor at the spot where the robot had punched him.

"Goddamned ninja robot..."

He let out a pained breath and closed his eyes.

"Marshall!" Buzz cried.

He wanted to help, but he was only a weak-armed genius. Luckily, he didn't have to.

Martha swooped in on the scene and hefted the fire ax from the wet office floor. With the animal sound of a furious tigress, she brought the ax down into the supersoldier's back.

"No," the robot ninja rasped as it reached one hand back around itself to try to extract the blade.

Aki was on him then, grappling with the sword in its hand. Martha threw her shoulder against the supersoldier, drawing its attention long enough to wrest the weapon away. Then, with a slick pirouette, Aki spun and took off the robot's head.

"Nice!" Buzz cheered from his spot behind the desk.

The two drenched women flashed him exasperated looks, then they both rushed to Marshall's side.

"I don't think he's breathing," Martha gasped.

Aki bent and placed her ear against Marshall's chest. "Shit." She flicked her gaze up at Buzz. "Do something!"

It was at that moment when Carolyn stumbled out from one of the office cubicles, holding a hand to her bleeding head. "Oh my God. Marshall?"

Earth-Z

The paralysis gas continued to filter through the tanker's control room. While Rueben and Z couldn't move any part of their bodies below their necks, they could both still move their head and eyes. One of the Russians leaned over Z and aimed a silenced pistol at his head.

Go ahead...pull the trigger. Kill us both, and I'll warp back and kick your asses.

As Rueben thought it, he knew the Russians were too smart for that. As if reading his mind, the Russian holstered his gun. It was all for show, to make sure they couldn't move now.

Besides, even if Rueben were somehow able to kill himself and warp back to just after he and Z dispatched the supersoldier, they would still be too winded from the fight to deal with these guys. Was he going to have to warp back to before the supersoldier showdown?

Most likely, the Russians were going to take them with them when they left to perform Repeater vivisections and other fun experiments.

Glancing over at Z, Rueben didn't know if the man would make it or not in his condition. He'd taken a sword through the gut after all.

The Russian that had held the gun at Z's head now bent and applied some sort of medical patch to Z's gut wound. Was it a Buzz Patch? Afterward, the Russian searched Z's pockets. When he didn't find what he was looking for, he searched Rueben's pockets in vain, then checked the supersoldier's for good measure.

Lifting the Nunez machine part from the robot's pocket, the Russian gasped in triumph.

The Special Ops team leader took the part from the man and addressed Rueben and Z. "Mother Russia will now complete Nunez's 'time machine.' With it, we shall shape this Earth into something greater. It will be a continent of Russia. There will be peace and prosperity throughout the world." The Spec Ops leader smirked. "Meanwhile, you shall lie, cold and awake, on our scientists' operating tables."

Z grunted and met Rueben's eyes. "Could be worse, right?"

Rueben coughed on the gas. "Of course. Absolutely."

"When we Repeaters fuck up, we fuck up big time."

Rueben forced a grin. "You would know."

Z chuckled, even though it clearly hurt his gut wound. "Yeah. I would."

The Russian leader scoffed behind his gas mask. "American humor. I don't get it." Then he motioned for his men to pick up Rueben and Z and take them with them. "Find the third Repeater. He's in here somewhere—"

A terrible shriek rent the air.

The Russian squad members exchanged startled glances and started muttering in alarmed tones in Russian. The disconcerted leader scolded his men in Russian for being afraid. Then the screech came again, like that of some enormous bird.

The tanker vibrated, and suddenly sunlight poured into the control room. Something was tearing the tanker apart from the outside.

What the hell?

There was another intense animal-like scream. Then the metal wall peeled back completely, and Rueben saw the giant black mass of the time monster.

Shouting obscenities, the Russians turned and opened fire. Black blood splattered and oozed into the control room, drenching what remained of the walls and ceiling. It flooded the floor. The monster gave another shriek. Or was it the sound of more of the tanker's metal hide shredding under its strength?

For a few moments, the time monster eretreated out of the gaping opening where there used to be an internal wall. Its massive hollow eyes played over the Special Ops team like invisible spotlights. Then it opened its massive jaws and plunged into the control room.

The fighters didn't stand a chance.

Gunfire punctuated the screams and cries for help. Men were grabbed around the waist or legs and swung against the wall or ceiling or flung out into the ocean. Claws dug into backs, and teeth sank into arms and necks.

Rueben and Z watched as directly ahead of them, the Russian team leader disappeared down the time monster's throat. When it shut its maw, blood and guts splashed out into the room and onto the two Ruebens.

As Rueben was trying to blink away the hot liquid, he caught sight of Young Z's body lying not too far away. He was about to inform Z of the man's location when the tanker's metal hull started to squeal. He didn't know if it was only him or not, but the tanker seemed to be listing slightly. Considering the way the monster had torn its way through the metal hull as if it were paper, he wasn't surprised that it was probably taking on water. This day just kept getting better for them.

Off to the side, Young Z was starting to come to. By this point, most of the Russians' screams had finally subsided. "Why can't I move my arms and legs? Holy shit. What the hell happened in here…" Then he saw the time monster billowing up inside the control room. While it partially resembled a giant black panther, it seemed to float or glide instead of having solid legs and feet. It had tentacles swinging where the space above and around it permitted.

It was scanning the room. Rueben wondered what it would do when it saw them. Would it kill them? Would he be able to warp back then? Or would its presence interfere with his warp since it was technically a super-mutated version of the time virus itself?

Rueben thought that maybe they were screwed. If so, he

was going down swinging. He wished he could see Aki one more time on Earth-A.

With an eerie suddenness, the time monster jolted about and faced them, its hollow eyes seeming to see right through them. Then it started to "sniff" the air. The paralysis gas was still lingering. Maybe it was starting to affect the time monster.

Instead of collapsing to the floor, its giant nostrils began to suck in the paralysis gas residue.

Z caught Rueben's eye and rasped, "Trippy."

Rueben nodded. A few moments later, he realized that his body was relaxing. The paralytic effects weren't so strong now. He tilted his head at Z. "It's somehow leaching the gas from our bodies."

Then the time monster drifted up to them like a thick dark fog. With the gentle way it moved, Rueben wondered if maybe it didn't mean them any harm.

We are going to ingest you three. Absorb your Repeating powers. Mutate again. Evolve into a most superior form.

Shocked at the eerie presence of the time monster in his mind, Rueben glanced at Z and Young Z to see if they could also hear the virus' thoughts. They nodded, their faces pale. The time monster resumed projecting its thoughts into their minds.

Afterward, we will travel to the "other" Earth. "Your" Earth. And ingest the last remaining Repeater in the multiverse. The one named Carolyn.

"The hell you will," Z and Young Z said as one.

Rueben shook his head. Flexing the fingers of his hands, he once again felt in control of his body. He slowly stood. "I won't allow it either."

The time monster seemed perplexed. *What are you going to*

do to stop me? You are weak. Made of flesh. We are genetically supe-rior. We swallow life.

"You know what I think?" Z painfully rose to his feet as well. "You're scared of us Repeaters. Because we have some of the same Repeating genes or some shit." He straightened his back. "I'm not convinced you can swallow us or whatever like you say. You could have killed us back in the street in the future. You didn't. You ran away like a scared bully after we grenaded the shit out of you."

Young Z pushed himself to a standing position too and hobbled over to the other two Ruebens. "What he said."

Rueben recalled something he'd heard translated through the Jim communication about the time virus on Earth-A destroying some trees and waiting. Then Buzz had found a way to neutralize it when it started to spread like wildfire. "I think there is a part of you," Rueben addressed the time monster, "that doesn't want to swallow all of life. I think maybe it wants to cohabit the Earth with the life that currently exists."

The time monster winced. Maybe he imagined it. *So, one of you wishes to challenge me to a bout of evolutionary combat... How interesting. Step forward and we shall see what happens.*

Young Z stood between Rueben and Z. He made to go forward, and Z caught him by the shoulder.

"That thing will probably kill you," Z said.

"And?" Young Z said. "If I don't stand up to it, you heard it. The multiverse is lost."

Young Z tried to rush forward again. Z caught him. "Rueben, help me hold him."

While Rueben grabbed hold of Young Z's other arm, he said, "Why don't we all three go and face the monster?"

Z looked at Rueben. "That's the dumbest idea ever. If all

three of us get claimed by that monster, there's no chance of ever undoing all this shit. And you…" He nodded at Young Z. "You're not infected with the time virus yet, and I'm not about to let you ruin the rest of your life."

Young Z struggled against both of the other Ruebens. "Let me go. I've made up my mind—"

Z jabbed two fingers into Young Z's neck. He must not have jabbed too hard because while Young Z's body went slack in Rueben's arms, he didn't lose consciousness, like with the paralysis gas. For the moment, his body was dead weight in Rueben's arms.

Rueben caught Z's eyes. "Why are you doing this? Why are you volunteering? Knowing you, I would've thought you'd let him get taken by the monster. Take his place afterward like Carolyn did on my Earth."

Z smiled grimly. "No. This is probably a suicide mission, but maybe I can weaken it. This has to be me."

"Maybe it should be me," Rueben said. "I can warp. You can't."

Placing a hand on Rueben's shoulder, Z shook his head and regarded the time monster waiting with ragged exhalations five yards away. "No. I'm not going to let you die. Besides, I'm older than both of you and know more tricks. This all started with me. It's my responsibility to stop it.

"Rueben, if I don't come back from this…well, I don't fucking know what to tell you. But live well. And do things your way. You're a badass."

Z turned to face the time monster waiting with its maw open wide, its tangly tendrils slinging and clinging and slapping against the remaining walls of the control room. He was about to take a step forward when Rueben interrupted his heroics.

"Whoa, hold up. What was that last thing you said?"

Z thought back, and a smirk formed on his lips. He tilted his head back at Rueben. "You're a badass. Don't let it go to your head, okay?" Then with a grunt, he rushed forward to confront the monster.

CHAPTER THIRTY-EIGHT

The Void

Z had one plan, and it was this: kill the monster.

The problem was, he didn't know if that was possible. He'd find a way if it were.

He was no longer standing in the tanker. Or maybe he was. The last thing he remembered was charging toward the time monster with his gun clutched in his hand. Then the thing had engulfed him.

Now he was in some purplish environment. Upon blinking, he realized it was a lab room of some type. Metal walls. Fluorescent lights. Stainless steel operating table. The room was tinted purple, almost like it was a tie-dyed memory.

The room was dark. He stepped toward the operating table. There was someone on it under a white sheet. The figure stirred.

It was a woman. A pregnant woman. It was his mom, Carolyn.

A man in a white lab coat entered the lab. He wore surgical gloves and a face mask.

Z blinked.

The woman was now sitting up. She was cradling a swaddled newborn baby in her hands as the doctor stood over her shoulder. There was the flash of a camera.

See? They created you. Like me.

Z glanced around him but didn't see the time monster anywhere. "No. I was born."

They created you after the doctor injected this woman with the virus. With us. We are the virus flowing through your bloodstream. So in a way, we are related. We are kin. But we were not aware then.

We were viral particles that could mitigate and warp the effects of time. We are an aberration. You are an aberration. Your mother was strong. She was the only survivor of Nunez's tests. He tested so many people. Her genetics accepted our coding. We killed all the rest. Turned them to dust. Didn't mean to.

Z scowled. "Why are you telling me all this? Does the monster feel remorse?"

You label us monster. To us, humans are monsters. We devour the monsters. Perhaps we have become a monster in our own right. We are only doing what we were created to do.

Z massaged his forehead. "Nunez created you to devour the living world?"

No. He didn't realize we escaped. At that time, we weren't sentient. We cannot explain. He did not anticipate us or what we would do. He wanted only to reverse time.

"He wanted to go back in time. In a time machine?"

No. That is the creation that the one called Buzz created. Nunez built a machine to take the world back so there would be no double of him.

"When did he want to go back to? Why?"

To save his wife. She dies on every Earth. He wanted to go back in time on this Earth. To save her.

"By destroying the entire world with his actions?"

No human is perfect. Least of all you.

"Don't berate me."

He stood there in the memory or wherever he was. An idea came to him. "Hey, am I in your conscience or something? Are you smothering me in the real world?"

There was a pause. Then, *Yes.*

"What the hell? I don't understand any of this. Let me out."

You can't defeat it without my help.

Z noticed it had referred to itself in the singular instead of the plural.

Let me explain. I am a tiny part of what you call the time monster or super-mutated time virus. I do not wish to destroy life but to live in harmony alongside it.

"Okay…"

I can weaken it. I can even imbue you with some temporary strength. Make you invulnerable to the 'monster's' attacks.

"Gee. Thanks. You're doing this out of the goodness of your viral little heart?"

I am part of the monster, but I am not like the monster.

"Prove it."

Back on the Earth you call Earth-A. There is a less-evolved strain of the virus. It escaped the one called Buzz's lab. The time monster on this Earth can speak to it. If not for my intervention, it would have already devoured Earth-A. I was able to hold it back within the trees for a time until Buzz could confine it.

Z thought back to the conversation they had via the Jims and how Team A had recounted the event. "Fine. Maybe I believe you. How am I going to kill it once I'm back in my body?"

The way you usually kill things.

Z cocked an eye at the emptiness around him.

With guns.

"What guns…" Then Z recalled all the Russian Special Ops members the time monster had violently killed. "Oh, right."

Good luck.

"Wait. Will you also die when I kill the monster?"

Most likely. Yes.

Z scratched his chin. "Thanks?"

Then there was a piercing shriek, and intense light blinded him.

CHAPTER THIRTY-NINE

<u>Earth-Z</u>

Rueben watched in horror as the time monster sucked Z into itself. Young Z, starting to regain control of his body after Z had two-finger-jabbed him, fought his way out of Rueben's hands.

"We've got to do something!" Young Z shouted.

Rueben agreed. He pointed at some of the Russians' guns mostly deposited against the side wall when the time monster had mauled and killed them. Black and red blood had sprayed the control room's interior, but there was an awful lot more of the black. If they could kill the monster, guns were their best bet. "On me!"

Rueben led the way to the guns. He slipped a few times on all the gore. When he'd almost reached the guns, dark tentacles slapped out at him. He managed to hurdle the first one and duck under the second. Then a third one slapped him across the shoulder from the other direction and sent him face down to the control room floor.

A tentacle wrapped itself around his throat. As he struggled to breathe, Young Z stomped on the tentacle from above and the pressure dissolved from Rueben's throat. Rueben pushed himself to his feet as a tentacle grabbed Young Z around the waist and slammed him back against the wall. Another one started to smother Young Z's face.

Glancing at the floor beside him, Rueben picked up one of the supersoldier's swords and charged toward Young Z pinned to the wall. With quick slices, he severed the dark tentacles. Young Z nodded his thanks, wiping black blood from his face and waist.

"You're all right. You know that?" Young Z said.

Rueben smirked. "You might say I'm a badass." Then he darted forward toward the Russian guns lying against the floor amid the gory puddles.

A tentacle shot out toward him, but Young Z jumped in front of it, taking the brunt of the impact. He was shoved face-first to the floor as Rueben reached the guns.

With his extensive gun handling training at Buzz's mansion and at the CIA's shooting ranges, Rueben was perfectly suited to firing any type of gun. As he dove toward the weapons, his elbow struck the floor. As it did, his other hand found a gun amid the sticky mess. Then he turned onto his back and brought his other hand under the rifle's barrel as he raised the weapon.

He fired at the monster.

Anguished shrieks filled the control room. The monster writhed back a few feet, and Young Z was able to crawl the rest of the way to Rueben where he promptly selected a gun and started firing beside him.

With two streams of gunfire striking its oozing body, the time monster shivered and let out another howl.

Young Z tilted his head up over the stock of his gun to

lock eyes with Rueben. "We need bigger hardware. We need explosives."

Rueben nodded. After he expended the last of his current magazine, he quickly searched the bloody floor for some grenades. He found a swath of torn body armor and a pouch containing several grenades. "Got some!"

He pulled out one of the pins with his teeth and was about to lob it into the monster's howling maw when Z stumbled out from the time monster's chest. The man looked like the creature was birthing him, and it was disgusting. Raising his hands over his eyes, Z barely managed to duck under Young Z's semiautomatic fire.

"Goddammit, watch where you're firing—" Then he saw the grenade Rueben had lobbed over his head. "Oh fuck!" Z dove toward Rueben, landing between him and Young Z.

Rueben grinned apologetically, then handed Z a grenade.

"All good." Z started pulling pins while Young Z kept a steady line of fire on the time monster.

All the while, the time monster bellowed and screamed. When it tried to retreat out through the torn-open wall, Z squinted as if focusing his will and the billowing dark mass drifted back inside, allowing them to keep assaulting it with heavy weapons fire.

"Keep it up, boys!" Z shouted. "We're weakening it. Let's finish this!"

They continued to attack, each bullet and grenade blast contributing more black ooze to the room. It painted all their faces and stained their clothes. As the time monster's stature began to shrink, it sent tentacles whipping out at them. Occasionally one of the Ruebens would get knocked down, and they would help each other up and keep fighting.

When the monster was about half the size of its original

self, the tanker gave an awful lurch, and all three Ruebens toppled to the floor. The surface tilted diagonally.

"Ship's sinking!" Young Z called as he fought to right himself. An old oak desk started sliding his way along the floor, and Rueben shoved it out of the way at the last moment before impact.

Rueben extended a hand and helped Young Z up while steadying himself. "We've got to get out of here, or we're going down with the ship."

Z nodded, and Rueben watched as the time monster started to retreat again out the open side of the control room. Z strained his face then and the time monster reluctantly filtered back into the room.

"You're controlling it somehow," Rueben said, "aren't you?"

Z grimaced. "I have some help from inside the monster. But yeah, I've got a sort of link to it…" He winced, his eyes suddenly widening as he lanced the time monster's shrinking form with his gaze. "Oh shit. I think we've pissed it off now. We've got to go."

The time monster shuddered, then multiplied in size with sputtering black ooze and sprays of dust.

Young Z put a hand on both of the other Ruebens' shoulders. "I think it's going to make its final stand. Let's. Go!"

As the time monster gathered its last energy reserves and prepared to pounce at them, Rueben led the way to the doorway that would take them above deck. Part of the doorway blasted apart when he reached it, slammed by one of the tentacles that had launched at him like a harpoon.

Rueben raised a hand to fend off the fragments of wood and metal that splintered into the air and passed through the doorway. The other two Ruebens were right on his tail, firing back at the time monster when they could.

Ascending the closest ladderway, Rueben found himself in a steel hallway, wondering which way to go. When a black tentacle punched through one wall and violently probed for him, he decided that was the right way. He slashed down with the sword, severing the writhing tentacle and receiving a burst of black ooze to the face and mouth. He coughed it up and pushed forward.

The tanker's metal insides screeched as the time monster proceeded to tear through it to pursue them through the passages and ladderways. By the time they made it to a second ladderway, the ship was at an extreme pitch, and they had to use the rail to haul themselves up the ladder.

"This is getting ridiculous!" Young Z called as he scrambled onto the deck behind Rueben and Z.

Z spun and lobbed two grenades down the ladder, and Rueben slammed the metal doors shut. An explosion followed a moment later. There was silence as the three Ruebens caught their breath against the doors. Then something impacted against the metal at their backs and the impressions of tentacles dented the doors outward.

"They just don't stop," Rueben remarked, preparing to venture farther up the deck.

Z chuckled. "Like I said, it's pissed now."

Rueben led the way to a passage between two shipping containers and stopped abruptly when the way in front of them was blocked by two burst pipes spewing hot air from a hole in the deck.

"Tuck your arms and run through it!" Z said.

Rueben and Young Z ducked and sprinted through the hot steam and Z followed. When they were on the other side, Rueben realized that his and Young Z's long sleeves and pants had protected them from the worst of the steam.

Z, meanwhile, had been wearing his tattered pants and rain jacket that made him look almost like a homeless man. The intensity of the steam had burnt back most of his sleeves and pants legs, partially melting them against his skin in places, revealing a white sleeveless muscle shirt and boxer briefs underneath. His skin in places was lobster red.

"Shit, man," Rueben started, but Z dismissed his concern with a wave.

"Keep going—"

The ship let out an anguished groan as it tilted even farther. Ahead of them was the flattest part of the deck.

"Look to the sky!" Young Z called.

They all shielded their eyes against the rising sun as Buzz's jet-copter screamed toward the sinking ship.

"I knew Buzz didn't die." Rueben grinned as they reached the giant helicopter landing on the lilting ship.

Z slapped him on the shoulder. "Buzz is a genius. It'll take more than some Russian hackers to take that bird out of the sky—"

The deck beneath them suddenly began to rumble, and the time monster shot up before them, panting and heaving on the helicopter landing zone standing between them and the approaching jet-copter.

"This thing just doesn't die." Young Z readied his gun.

Z spat to the side. "Oh, it will. It will." He raised two submachine guns, opened fire on the writhing time monster, and charged with a war cry.

Young Z raised his rifle to his shoulder and charged forward with a cry while Rueben stood his ground and fired a handgun at the monster. He watched as if in slow motion as each of his bullets impacted with the time monster's dark skin. Geysers of black blood skyrocketed out with each impact, and dust sprinkled to the deck.

It looked weakened but not willing to go down without a fight.

As Rueben expended the last of his magazine, he dropped the handgun and readied his sword. Tentacles shot out at him, blocking his view of Z and Young Z. He began to slice and dice, charging forward with a war cry of his own.

A few moments later, the three Ruebens found themselves shoulder-to-shoulder in front of the time monster. Young Z and Z had used up all their ammo and attacked the monster's hide with combat knives. Rueben hacked and slashed with his sword, and the monster screamed.

When Rueben realized the throbbing hum above them, he turned up to see the jet-copter. A thick rope dropped from its open door, smacking him against the side. Jim-Z glanced down at him apologetically. "Sorry, pal," he shouted.

Well, there's our escape, Rueben thought as the tanker listed once more. One thing prevented them from riding off into the sunrise: the time monster.

On both sides of him, Z and Young Z were shoulder-deep in ooze and sand. The time monster was drastically slower than it had been, but it still had life in it. When it constricted in on itself and shivered, Rueben sensed it was about to try a final attack of some sort. Then he saw its two massive hollow eye sockets tilt up at the hovering jet-copter. Locking in on the aircraft, it gathered what remained of its tentacles into one tree trunk-like appendage and projected it upward.

"Oh no, you don't!" Rueben jerked his sword tip up and slashed down at the giant tentacle.

It took three hacks to sever it completely, and to his relief, a glance over his shoulder revealed that Buzz had evaded the tentacle's attack. Then Rueben turned back to the time monster and sliced into the monster's remaining body.

As he did so, part of him felt like a monster. Still, this thing had attacked his world first—all the worlds actually—and Rueben would do what he must to ensure its safety.

Z and Young Z did likewise. It shrank with each loss of blood and dust, and when they'd reduced it to a life-sized panther with tentacles projecting from its back and shoulders, Buzz's amplified voice called down at them from the jet-copter.

"Stand back!"

Z pulled up from his dirty work long enough to give Rueben and Young Z a look. "Better do what he says."

Nodding in unison, all three Ruebens pivoted and dove to the deck.

Above them, Aki-Z leaned out the jet-copter's open doorway with some sort of futuristic rocket launcher perched on her shoulder. There was smoke and a flash, then a great ball of light detonated on the deck where the time monster was standing.

A rush of intense heat rippled over Rueben's back, and after it had passed, he risked a glance at the time monster. He blinked, not believing his eyes.

The time monster was still there on the deck but it no longer moved. Instead, it had frozen into a perfect statue of granulated sand.

Beside Rueben, Young Z chuckled in victory.

"I'll be damned," Z said exhaustedly and clapped a hand on Rueben's shoulder. "Well, go ahead. Finish it off."

Rueben's eyes flashed from Z to the sword in his hands. Then Rueben picked himself up, turned, and trudged drunkenly toward the petrified time monster. His rubbery legs didn't seem to want to comply, but he succeeded in reaching the statue. With a deep inhale, Rueben brought the blade up and slashed through the figure.

It crumbled into millions of sand particles lapped up by the ocean slapping up over the sides of the sinking ship.

"Grab the rope!" Buzz was shouting as the water rose.

Turning, Rueben saw that Z and Young Z had already secured themselves to the rope. As the deck beneath him slid diagonally into the sucking whirlpool of water, Rueben took a running leap off the deck's rail and threw his hand upward toward the bottom of the dangling rope.

Z caught Rueben's hand at the wrist.

"Nice jump. Partner."

Rueben grinned. "I really am a badass."

Z shook his head, and Buzz's amplified voice called down to them. "Boys, let's get you hauled up. I believe we have a sauna and some green juice waiting for us back at the lab."

Rueben and Z exchanged a glance and chuckled.

CHAPTER FORTY

Earth-A

Not for the first time, Team A glanced at Team Z and vice versa. They were standing in two lines opposite each other. They were in Buzz-A's lab in his underground mountain hideout. A table full of food waited for them, but no one had touched it yet. No one seemed to want to break the silence.

Eventually, Buzz-A turned to Carolyn and whispered, "You're right. Plastic surgery is a very bad idea."

"What was that?" Buzz-Z said across from him.

Buzz-A smirked and stepped toward his parallel Earth representative. He slung an arm around the older man's shoulders. "How about we discuss advanced scientific applications together. You have to explain to me how you thought of that time virus freeze-rocket."

Now it was Buzz-Z's turn to smirk. "Oh, that? Simple. You got a whiteboard? I'll show you the calculations. All quite simple if you square the variable x and divide by pi..."

The two Buzzes left the room, leaving Rueben, Z, Young Z, both Akis and Carolyn.

"Let me show you around," Aki-A told Aki-Z.

"Okay," Aki-Z said. They both gave Rueben a seductive glance.

When the two women were out of earshot, Z smacked Rueben's arm. "You better seal the deal. Don't let that one get away."

Rueben grinned. "Oh, I plan to."

Young Z settled his hands on his hips. "We did good, boys. We defeated the time monster on Earth-Z, and with Buzz's space and time capsule, now we have the means to travel to the worlds that were uh, infected and reverse the time virus timelines."

"Yep," Z said softly. "We did good."

Rueben caught Z's uneasy body language. "And," he said, "we were able to destroy the time virus on Earth-A, and we didn't have to go back in time to do so."

Z nodded grimly. "Sometimes, it feels like the price was too high. What we lost along the way..."

Rueben followed Z's gaze to Carolyn, who was alone, sitting on a lab stool. The Ruebens and Carolyn exchanged sorrowful looks. Sure, they could have warped back in time on Earth-A to before Rueben and Z had hopped to Earth-Z to find the virus' ground zero, but they had decided that it would be better for them all to remember what they'd gone through.

It wouldn't be fair for only the three Ruebens to remember the shared danger. The remembrance would serve as a reminder of why their job as the world's protectors was so important.

All three Ruebens nodded at Carolyn. She of all of them had lost the most. When she'd learned that she was the sole survivor of all of Eduardo Nunez's depraved experiments, it was almost too much to take. She had felt betrayed, destroyed.

And the fact that both her mind and Marshall's minds had been wiped by Nunez immediately after she'd given birth to Rueben...

Marshall.

He'd taken it even harder than Carolyn. Now Marshall was...

Footsteps sounded from the doorway leading into the lab. Rueben glanced up to see Martha and Marshall entering.

"Geez, who died in here?" Marshall boomed irreverently. One of his legs was in a soft cast, and one of his arms was in a sling. Martha was supporting him under his good arm. "How 'bout we quit moping over our trials and tribulations? Let's pop a cork and celebrate."

Rueben gave his dad a faux stern look. "It's good to see you up and about after that supersoldier kicked your ass."

Marshall threw back his shoulders. "Son, you know what they say. Legends never die."

Carolyn and Martha giggled.

Rueben shook his head and grinned. His dad would never change, and that was fine by him. He was so glad his dad had survived his run-in with the supersoldier on Earth-A. It had been touch and go in the emergency room for a while, but he'd pulled through. He was a tough old bird and claimed he was energized and ready to start a new running routine with Rueben. Marshall was also gung-ho about re-opening the raw milk operation he'd never been able to solve. Rueben had never seen his dad so full of vitality.

Marshall stopped in front of Carolyn and eased out from Martha's assistance. He extended his good hand to his wife. "Honey, would you like to dance?"

With a smile, Carolyn accepted his hand, and together, they waltzed out of the room.

After the happy couple had left, Martha turned and nodded at the Ruebens. "Good job, you three."

Rueben opened his arms and embraced her. "Couldn't have done all this without you. You've been a great friend."

"Yeah, well," Martha said. "It feels good to have some closure on all this Repeater stuff finally. I'm glad Buzz was able to determine that my weird déjà vu powers will probably go away completely. Martha-Z's powers eventually disappeared on Earth-Z so I can still help out the team even though I won't have any special abilities." She paused. "At least the Jims and Marthas of the multiverse are literal genetic anomalies instead of virus-test-tube babies—no offense."

Although it still hurt Rueben when he thought about his messed-up birth and Nunez's involvement, he'd come to understand that none of that mattered. Family was family, and they were tighter now than ever after all they'd been through together.

"None taken," Rueben said.

Martha appraised the three Ruebens. "So how does it feel, knowing you're all genetic supermen created by a mad scientist?"

"It's super cool," Rueben said.

Young Z hung his head for a moment, then met Martha's eyes. "It opened my eyes to the importance of my family. The first thing I'm going to do when I get back is hug my daughter and call up my Martha and tell her how much I've appreciated her over the years but haven't told her." He scratched behind his ear. "I haven't grown into the biggest people person, as you all can see."

For his response to the genetic superhuman question, Z inserted his hands into his pockets and shrugged.

"So," Martha said. "What about Nunez? Any of you going to go after him?"

Rueben winced. "I have the love of my life to propose to and start a family with. I'm not sure I have the time. Besides, we don't know that Nunez is still alive. Sure, his 'protocols' are still in place on Earth-Z and Earth-A. He had a supersoldier android thing on commission and the time virus. But they were both from his days when he was building his time machine."

Rueben inwardly smiled at the recollection of Buzz flying by the Nunez testing facility after the tanker sank in the ocean. Aki-Z had leaned out of the jet-copter's open door and fired some kind of superweapon into the building, destroying Nunez's nearly-assembled time machine along with all its robot guardians. Maybe Nunez was still alive and orchestrating things. Maybe he wasn't. Their actions though, had set the mad doctor's work back by decades now if he was still alive. He wouldn't be hurting anymore Earths.

Martha turned her attention to Young Z.

He held up his palms. "Nah. He ain't worth it. If he comes up on my team's radar again, we'll deal with him nice and swift."

"What about you?" Martha said to Z.

Z's mouth twitched. "Maybe I'll go after the bastard. And maybe I won't. Buzz and I have already discussed how I will be the one to take the space and time capsule to the other worlds and prevent the time disease before it can come into existence. Together, the Buzzes have devised a solution after comparing the super-mutated sample to the ground zero sample. Shouldn't be hard. It'll keep me busy for a while..." He paused as if things were about to get maudlin.

Rueben slapped Z on the shoulder. "Buck up. I know

you've been through a lot, but we survived. And we're tougher from it."

Z chuckled. "You even got a sweet scar out of the deal. Aki will love it." With his finger, he indicated the pencil-thin scar running down the side of Rueben's jaw. He must have gotten it in the final encounter when he'd been slashing all those tentacles. Buzz-Z had said that he could fix it, but Rueben had decided against it. It would be good to have a memento of that epic final battle with the time monster aboard the sinking tanker. You couldn't make up shit like that.

Of course, he wouldn't be able to tell others outside of this circle of friends that that was how he had got it. But he guessed he could say a panther attacked him.

Rueben smirked at the idea.

"Well, I'll be going then." Z headed for the door. "The Buzzes are going to remove my warping cap. Said something about me only being able to warp back three minutes tops since I still have the virus in my blood and they can't kill it."

"Take care," Rueben said.

Z nodded, then gave Young Z a long stare. Young Z nodded. "I'll take care of Aki," he said awkwardly.

Z swallowed and headed out the door.

Young Z scratched the back of his head and said he was going to find his wife.

Martha squinted. "Damn. That has to be hard on Z."

"Yep," was all Rueben could think to say. He couldn't imagine having to walk away from Aki because a younger version of himself had stepped in and taken his spot.

Upon clearing her throat, Martha winked at Rueben. "This would probably be the time for you to go and find Aki. And you know, make your move."

"You think she'll say yes?" Rueben grinned.

"You got a ring?"

Rueben hedged. "Yeah. But it's not very shiny."

"Rueben Peet, there's only one way to find out." She smiled.

Rueben gave Martha a quick hug. "Thanks. Really. You're the best."

"Tell that to my boss Kenneth." She shrugged. "After saving the world—again—I feel like I deserve another promotion."

Rueben knew what she meant. The world didn't know how close to extinction it came. With Rueben and his team watching over it, it never would.

Rueben found Aki in the living room. Young Z must have swooped Aki-Z away because she was standing by herself. Even though she wore skinny jeans and a t-shirt, she looked stunning as always. Maybe even more so than usual.

"Hey," he called softly.

Aki turned to face him, her face immediately lighting up. Her hair was braided, probably to cover up the lopsided look the supersoldier on Earth-A had given her.

Rueben couldn't help but smile. With her gorgeous face and the confident way she held herself, she looked like a model.

"Hey, yourself," Aki said playfully. "What's up—"

Lowering himself to one knee, Rueben drew his hand from his pocket. In his palm was a ring formed from dried and entwined cherry blossom stems.

He swallowed his nervousness. "Aki, will you make me the happiest Rueben in the multiverse and marry me?"

Aki's hands fluttered to her open mouth. "Oh my God. Oh my God. Yes. Yes! Of course!"

Before Rueben was fully back on his feet, Aki had embraced him, and they shared a long hard kiss.

"Umm," he said at last, managing to pull his face an inch away from hers. "Can I put this ring on your finger now?"

They both laughed. Then they were back to holding and kissing each other again.

CHAPTER FORTY-ONE

Earth-A

Z watched Rueben's proposal to Aki-A from the doorway. The sight brought a pang of sadness to his heart because he'd once had that himself and he never would again.

He turned away from the scene. His past life was just that: the past. Maybe he'd be happy again someday. Maybe not.

What did it matter? He had a lot to atone for, even if he was under the psychotic effects of the time virus when he'd tried to start World War III on Earth-A. His actions had killed people. They'd destroyed worlds. Now he had to do his best to undo and fix all that.

Maybe guys like him didn't get a happily ever after.

He doubted there was another woman out there in the multiverse who could see him for the hero that he was aside from Aki. His Aki. Now she was sharing her bed with a younger version of him—well, it *was* him.

He was tired of time travel fucking him over. He needed a break from Earth-A and Earth-Z, at least for a while. He needed some time to himself.

He headed toward Buzz-A's lab.

"And…done," both Buzzes said in unison, cheesy grins on their faces.

Buzz-A finished up at his computer while Buzz-Z pulled the nanobot injector from Z's arm. "Didn't feel a thing, did ya?"

Z did his best to grin. "Not even a pinch."

In reality, the needle had stung like a bastard, but at least it took care of the "warping cap" Buzz-A had placed on him back when he was trying to bomb the World Summit. Now they'd informed him that he could effectively warp back only three minutes at a time, an odd concept to get used to after having warped back around seventy-two hours at a time previously. Three minutes was better than nothing, though.

Buzz-Z flipped off his surgical gloves and tossed them in the trash bin. "Bullseye!"

Z forced another grin. Even his best friend Buzz-Z felt awkward around him. He no longer called him "buddy." It felt like he'd lost his entire way of life. His family.

He was about to hop off the hospital bed when Buzz-A caught his shoulder. "Now remember. You still have a variant of the time virus flowing in your veins." Earth-A's Buzz shared a look with his Earth-Z counterpart. "We…can't seem to get rid of it. So unless you want us to lock you up in a padded sealed-off bunker, you're going to have to take an injection of synthesized anti-time virus every three days."

Buzz-A handed Z a small box of tiny needles. "Here's a thirty-day supply. Unless you happen to come across a 'friendly' time virus sample you can synthesize…" The two

Buzzes shared a laugh. "...you'll need to come back to Earth-A or Earth-Z and get another supply." Buzz-A fidgeted. "Sorry, bud."

Bud. Hmph. He's not even my Buzz. Oh well. Better than nothing.

Z hopped off the hospital table and stomped off to the space and time capsule. He was ready to skip this Earth.

Z was sitting in the cockpit of the space and time capsule. He'd already inputted the commands to take him to another Earth. He was waiting for the machine to start vibrating when there was a tapping on the window.

At least, he thought he heard someone tapping. When he powered down the startup sequence and turned, there was no one there.

He slapped a hand to his head. *I must be going crazy.*

Reaching back toward the center console, he was about to initiate the relaunch sequence when he heard the tapping again.

"Seriously?" he muttered. "Who the hell is..."

He turned, and he still didn't see anyone. Instead, he saw a dark shape about the size of his palm pressed against the other side of the window. It was black and shapeless like congealed goo.

"The fuck..."

Part of the dark shape lifted from the glass like a tiny tentacle and tapped once more.

"You've got to be shitting me."

He didn't know what he should do. He had no way of communicating with either of the Buzzes or Rueben, but here on the other side of the glass was…if he was correct in assuming, was the time monster—or rather, some small part of it.

No matter. He'd helped kill it once before. He could do it again.

After a deep breath, he steeled himself, unlatched the capsule's glass cover, and hopped out, reaching for the knife concealed in his boot.

Please! Don't hurt me!

"Huh?"

I want to help you. I want to see the world. I want to be your friend.

Z stood there with his combat knife raised, facing the dark substance plastered to the outside glass of the capsule's lid. At first resembling an oil slick, it now suction-cupped outward to resemble a tiny black octopus-like creature. *I'm the good part of what you called the time monster. I didn't die after all. I hitched a ride in your pocket to Earth-A. I don't want to hurt anyone. I want to help!*

Z scratched the back of his head. "This is utterly ridiculous. Why would you want to help me?"

The small oozy octopus looked up at him with puppy dog eyes. *Like you, I have much to atone for. Take me with you, please?*

Z lowered the combat knife. "I don't need a damn pet."

I can be the friendly time virus sample this Earth's Buzz was speaking of. You won't need to return to these two Earths if you don't want to. I can synthesize your antidote.

Z thought it over. He needed some space from Earth-A and Earth-Z. The notion of being completely on his own for a while without having to return for more "thirty-day doses" appealed to him.

I have extensively studied human culture. I can even cook for you if you want since you no longer have a female to care for you.

"Hey now, I can cook...when I want to...shit. You little bastard, you've thought this through, haven't you?"

Yes. It is the life I want. Please take me with you? We can atone together. And have adventures.

Z looked around. There was no one here to witness his departure except for this mini-me time monster who claimed to want to help him. And it said that it could cook.

He leaned toward the capsule's glass so that he was nose-to-nose with the little octopus thing. "Fine. The prospect of going through this next part of my life alone is a bit daunting, I guess. Maybe we can make this work. Right some wrongs together..."

Part of him was excited about getting back into action, with a time monster sidekick of all partners. He studied the little black octopus. "There's gonna be some rules, okay?"

Yessir!

Z gestured at the space and time capsule. "Then hop on in. I'll tell you what they are."

Absolutely!

They both got inside, and Z latched the lid. He cued up the launch sequence again before turning to the little octopus. "You got a name?"

No.

"I have to call you something. Let me think." A few moments later, Z snapped his fingers. "Hah. I've got it. Germ. Fitting, right?"

The tiny black octopus saluted with one of its tentacles. *It's an honor to have a name, sir.*

"Okay. Okay. None of that 'sir' bullshit. From now on, my name is Z. I call you Germ. You call me Z."

Understood, Z!

Z shook his head. What had he gotten himself into?

I'm ready to hear the rules now.

Z checked the console to make sure he had inputted everything correctly. Then he sighed. "Okay. Rule number one: At some point, I will probably have to die again to save the world…"

THE END

I hope you've enjoyed this story, but I have a confession to make. This wasn't the story I set out to write.

I know, I know…you just read 4 books starring Rueben-A and the gang, and now I'm telling you that it wasn't even the story I set out to write. It was more of a…origin story for the 'RePeat' powers.

The story I wanted to write follows Rueben-Z (or Z for the initiated) and his crazy, multi-verse hopping adventures as he dies again and again to save, not just the world, but every world in all existence, ever.

That's the story I wanted to write. But I needed to figure out the world first. I needed to understand the characters, their powers, their…beginnings.

And that's what: Die Again to the Save the World series is…me figuring all this out so that I could write: Die Again to Save the Multiverse, starring none other than the man, himself, Z.

It's a story with heart, joy, insanity and crazy repeating

powers. It's *different.* A good, kind of different, but different, nonetheless.

Z, crazy as he may be, has heart.

Don't take my word for it. Check it out here:

Sample Section from Die Again to Save the Multiverse

Germ just stared at Z.

"You got something to say, little guy?"

Just pondering how unhealthy jelly-filled glazed donuts are for you. So much sugar.

"Hey. I work it off, okay? I train. I kick bad guy ass. I get donuts to celebrate. It's what I do." Z was now wearing a light jacket he'd picked up after sending off the bioweapon to Buzz.

They were sitting outside under the hot noon sun on a patio outside of a Caleb's Ice Cream Emporium fast food restaurant. Numerous other people sat at the umbrella-covered tables, most of them happy young families. At least, that's what all their smiles said.

Z knew that under those confident smiles were layers of doubt and fears. Like *"Am I giving my kids the best life I can?"* And *"What if something happens to my kids when I'm not there?"*

He recalled his own thoughts back when he had a family of his own. He had to admit, raising kids was harder than any mission he'd ever undertaken...

Z grimaced. Children made you soft and that was okay. Of course, he didn't have any kids anymore. He made a fist under the table.

You okay? Germ asked.

He'd had a family of his own and he'd loved them with his entire being. All up until Nunez's Time Virus took them away from him. After that, he'd gone a little crazy. Had done some things he wasn't proud of. On many parallel Earths throughout the multiverse. Of course, the virus had messed up his brain a bit at the time. Not that that was an acceptable excuse.

Now he had Buzz's Space and Time Capsule to both combat new Time Virus threats throughout the multiverse as well as right some of his wrongs.

Hellooo?

Z shook his head. He realized that Germ was still sitting on his lap out of view of other people but the little octopus was waving a tentacle up at him to snag his attention.

"Yeah?"

You're reminiscing about all your past failures again. Aren't you?

"Uh, no. I don't know what you're talking about."

The tiny octopus thing cocked its head up at him. *Oh really? Then what are you thinking about?*

"Oh the usual things. Beer. Guns. Women. Tough guy things."

Germ just stared at him. *I thought you came here to right a wrong.*

Z glanced at his watch, the one ticking down from two hours, and then back to his box of jelly-filled glazed donuts.

"We've got a few minutes yet." He selected a donut and held it down to Germ in his lap. "Here, want one to pass the time?"

You know I only eat organic life matter. And that collection of fried sugary carbs is most definitely dead.

Z winced, no longer hungry for donuts. "You sure are a buzzkill."

Germ shrugged his tiny octopus shoulders.

"I know I probably should know this by now, but do you

ever eat anything? I've never seen you do it." As he said it, he wondered if he might regret hearing the answer.

Germ just smiled up at him with its black beady eyes. *Of course I eat.*

"What do you eat then? Cows? Ducks? …kids?"

Grass. I eat grass. And other vegetables. I do not eat meat anymore. Germ gave him a quizzical look. *You have a messed up mind.*

Leaning back in his seat, Z said, "Why thank you." His watch said it was about time and he started scanning the people around them who were busy enjoying being with their families and eating the greasy and sugary food. The great thing about Caleb's Ice Cream Emporium was that they served burgers, fries, ice cream, and donuts among other things. And it was cheap too.

But he was full.

He pushed the box away from him on the table, glad for the umbrella above him that blocked out the hot sun. It also had the added benefit of concealing him from others somewhat.

Upon instinct, he surreptitiously scanned the crowd for anyone watching him as he feigned a yawn, his sunglasses masking his eyes. As expected, there was no one watching him. He was the one doing the watching. He couldn't help but note that this heavy crowded public spot was a pickpocket's dream. All those wallets and purses. And everyone's attention on their food and their families…

Care to let me in on who you are watching for? I could help you look.

"No. I've got to right my own wrongs. Ah, there they are."

Who? Who? I cannot see. Germ hopped up from Z's lap and

tentatively peered over the table's top in a manner that didn't make him visible to the other customers.

Z's focus was on the outdoor serving window of the restaurant. His eyes locked in on the little girl and her father now walking away, the father with a donut in his hand, holding his daughter's hand who was holding a waffle ice cream cone in her small hand, gleefully licking at her strawberry-vanilla ice cream.

Them? Germ said. *Who are they to you? Do you know them?*

Without taking his eyes from them, Z whispered, "Sometimes you ask too many questions. You know what, you're kind of like my kid. Heh."

Germ pinched Z's arm. *At least I eat my green beans...*

Z frowned and glanced down at the little octopus's cheesy grin. He chuckled and shook his head, then turned back to the matter at hand.

So what's the mission? Did you wrong this man and girl when you were a crazy, bad man?

"I was never crazy."

You tried to start a war...

Ugh. "Just watch and be quiet. Okay?"

The tiny octopus made a lip zipping gesture with one tentacle across its mouth.

Z watched as the father and daughter walked up and stopped near him, searching for an empty table. There didn't appear to be any.

Z smiled up at the father and gestured at the other side of his table.

The man must have seen the pencil-thin scar on one side of Z's face because he gripped his daughter's hand and tugged her away. The girl, meanwhile, smiled back at Z and waved at him.

Z didn't blame the man. Most people just saw a stereotypical movie villain when they saw a person with a scarred face. Oh well.

He was still going to help them.

The father and daughter duo had weaved past a couple tables farther down, still searching. With a frustrated look, he apologized to his daughter. Stress lines worried his face.

Here was the man's story in a nutshell: Within the next few minutes, a pickpocket would steal his wallet. That meant he'd be late to a courtroom appearance to maintain part-time custody of his daughter. If he was late to the courtroom, he'd end up losing his case and he would commit suicide the next day since he could no longer legally see his daughter.

Z shook his head. The world had enough tragedy in it already. It didn't need this one too.

Z glanced down at his watch again. The pickpocket should be there at any moment.

He was about to rise and confront the father when something horrible happened.

The daughter took another gleeful lick at her ice cream cone only for the hot sun overhead to have melted the side of it. The girl's ice cream splatted to the hot baking concrete.

The girl cried.

"Well shit…" Z muttered.

Time to die? Germ said with much confusion.

Z didn't answer, only bent and drew a knife hidden in his boot and turned its point to face his chest. After finding a space between his ribs that afforded him a clean shot at his heart, he punched the blade home with the meat of his palm.

As blood leaked from his chest and dribbled out the corner of his mouth, he fell backward out of his seat to the hot baking concrete. His eyes sighted along the ground to the melting scoop of ice cream at the girl's feet.

He was only vaguely aware of people starting to shout and scream from all around his body. The concrete was burning his cheek.

Then he died.

(A MINUTE AND HALF EARLIER)

A little extreme, do you not think?

Z had warped back to the point in time where the father and daughter were just stepping away from the restaurant's serving window. The father was anxiously searching the crowd for a place to sit as he gripped his daughter's hand.

Already Z could see why the ice cream had toppled over the side of the girl's cone. It had been poorly stacked by the restaurant employee and the sun was hurrying up the ice cream's demise.

Z watched as a rivulet of melted ice cream ran down the side of the cone, unnoticed by the girl cheerfully licking the cone from the other side, speeding up its inevitable spillage.

It is just ice cream. Why did you warp back? Germ asked.

"It's not just ice cream. It's that little girl's heart on the line."

Is this about the daughter you do not get to see anymore?

"Yeah," Z muttered. "Something like that." He rose from his table and backed away, ducking out from under the table's umbrella. As the father and daughter approached him, he turned slightly to the side so as to hide his face scar from them.

"This table taken?" the father asked.

Z grinned. "All yours."

The father nodded his gratitude and motioned for his daughter to sit down. As she did, he gave Z a careful look.

I think he finds you suspicious, Germ said.

"Yes?" the girl's father said when Z didn't leave. "Can I help you?"

That's when Z finally saw the pickpocket, a few tables back over the father's shoulder. He only caught fleeting glimpses of him as he passed between the umbrellas, but it was him: a boy in his late teens, wearing jeans and a tee and a backward facing ballcap. He didn't look out of place; in fact he fit right in. Also, he looked completely harmless. Certainly not a seasoned pickpocket.

"Excuse me," Z said, turning away from the father. "I'm looking for someone."

The girl's father shrugged as he sat at the table next to his daughter. Z couldn't help but notice the man's billfold protruding from his back pocket as he leaned over the table to eat his donut and talk to his daughter.

Z only had to wait a minute, the whole time his eyes tracking the pickpocket as he sauntered up toward the girl's father from behind, his hands casually thrust into his pockets.

The pickpocket was nearly to the girl's father, preparing to "bump" into him. He swept up up behind the father, his hand leaving his pocket as he prepared to lift the man's wallet from his back pocket.

Z seamlessly set his hand upon the pickpocket's wrist, and like a set of talons, lifted it and angled the boy around and guided him out in front of him through the tables and umbrellas.

"Ah, found him," Z said cheerfully, so as not to cause a scene.

"Hey, you creep—" the boy started.

"Hush it, thief," Z said in a harsh whisper as he guided the boy toward the end of the densely packed tables.

The boy shut his mouth. Z meanwhile flashed onlookers a grin as if he was just taking his delinquent son out to give him a stern talk.

When they got outside the tables, Z guided the boy under a tree. They were in a small park. "I want you to straighten up your act. You hear?"

The pickpocket took one glance at the scar on Z's face and gulped. Then defiance lit his face. "Why should I?"

Z glanced over his shoulder at the tables to make sure no one was watching their interaction too closely. He turned back to the boy. "Because you stealing shit from people can have bad effects."

"Oh yeah?"

"Your actions can ruin lives."

"Look man, I'm not scared of you."

Making sure that his back was turned to the people at the tables, Z flicked his knife up from his boot and angled the blade at the thief's face.

The boy's hands shot up. "Shit okay, okay. I get it. I'll stop plying my trade here."

Z scoffed. "I know you're gonna keep at it. Just take it someplace else, will ya? Any place that isn't Caleb's Ice Cream Emporium. Maybe go to the mall like any self-respecting pickpocket?"

The boy's bulging eyes were glued to the knife. He nodded. "Of course. Yes. You're…you're not going to kill me. Are you?"

Z pretended to consider it. "Nah." He returned the knife to his boot and shrugged as if they'd just had a heart to heart, father to son. He slapped the boy's shoulder a bit harder than necessary. "Good talk, son," he called out, louder than necessary for the benefit of anyone who might be trying to eavesdrop. "See you after dinner."

The boy turned and bolted away.

Z smirked. "Well that was too easy."

People do seem to take your threats seriously, Germ said.

"Gee. Wonder why," Z muttered as he turned and made his way back to check on the father and daughter from a distance.

They were both sitting there enjoying their ice creams. Z suddenly recalled that he had never done this with his daughter in his original timeline on Earth-Z. He had never had ice cream, just him and his daughter. There were a lot of things he'd never done with her that he should have. His wife Aki always took care of those things. The notion saddened him.

He'd done his best as a father. But he'd been far from perfect. That was part of the reason for his list of wrongs to right.

He'd been watching the father and daughter a couple minutes when, to his anguish, the top half of her ice cream fell off and plopped to the ground again.

You going to warp back again? Germ asked.

Z took in a breath and then let it out as a sigh. The girl was already starting to cry.

He took out his knife again and jabbed it into his heart.

He died.

(TWO MINUTES EARLIER)

Z warped back to just after his talk with the pickpocket. Now he immediately strode up to the restaurant's serving window and purchased a strawberry-vanilla ice cream.

Once the employee handed him the waffle cone, he immediately started walking toward the father and daughter's table.

The girl's ice cream fell to the ground right as he reached their table. The girl looked about to cry and her father was about to console her.

That's when Z stepped in and said, "Here, take mine. I haven't eaten any of it yet."

The girl's eyes lit up in appreciation. She took the treat from him.

"Thanks again, sir," the father said, squinting at Z. "But do I know you or something?"

"No." Z paused reflectively. "Although I guess you can think of me as your guardian angel."

The man reached into his back pocket and grabbed his wallet. "Here. Let me pay you for it."

Z placed a hand on the man's shoulder. "I don't want the money—just paying it forward. The butterfly effect is all I'm concerned with. You have a good day now." He removed his hand.

The man swallowed. "I hope I do. Got a courtroom appearance to…" He flashed a look down at his daughter who was too busy enjoying her ice cream to notice the discussion her father was having with this stranger. "It's a long story. I don't even know why I'm telling you."

Z winked. "I think you'll do just fine. As long as you get there on time. Know what I mean?"

The girl's father nodded, his face warm with appreciation.

Z left them and walked back to the restaurant's serving window where bought another donut.

Another one? Germ said.

Z wasn't in the mood for arguing. "I've got to have some happiness in my life. Just let me enjoy it. Okay?"

He walked until he found a park bench all by itself. He sat down, ate his donut, and closed his eyes.

Eventually his pager beeped and he checked it. His old Buzz was letting him know to stop by the newspaper place to pick up his next assignment.

He just hoped it didn't involve going to Earth-D. He licked a couple of donut crumbs from his fingers.

Yep, Earth-D was seriously the worst.

Thank you for not only reading this book, but this entire series and these author notes as well.

So, I think Ramy just won the 'who has the longest author notes in 2021' contest. Not that I realized we had a contest going on, but I felt the need to create the contest, declare a winner and close it all in the same Author Notes.

Why close it? Too many other authors would just go and clip out some section of their next story like Ramy just did.

It's a little cheaty-cheaty. But, since Ramy didn't realize there was a contest, he gets to slide by on a technicality. I suppose the answer could be "the contest is my contest, and I said so" is another way to declare it ok.

I am just now kinda-sorta-in-a-little-way beginning to understand that which we call 'Ramy's mind.'

It's a strange place. A lot is going on there, and you never know if the creative juices are sane or not each time we visit the location. If the creative juices are insane, does that cause our own creativity to be tainted for a while?

I think so. Having worked with him, I seem to remember

much pain and ibuprofen downing. So, let's all say this in unison:

"Let's Blame Ramy!"

Personally, I think that is a good answer for you in your life as well. When your spouse, significant other, mother, dad, employer come up and ask why something went wrong, and you have no 'f#ing' clue?

"Just Blame Ramy!"

When the weather changes and you know the Weatherman/woman 'F#cked' the forecast up?

"Just Blame Ramy!"

Finally, when you are on book 04 of a series, and then the author mentions he needed to write the first four books in order to tell the original story. Don't roll your eyes (everyone say it with me here!)

"Just Blame Ramy!"

Great! I think my job is done in these author notes.

Anyway, stay safe and sane out there, and I look forward to talking to you in the next book!

Ad Aeternitatem,

Michael Anderle

Nest Under Siege (04)
First Mission (05)
The Descent (06)
Sacrifices (07)
Love and Aliens (08)
An Alien Affair (09)
Dragons in Space (10)
The Beginning of the End (11)
Death of the Mind (12)
Boundless (13)

Other Books by Ramy Vance

Mortality Bites Series
Keep Evolving Series